Fiction
FARLEY
Ashley

Farley, Ashley.

Lies that Bind.

D0473442

lies
that
bind

ASHLEY FARLEY

Leisure Time Books
a division of
ahb publishing

ALSO BY ASHLEY FARLEY

Life on Loan

Only One Life

Home for Wounded Hearts

Nell and Lady

Sweet Tea Tuesdays

Saving Ben

Sweeney Sisters Series

Saturdays at Sweeney's

Tangle of Strings

Boots and Bedlam

Lowcountry Stranger

Her Sister's Shoes

Magnolia Series

Beyond the Garden

Magnolia Nights

Scottie's Adventures

Breaking the Story

Merry Mary

Copyright © 2020 by Ashley Farley

All rights reserved.

Cover design: damonza.com

Editor: Patricia Peters at A Word Affair LLC

Leisure Time Books, a division of AHF Publishing

All rights reserved. No part of this book may be used or reproduced in any manner
without written permission from the author.

This book is a work of fiction. Names, characters, establishments, organizations,
and incidents are either products of the author's imagination or are used
fictitiously to give a sense of authenticity. Any resemblance to actual persons,
living or dead, events, or locales is entirely coincidental.

ISBN: 978-0998274195

To Alison Fauls,
with appreciation for your continued support.

MAGGIE

*E*arly morning traffic approaching the Portland International Airport is more stop than go. With a glance at the dashboard clock, Valerie lays her hand on the horn, the loud blast setting Maggie's teeth on edge.

"Mom! Geez! That's not helping anything."

"Sorry, honey," her mother says, and blows the horn again, two short successive toots. "I don't want you to miss your flight."

Maggie wishes she would miss her flight.

The stoplight overhead changes from yellow to red, leaving them stranded in the intersection behind a line of unmoving cars. When angry honks from cars to her right urge them onward, Maggie avoids eye contact with the drivers. What can she do? She's only the passenger. The minivan in front of them finally gains clearance, and Valerie inches her Subaru forward.

Maggie studies her mother's profile, memorizing her features for later when she's living three thousand miles away. What will she do without her mother? Her rock. Her best friend. She's seen Valerie nearly every single day for the past twenty-eight years. Who knows when they will be together again? Easter? Maggie's birthday in June?

Valerie's hair is the same mahogany color as Maggie's, gray roots dyed and cut to shoulder length. Her mother is a no-frills woman devoted to her family. They live a modest life on her father's plumber's salary. But what they lack for in possessions, her parents make up for by showering their children with love and support. Her mother volunteers in their church's office and provides food and care for sick parishioners. While Maggie admires her mother, she wants more out of her own life. Sure, she wants a family. But only when the time is right. Career first, and then come the children.

"Say, Mom, did you ever have any doubts about Dad?"

Valerie, her head on a swivel, shoots Maggie a concerned look. "Not serious doubts, no. Why do you ask? Are you having doubts about Eric?"

Maggie bites on a hangnail as she thinks about her answer. "I wouldn't call them doubts exactly. More a feeling of unease."

Valerie's expression softens and she returns her gaze to the road. "Which is understandable considering you're moving all the way across the country to Virginia."

Maggie sighs. "I'm sure that has something to do with it. But I never had doubts about Daniel. Obviously, he had doubts about me."

"Daniel got cold feet," Valerie says. "He would've come to his senses if you'd given him some time."

"Some time?" Maggie scoffs. "Daniel and I dated for six years. I was expecting an engagement ring. Instead, he breaks up with me out of the blue and flies off to Europe. Exactly how much time do you think I should've given him?"

Tightening her grip on the steering wheel, Valerie mumbles, "More than six months for sure."

Maggie met Eric a week after Daniel dumped her. They got engaged seven weeks after their first date and married four months later. She started dating him to prove to Daniel that she was moving on with her life. She never intended to fall for Eric, but she discovered qualities in him that appealed to her. He's everything Daniel is not. Older than Maggie by five years, he's mature and secure, a successful real estate developer who can more than adequately provide for her and their future family. Most importantly, she knows she can count on him not to run out on her.

"Marriage isn't what I thought it would be," Maggie says, chewing harder on the hangnail as she stares out the window.

"I warned you, marriage is hard work."

Maggie wonders why she opened this can of worms. "Correction, you warned me not to marry Eric."

"We warned you it was too soon after Daniel," Valerie says. "Despite what you think, we don't dislike Eric. We're concerned because we know so little about him. He only invited three people to the wedding, not family or friends but coworkers. You claimed you investigated him, but . . ."

"But what, Mom? He's from Topeka, Kansas. His parents are both dead. He graduated from Seaman High School and Kansas State University."

"You already told me all this."

Maggie crosses her arms over her chest. "Then what are you saying?"

The line of cars comes to a complete stop again, and Valerie shifts in her seat toward Maggie. "As a child, you interrogated every new kid on the block before you'd let them in our house." She laughs. "You turned more than one poor child away when you thought they were lying. You knew the names and ages of their siblings. The breeds of their pets. Their mother's and father's occupations. What kind of cereal they ate for breakfast—"

"What's your point, Mom? I have an inquiring mind. I'm an investigative journalist."

"That *is* my point. Your genuine interest in people's lives is what makes you so successful at your job. But it's different with

Eric. You confirmed what he told you about himself, but you haven't learned much else. It's like you're in denial, afraid of what you might find out about Eric, that your new husband isn't the man you want him to be."

"You're wrong," Maggie says with a stiff upper lip. "Eric *is* the perfect man for me."

Maggie admits, though, that she didn't try very hard to find out about his past. She's never seen a photograph of his parents, and whenever she quizzes him about his family, he gets visibly upset, as though some horrific tragedy happened to him during his youth. She doesn't want to know more about his past. Her mother is right. She's afraid to find out he isn't the man she wants and needs him to be—steady, caring, good provider.

She's seen a different side of Eric in the nine weeks since the wedding. He's more controlling. He insists on things being a certain way. And he's not as much fun as he used to be. Was he ever fun loving? Or were those good times from early in their relationship a figment of her imagination? In hindsight, they should've lived together before rushing down the aisle. But this real estate deal came up and Eric wanted her to move to Virginia with him, not as his live-in girlfriend but as his wife. Maggie will be thirty in sixteen months. Most of her friends are married. Some already have kids. She wants what they have, and Eric is her best option for getting it.

Her throat swells at the sight of the overhead sign directing them toward departures. She will make her flight after all. She straightens in her seat. "I'm sorry if I worried you, Mom. I'm just anxious about the move. Eric and I will be fine."

Valerie pulls to the curb in front of the United Airlines counter and puts the car in park. "In order for you to make your marriage work, you'll need to stop pining for Daniel."

"I'm not pining for Daniel," Maggie snaps, because the truth hurts. She is totally pining for her old boyfriend. "Daniel's engaged now, anyway, to a blonde Swedish woman named Ingrid."

"Oh. I see." Valerie's face registers disappointment. "I hope he'll be happy."

Maggie suddenly wants, more than anything, for her marriage to work. For her parents to accept Eric, to love him as much as they loved Daniel. "You'll come visit, right?" She unbuckles her seat belt. "I can hardly wait for you to see my new house." She giggles. "*I* can hardly wait to see my new house." She grabs her mom's hand and squeezes it hard. "How blessed am I to have married a man who bought me a house?"

"You're very blessed, sweetheart. And I'll come visit as soon as you're settled." Valerie brushes a strand of hair out of her face. "More than anything, darling, I want you to be happy. You're an intuitive young woman. Trust your instincts. Remember, you can always come home. Or, if you ever need me to come to you, call me, and I'll be on the next flight."

MAGGIE

*R*ows of historic homes stand tall and erect on both sides of the tree-lined street like medieval sentries protecting their inhabitants. Most feature slate roofs and Queen Anne towers. Some of the facades are painted handsome shades of taupe and gray while others bear the original century-old crimson brick. Wreaths of dried Christmas greens adorn many of the front doors, even though the New Year is already fourteen days old. Tricycles, toys, and strollers litter the porches of families with small children. Boxwood topiaries in iron urns grace the entryway at the home of a gardening enthusiast. Farther down the street, peeling paint and rotten shutters suggest a homeowner too strapped for cash to make repairs.

"West Avenue," Maggie says, liking the sound of the name on her tongue. "A generic name for a charming street. I couldn't have chosen better myself."

She meant it as a compliment, but the tightening of her husband's jaw warns her she's irritated him.

Eric had insisted on following the moving van across country. He wanted to arrive in Richmond ahead of her to have the house ready when she got there. Something in him had shifted during the two weeks they'd been apart. She sensed it in the car on the way home from the airport. Something under the surface that he's having to work hard to control. Obvious irritation, but is it anger as well? Maggie couldn't put her finger on it. Did she do something to make him mad?

Eric opens the wrought iron gate and motions her up the brick steps to the columned stoop. At the front door, he hooks his arm around her neck, covering her eyes with his left hand while he unlocks the heavy black front door with his right.

"Why all the suspense?" she asks.

"It's a surprise. Watch your step," he says, and holds her arm as she crosses the threshold.

The smell of fresh paint greets her inside the foyer. When he drops his hand, she takes in the white walls and bare hardwood floors. Letting out a nervous giggle, she says in a teasing tone, "What's so surprising about a flight of stairs and a narrow hallway?"

"You haven't seen anything yet. I hired a decorator."

Her brown eyes widen. There's seemingly no end to the brokerage account Eric is always talking about. "A decorator? Can we afford that?"

Indignation crosses his handsome face. "I told you, Mags. You don't have to worry about money."

"Easier said than done for a girl who put herself through college."

He hangs his fleece on the wooden rack by the door, but when he moves to take off her coat, she snuggles inside the warmth of her down parka. "I'll leave it on for now. It's chilly in here."

"Better get used to it. Old houses can be drafty."

She smiles at him. "I guess I'll have to buy more sweaters."

He sweeps his hand at the wide doorway to his right. "After you."

She takes tentative steps down the hallway, stopping short in the doorway. Hard edges and glimmering surfaces make up the decor in the living room. Everything is white—upholstery and carpet and walls—with the exception of an abstract painting in bright colors above the fireplace mantel. The übercontemporary style is a drastic departure from the eclectic mix of furnishings in their apartment back home.

Beside her, Eric asks, "Well? What do you think?"

"It's pretty. Although not exactly what I was expecting." She searches the room for a familiar lamp or framed picture or knickknack. "Where's all our stuff?"

"I got rid of most everything," he says. "None of it fit with our new style."

Maggie drops her head, staring at him from beneath a heavy brow. "*Our* new style? This is all so contemporary. My tastes lean toward traditional."

"Your tastes lean toward tacky." He laughs, as though he's joking, but she can tell he's dead serious.

Maggie stiffens. "That was uncalled for."

She's expecting an apology. Instead, he brushes past her into the living room. Standing at the fireplace, he stares up at the painting, which Maggie now sees is a school of fish. All of the fish are red with the exception of one lone yellow fish swimming against the others. She wonders if the decorator chose the painting or if Eric picked it out himself. Does he identify with the yellow fish in some way? Does he consider himself the odd man out, swimming against the school of norm?

"We have a certain image to uphold, honey. I want to make a good impression on my new business associates. Your collection of yard sale furnishings wasn't cutting it."

She trails him into the room. "We're married now, Eric. We're a team. I'm hurt, and more than a little annoyed, that you made all these decisions without consulting me. You can't go throwing my belongings away without asking me. I had sentimental attachments to my possessions."

"Then you'll have to develop sentimental attachments to your new possessions." He waves his hand above his head. "Like this painting. I paid a small fortune for it. Isn't it cool?"

"It looks like a kindergartner painted it." Maggie turns away from him, crossing into the adjoining sitting room where she's relieved to see her treasured collection of biographies and historical accounts of world events organized alphabetically on shelves that line one wall. She proceeds into the kitchen. The clean look continues here with white walls and cabinets and stainless-steel appliances. A round black table and four chairs nestle inside the bay window. As she stares out into the courtyard garden, she imagines summer barbecues on the slate patio with new friends. Being able to buy a house is the bright side of having to move three thousand miles away from her family.

Eric rejoins her as she continues her tour on the second floor. At the top of the stairs, he takes her hand and leads her into the master bedroom. The marble-top oak bureau from their apartment in Portland made the cut, but Eric has replaced her four-poster mahogany queen from childhood with a king that has a tufted headboard.

Sunlight streams in through a bay window identical in size to the one in the kitchen. Moving to the window, she watches an elderly gentleman on the sidewalk below walking his three corgis on leashes. Closing her eyes, she imagines the maple trees lining both sides of the street when they leaf out in the spring and turn golden orange in the fall.

"Come, let me show you the biggest surprise of all." Bracing her shoulders, he marches her out of the master bedroom and down the hall to the back of the house.

"What's in there?" she asks as they pass a closed door on the right.

"An empty room. We can either use it as a guest bedroom or a home office."

He swings open a door at the end of the hall, revealing a

nursery decked out for a newborn—with crib, comfortable rocker, and chest of drawers doubling as a changing table.

Maggie doesn't trust her eyes. She blinks hard, but when she opens them again, the scene in front of her hasn't changed. "We agreed to wait a few years before starting a family."

"True." He turns to face her, brushing back a strand of her long mahogany hair. "But I don't see why we need to wait. I have plenty of money. You don't have to work. Let's have a baby right away. Let's start our family now, Mags. With your looks and my brains, our children will be superstars."

"But I'm not ready to have a baby, Eric. My career is finally beginning to take off. The job I'm interviewing for on Friday could be my big break."

Eric's arms fall to his sides. "I don't want my wife traipsing all over town, chasing after two-bit news stories."

"I can take care of myself." She studies her husband's chiseled facial features for clues as to where this sudden change of heart is coming from. He knows how important her career is to her. Before she agreed to marry him, she'd made him promise he wouldn't interfere in her professional life.

"I'm not planning to be a reporter forever, Eric. The news anchor is going on maternity leave in May. If I do a good job, I'm hoping they'll offer me the position."

"That would only be temporary, until the anchor comes back."

"*If* she comes back," Maggie says. "She might decide to stay at home with her baby."

"Home with her baby is where she should be." Eric leaves her in the doorway and moves to the crib. "Aside from the obvious charm, there's a reason I chose West Avenue. It's known as Stork Alley, has been since the first houses were built on the street, because of the abundance of young families who live in them." He stares at the mobile of knitted safari animals. "I was hoping you'd be pleased with the nursery. I thought you'd be excited about the prospect of having a baby. I'm not getting any younger, you know." He swats at the mobile. "I was an only child of parents who fought all the time. As you know, I don't like to talk about it. Suffice it to say, my childhood was miserable. I've always dreamed of having a big happy family. You're a wonderful wife, Mags, and you'll be a loving mother. We'll be good parents to our children."

This is the most he's ever shared about his past, and Maggie can't help but soften toward him.

What's so wrong with him wanting to start a family, anyway? Most women would be overjoyed to be in your shoes. Look at this lovely home. He can afford the kind of life you always dreamed of. His desire to be a father isn't a bad thing. It's sweet that he wants kids. And he'll be a great dad.

"Look, Eric." She goes to stand beside him at the crib. "You're throwing a lot at me at once. New city. New home. New decor. Give me some time to adjust to the idea of starting a family earlier than we agreed."

Leaning into him, they walk back down the hall to their bedroom. Inside the doorway, she turns to face him. "Why don't I cook us a nice dinner to celebrate our first night in our new house. I'll unpack first and then go to the grocery store. Where's my car, by the way? I didn't see it on the street when we came in. Is it parked around the corner?"

"About that . . .," he begins.

A sickening feeling in her gut warns her of what's coming. She'd last seen her Chevrolet Malibu as the moving van left Portland, her car in tow.

"The movers ran into some trouble when they were towing your car. We had to sell it in Wyoming."

Her mind races as she considers the logistics. "What kind of trouble?"

"Let's see." He rakes a hand through his thinning dark hair. "First, they blew out a couple of tires on the trailer. Then some other stuff happened. I'm not exactly sure what. I'm a builder, not a mechanic. Towing the car was slowing them down."

"So, you sold it. Without my permission." She levels him with a cold stare. "How'd you do that, anyway, without the title?"

"You gave me the title, remember?"

She remembers. For safekeeping. He personally transported their important legal documents to Virginia. "Still! It would've been nice if you'd consulted me before you sold my car. How much did you get for it?"

"Pocket change," he says. "Your 2001 Malibu had more than a hundred thousand miles on it."

"I loved my Malibu. I paid for it myself with money I earned waitressing in college."

He tilts his head to the side, grinning down at her. Dressed in jeans and a green plaid flannel shirt, Eric reminds Maggie of her three older brothers, as children, returning home from spending the day in the woods. "We'll go shopping next weekend. I'll buy you a new car. Maybe something like a Volvo SUV with a third seat for when you have to drive carpool."

She lets this latest reference to starting a family slide. "How am I supposed to get to my job interview on Friday?"

"I'll drop you on my way to work, and you can Uber home." Taking her face in his hands, he kisses her, his teeth nibbling at her lips. Their sex life isn't bad. But it isn't great either. Not like with Daniel.

You need to stop pining for Daniel.

She tolerated the kiss a little longer before pushing him away.

He holds her at arm's length. "I'm sorry if I've upset you, Mags. You'll see. We're going to have a beautiful life together. You need to trust me to take care of you."

Eric's eyes are so crystal clear and aqua blue most people mistake them for colored contact lenses. When they first met, Maggie found them mesmerizing. Hypnotic. She felt as though he was seeing inside her soul. But now, his penetrating gaze makes her squirm. It's like he always knows what she's thinking. And at the moment, she isn't thinking very kind thoughts.

He plants another peck on her lips before leaving the room. She hears his footfalls on the bare steps followed by the closing of the front door. He returns minutes later with her suitcase, parking it just inside the door. "I'll be downstairs. When you're finished unpacking, I'll drive you to the grocery store."

Maggie slips off her coat, draping it over the back of a slipper chair, and sets her phone on the bureau. Opening her suitcase on the bed, she removes her favorite sweater, a thigh-length, pale-gray cashmere cardigan, and hangs it in the closet with the rest of her wardrobe, which is still organized according to type—blouses, slacks, skirts, dresses—the way she'd packed them in Oregon.

Gathering up her bras and panties from the suitcase, she opens the top drawer of the bureau and is taken aback at the sight of neatly folded gowns and teddies in slinky fabrics with lace trim. She thinks there's been a mistake, that the movers mixed up their possessions with another client's. But then she realizes this is yet another one of Eric's surprises—seductive lingerie intended to spice up their sex life in order to produce a baby for the crib down the hall, another child to play hopscotch on the sidewalks of Stork Alley.

Most brides would be turned on by the thought of their new husbands buying them sexy lingerie. But all Maggie feels is repulsed. She drops her bras and panties on top of the lingerie and slams the drawer shut.

Staring at her phone on the bureau, she wants desperately to call Valerie. But how childish of a twenty-eight-year-old woman to complain to her mother about her husband. *You're an adult now, Maggie. Suck it up. Your family is expecting your marriage to fail. Prove them wrong. Try harder. You can do this.*

EVA

*E*va locks the door behind her last customer of the day. With tears in her eyes, she turns to her associate of twenty years. "How will I ever manage without you?"

"Oh, honey, come here." Annette reaches for her. "My offer still stands. Florida can wait. I'll postpone my retirement."

Eva sags against Annette's stout frame, the familiar arms comforting her. She's cried many tears on Annette's shoulder throughout the years. "I can no longer afford to pay you, and I can't let you work for free. Besides, if not for me, you would've moved years ago."

Annette strokes Eva's cropped salt-and-pepper hair. "You're gonna be fine. You're in a good place now."

Pushing Annette away, Eva faces the showroom. "There's a good chance I'll have to close the shop. What will I do then?"

Annette stands close enough behind her for Eva to feel the heat radiating from her body. "You'll close the shop. And you'll do what I've been telling you to do for years—you'll sell that mausoleum you live in. It'll be good for you to leave all these sad memories behind and start over somewhere new."

Feeling the onset of a headache, Eva pinches the bridge of her nose. "The memories are all I have left. I can't leave Richmond. What if Reese comes home and I'm not here?"

Annette exhales, her breath tickling Eva's neck. "I've never said this to you, but I've thought it many times. You would've heard from Reese by now if she were still alive. Or someone would've spotted her. Or the police would've received a lead. It's time for you to face reality, Eva. Reese is never coming home."

Eva shakes her head. "You're wrong, Annette. My daughter is out there somewhere, and one day she'll come home. And when she does, I'll be here waiting for her."

"At least come visit me in Florida. Do you think you can leave Richmond for a long weekend?"

"Maybe," Eva says, but she knows she won't leave Richmond for even a day. "Although it'll be difficult with no one to cover the shop now that you're gone."

"Why don't you close Claudia's Closet in early August when everyone in town goes to the beach. Tape a note to your front door in the extreme off-chance Reese picks that week to return home. And tell your crazy neighbor . . . what's his name . . ." She snaps her fingers until the name comes to her. "Ian! You tell Ian where you're going in case he needs to reach you."

"We'll see. But I can't think about that now." Eva glances at her watch. She's ready to be alone with her ghosts. "I'm sure you have packing left to do."

Annette leaves her side and moves about the shop, her white New Balance running shoes squeaking against the wooden floorboards as she makes her final lap. When she's ready to leave, Eva walks her through the shop and the adjacent stockroom to the back door. A lump fills her throat. If Annette lingers, Eva will break down.

Annette hands Eva her dull brass key to the shop. "You'll need this for my replacement. Hire someone, honey. You can't run the shop alone."

"I'll think about it." Eva takes the key and unlocks the door.

"Good luck with the move."

Annette palms her cheek. "You'll remember to eat. You can't afford to lose any more weight."

Eva nods. "I'll remember to eat."

Annette wags her finger at Eva. "No pills, and you'll limit the drinking."

Another nod. "I promise."

"We'll FaceTime every day."

Eva lets out a moan. "You know how much I hate technology." But staying in touch is important to Annette and she quickly adds, "We'll do it all—text, talk, and FaceTime."

A sudden gust of winter wind causes both women to shiver. "I should get going."

They embrace for a long moment. When Annette draws away, she has tears in her eyes. She presses her fingers to her lips. She wants to say something, but she's too choked up to speak. Her hand shoots up in a parting wave as she hurries out to her car in the gravel parking lot.

Closing the door behind her, Eva drops the spare key in the desk drawer in the stockroom and returns to the showroom. Eva has big shoes to fill. Annette, a master of organization and inventory control, always kept mental lists with detailed notes of every item of vintage apparel. She knew their regular customers well and, at any given moment, could find the perfect item to fill a shopper's wants and needs. Eva was content to let Annette take charge of the retail side of the business while she handled the accounting and purchasing. But now, with Annette's departure, all of the responsibility will fall on her.

She'll give it until May. If business doesn't improve, she'd sell the shop and cut her losses before she blows through the remainder of her savings.

Eva inhales a dusty breath, feeling better having set a deadline. Removing her clutch from under the front counter, she turns out the lights and exits the back door. As she weaves through the streets of The Fan, her thoughts drift to the vodka and soda waiting for her at home. She only allows herself one, but that *one* is the highlight of her day.

Eva finds every house on her block charming in its own way, but she thinks hers is the most cheerful with brick painted soft gray and double front doors a lemony yellow. As she parallel parks her old Volvo wagon on the curb out front, she notices a lone figure, a woman, standing at the second-floor window of the house across the street. Her new neighbor. She turns off the engine, and as she gets out of the car, she waves up at the woman. The woman lifts her hand in response. From the distance, it's difficult to tell her age, but Eva guesses she's in her late twenties. The same age as Reese. Maybe Eva will bake a cake to welcome her to the neighborhood.

She is reaching for the brass knob on her paned storm door when she hears a familiar voice. "I made Brunswick stew this afternoon. I thought you might like some for your dinner."

She looks up to see Ian, her next-door neighbor, on the porch beside her with a plastic container in hand. She's known him for thirty years, as long as she's lived on West Avenue. Eva's husband, Stuart, was out of town on business the night she went into labor, two weeks before the baby was due. Ian drove her to the hospital and stayed with her until Reese was born. With no children of his own, he doted on Reese like an uncle and she worshiped him in return. He was distraught when she went missing.

Ian now fusses over Eva like a mother hen. He takes her trash to the street on pickup day. Goes to the pharmacy for medicine when she has the flu. Helps with rodent and plumbing problems. Not to mention, he's a fabulous cook, bringing her goodies several times a week.

Behind him, Mack waves at Eva from Ian's front porch. Both men are wearing cowboy boots, plaid shirts, and Stetson hats. Ian changes his style as frequently as he changes live-in lovers. Mack is the son of a cattle farmer from Texas. Before him was Nathan, a florist who displayed breathtaking arrangements of fresh flowers and orchids around the house. Then there was Chester, the artist, who adorned Ian's walls with canvases splashed with bright colors. But Eva's favorite, Santiago, the musician, had been Reese's favorite as well. Reese had taken guitar lessons for years, but Santiago taught her how to play with heart.

"Bless you," Eva says, taking the container of soup from him. "I haven't given the first thought to dinner."

His eyes narrow as he studies her closely. "Bad day? You look like you lost your best friend."

"In a manner of speaking, I did. Today was Annette's last day. She's moving to Florida tomorrow."

He sighs. "I'm sorry, Eva. I know how much you rely on her. I hope you're planning to hire a replacement."

She stares past him at the dormant patch of grass between her house and the sidewalk. "I'm going to wait and see what business is like this spring before I decide."

"I'm happy to help out if you get in a bind." He holds her door open while she steps inside.

Ian is a trust fund kid. While he's never had to work, his high energy level dictates that he stay busy. He's worked too many jobs for Eva to count, including caterer and shoe salesman and waiter. He currently works as a clerk at a local wine and cheese shop.

"I'll keep that in mind, Ian. Thank you. And thanks for the soup," she says, pushing the door closed with her foot.

She hangs her down jacket on the coat rack by the front door and takes the container of soup to the kitchen. Setting it on the counter, she opens the cabinet to the right of the stove and removes a half-gallon bottle of Absolut Citron vodka, the only alcohol she keeps in the house with the exception of a bottle of red wine a neighbor gave her for Christmas. She fills a tumbler with ice and vodka, adding a splash of soda for good measure. She doesn't bother turning on any lamps as she makes her way to her dark-paneled living room and settles into her husband's leather recliner. The gas logs in the fireplace to her right no longer work, nor do the lights on the eight-foot artificial Christmas tree to her left. The cheap tree, purchased at Home Depot the December Reese went missing, long outlived her expectations. Every night for three years after the accident, a thousand mini white lights glistened in the window, a beacon to guide Reese home. Even though the lights are burned out, Eva can't bring herself to take down the tree. Once a month, she blows off the dust with her hair dryer and rearranges her daughter's and husband's gifts underneath. Stuart will never open his presents, and he'll never again wear any of his clothes hanging in their master bedroom closet upstairs, but she can't bring herself to donate them to Goodwill.

Her drink goes down too easily, and she's thirsty for more. Staring into her glass, she clinks the ice cubes as she fights the temptation. She refuses to go down that rabbit hole again. She sets her glass on the table next to her, beside the framed black-and-white photograph of Reese from her senior year in high school. The vignette image is classic, a lovely young woman with bare shoulders and a single strand of pearls draped around her neck. She picks up her cherished porcelain figurine, a black Scottish terrier wearing a blue-and-white checkered vest, and cradles it in her hands. Stuart and Reese had given her the figurine for Christmas fifteen years ago, the year she lost Bailey, the Scottie she'd loved so dearly.

Taking her empty glass to the kitchen, Eva places it in the sink and reheats Ian's Brunswick stew. Back in the living room, with her soup bowl on a tray in her lap, she channel-surfs until she finds an old Julia Robert's movie. When the movie ends at ten, she returns her tray to the kitchen and slowly climbs the stairs, traipsing down the hallway past the closed doors of the master bedroom and her daughter's room to the guest room at the back of the house.

She crawls fully clothed beneath the bedcovers. She is always on alert for the ringing of the phone or the doorbell. Flat on her back with hands behind her head, she stares at the ceiling. Rays from the moon stream through the open window and create dancing shadows on the ceiling. The shadows are ethereal, like ghosts. Stuart's ghost. But not Reese's. Because, despite what Annette thinks, Eva refuses to believe her daughter is never coming home. While there's a slim chance a madman is holding Reese captive, or that she's suffering from amnesia, Eva suspects she's living somewhere under an assumed identity. And it's all Eva's fault for making Reese's life a living hell during her teenage years.

Eva tried drinking away the guilt, and when booze wasn't enough, she resorted to narcotics. Which drove her to lose nearly everything. Not that anything she has left is worth living for without Reese and Stuart.

She flashes back ten years to the night before Reese left for college. Eva can still see her daughter's mountain of gear accumulating by the front door to be packed in the car the following morning. Suitcases, crammed with clothes; plastic bins, full of linens and towels; bulletin boards and cardboard tubes of posters and paper shopping bags of school supplies. On top of the pile was Reese's beloved acoustic guitar, Max, the name she'd given it when she'd purchased it three years ago with money earned from several summers of babysitting.

Eva cornered her daughter in the upstairs hall during one of Reese's many trips up and down the stairs. "I know it's been a difficult summer, but I'd like to put all that behind us and enjoy our last evening together. Daddy and I are planning a going-away celebration dinner. He's cooking steaks on the grill, and I'm making your favorite potato casserole."

With an armful of decorative pillows, Reese brushed past Eva on the way to the stairs. "Fine. But can we eat early? I have plans with Shannon."

From the railing above, Eva looked down at the top of her daughter's honey-colored head. "But it's your last night in Richmond."

"That's why I'm going out with my friends." Reese dropped the pillows on top of her pile and disappeared down the hall toward the kitchen.

Much to Eva's dismay, Reese wore her headphones and brought her surly mood to the table when they sat down for dinner at six thirty that evening, a half hour earlier than they normally ate.

Eva yelled at her, "For God's sake, Reese, take off the headphones."

"What?" Reese asked, although Eva was sure she'd heard her.

"Take off the headphones," she repeated, pointing at her ears.

Reese tugged the headphones off and set them down beside her plate.

"We agreed we'd leave at six in the morning," Eva reminded her. "We have a long drive ahead of us tomorrow. I hope you're not planning to stay out too late tonight."

Reese stared at her plate, not touching her food. "I can sleep in the car."

"Are you excited about decorating your dorm room?" Eva asked as she carved off a chunk of steak. "I can't wait to meet your roommate."

Reese dragged her fork through the potato casserole. "Can we please not talk about this right now?"

Eva looked to Stuart for help. "Your mother spent all afternoon preparing this nice dinner for you," he said. "The least you can do is give us your attention for a few minutes."

"Sorry. I'm not hungry. And Shannon is waiting for me." Reese pushed back from the table, dumped her untouched steak down the disposal, snatched her headphones, and stormed out of the house.

Reese had stayed out late every night that summer. Always

past midnight but never later than two o'clock. At two thirty, Eva texted Reese to come home. At three o'clock, her anger morphing into fear, Eva tried calling Reese—three, four, five times. And when those calls went to voice mail, she tried Shannon's cell and Shannon's family's house line. All of her calls went unanswered. Eva was frantic when she woke Stuart at five. At five thirty, they were heading out of the house to drive by Shannon's when their daughter came strolling up the sidewalk from the corner with her guitar slung across her back.

Eva followed Reese into the house. "Where have you been, young lady? I've been worried out of my mind. Do you know what time it is? And why are you walking home alone in the dark?"

"It's not dark anymore," Reese said. "The sun is coming up. And Shannon just lives around the block."

"Around the block, a mile away," Eva said.

"Whatever. At least I made it home in time." Reese headed for the stairs. "I'll take a quick shower, and we can pack the car."

Eva ran after Reese and grabbed her by the arm, preventing her from mounting the stairs. "I can smell alcohol on your breath," she said, sniffing near her daughter's mouth. "And your eyes are bloodshot. Have you been smoking marijuana?"

Reese glared at her with pure hatred in her eyes. "We go through this every single night, Mom. I've told you a million times, I don't drink and I don't smoke weed. My eyes are bloodshot because I just woke up. I fell asleep on Shannon's couch."

"And who were you sleeping with on Shannon's couch? Are you having sex?"

"I don't have to listen to this." Jerking her arm free, Reese dashed up the stairs.

"I'm warning you," Eva screamed. "If you get pregnant, don't come crying to me. I'm done raising children."

REESE

Ten Years Ago

*T*he more Eva gushed over her new roommate, the more the walls of her dorm room caved in on Reese. Mary Beth was her mother's dream daughter—blonde, beautiful, and undoubtedly popular with her peers. The musical was *Grease*, and Mary Beth was in the lead as Sandy. Which was fine by Reese. Olivia Newton John was boring. But Stockard Channing was badass.

Reese had played the supporting role of Betty Rizzo in a high school production of *Grease* her freshman year. Eva had missed opening night. Missed all the other nights of all her other performances throughout high school as well. Eva was more interested in seeing Reese on the athletic fields than on stage. Unfortunately for her, Reese sucked at sports. Reese was done with acting, anyway. She'd chosen Erie State College for their contemporary music program.

"Are these originals?" Eva asked Mary Beth about her black-

and-white posters of iconic movie stars like Audrey Hepburn and James Dean.

Mary Beth looked at Eva as though she was the dumbest person on the planet. "Um . . . No . . . They're copies."

Reese took her mother by the arm. "Time for you to leave now, Mom," she said, dragging her to the door.

Eva protested, "But we just got here. I want to help you set up your dorm room."

"I'll send you a pic." Her eyes pleaded with her father for help.

"We should probably hit the road," he said to Eva, and to Reese, "Walk us to the car?"

"Fine." Reese stomped off down the hall ahead of them. When she reached her father's ancient Land Cruiser in the parking lot, she turned to face her parents. "It's been real. Have a nice life."

"Please, sweetheart," Eva said. "Can we not argue? I'm so excited for you. You're off to a great start with your roommate. Mary Beth seems like a nice girl."

Reese brushed her mother's hand away. "Oh really? How can you tell? You've known her for what, five minutes?"

Eva smiled. "I can just tell. She comes from good breeding."

Reese felt like smacking some sense into her mother. "Contrary to what you believe, Mom, plenty of good people come from bad breeding."

"If you're talking about Shannon, you're mistaken," Eva said. "She comes from bad breeding, but she's not a good person."

"You don't even know her." Reese didn't like Shannon either. She used the situation to piss her mother off.

Mother and daughter glared at each other with two identical pairs of gray eyes, the only feature they shared in common. Eva was fair skinned and petite with pointy features while Reese was darker skinned like her father and bigger boned. Bigger everything, actually.

"Shannon is beneath you," Eva continued, because she never knew when to stop. "I've warned you time and again, people will judge you by the company you keep." She lifted Reese's chin. "Listen to me, sweetheart. You have a chance to reinvent yourself here, to be whoever you want to be. To associate with the right kind of people. Take advantage of that opportunity."

"You're the only one who doesn't like me the way I am. I'm really not such a bad person, Mom. I'm just not the person you want me to be." Fighting back tears, Reese stared up at the cobalt sky. "You're such a hypocrite. Take a look in the mirror. You're not so perfect either. All the things you've been accusing me of—drinking and doing drugs and having se—"

"Don't talk to your mother that way," her father snapped. He almost always took Eva's side. If only he knew the truth about his wife.

Reese swiped at the tears spilling from her eyelids. "God! I'm sick of the arguing. Whatever. I need to go unpack. Enjoy your empty nest." Turning her back on them, she walked away from her old life and into her new, feeling lighter with each step toward her dorm.

In the room, she found Mary Beth strumming Reese's guitar. She took the guitar away and laid it on her bed. "Sorry about my mom. She can be over the top sometimes."

"No worries. I think she's kinda cute." Mary Beth gave her the once-over, as if to say, What happened to you?

Silence fell over the room. She had nothing in common with her new roommate. That they would never be friends was mutually agreed upon, no discussion necessary.

That afternoon was busy with orientation meetings. When dinnertime rolled around, the roommates walked to the cafeteria together, parting inside the door—Mary Beth heading off to the salad bar and Reese joining the other students waiting for a hot meal. By the time Reese exited the line with her tray, Mary Beth was already seated at a table with other freshman students. Mary Beth had not saved a chair for Reese, but Reese didn't care. She was used to being invisible. Locating a vacant table by the window, she moved her headphones from around her neck to her ears and ate her dinner in the company of the Rolling Stones.

Reese loved the Erie State campus with its impressive stone buildings, lily ponds, and green common areas, but the academics were harder than she'd anticipated. While she'd gotten Bs in high school without having to study, she'd come to college prepared to work hard in order to excel. But she was finding that difficult to do, even though she spent every free minute of her time in the library.

At the end of September, she received her first opportunity to perform in her Introduction to Vocal Studies class. Professor Hunter—wavy dark hair, scruffy beard, and blue eyes twinkling behind heavy black eyeglass frames—stood in the doorway of their classroom directing students as they arrived. "Down the hall to the auditorium."

So, the rumors about Professor Hunter and impromptu performances are true, Reese thought.

When Hunter joined them in the auditorium five minutes later, he climbed the sidesteps to the stage and tapped on the microphone. "Today is karaoke day. We'll play by my rules with no lyrics and no recorded music. Instruments are allowed. Otherwise, you sing a cappella. I'll pick students at random. Starting with . . ." He drew imaginary circles in the air before landing his finger on Reese. "You, Miss Carpenter. Give it your best shot."

Reese's mind raced as she took her place on stage with her guitar. She had an extensive repertoire to choose from, but she picked one of her all-time favorites—Tina Turner's rendition of *"Proud Mary."* Strumming a few chords on her guitar captured her audience's attention, but when she began to sing, they sat up straight in their chairs, all eyes on her. She hit all the notes and when she'd finished, her classmates were on their feet, their loud clapping ringing throughout the auditorium.

"Very nice, Miss Carpenter," Professor Hunter said. "You just set the bar very high for your classmates."

Reese listened with rapt attention as, one by one, her classmates performed knockout performances, off the cuff in a variety of genres from pop to country to classic rock. She'd suspected they were gifted. Everyone had to audition in order to be accepted to the music program. She just wasn't expecting this level of talent and would have to step up her game if she wanted to outperform the others.

Reese's stomach knotted when Professor Hunter asked to speak with her after class. Had she done something wrong? He'd complimented her performance, but she'd gone first, ahead of twenty other stellar performances. Was he going to tell her the competition was too stiff, that she didn't have what it took to compete at this level?

They stood together in front of the stage until the last student had left the auditorium, and then he turned to her. "You're a natural."

Her belly tingled with excitement. "Do you think so, really?"

He smiled. "I do. Really. You picked a great song to show off your vocals. You're obviously comfortable on stage. But I want you to work on developing your own style instead of adopting the personality of the vocalist whose song you've chosen to sing. Does that make sense?"

"Yes, sir." He wasn't telling her anything she hadn't been told a million times before. She had no stage presence.

"Do you always sing R&B?"

"When I have a choice. My voice coach at home says I remind him of Teena Marie."

Hunter considered the comparison to the singer and songwriter from the 70s and 80s era known as the Ivory Queen of Soul. "I can see it. And there's nothing wrong with vintage R&B.

Personally, it's one of my favorites. But I'd like to see you try some music from contemporary artists. Like Mariah Carey."

Reese groaned inwardly. She didn't particularly care for Mariah Carey, but she was willing to do whatever it took to find her place in the modern music world. "Yes, sir."

"Next time, I'll give you a chance to prepare for your performance. I'm happy to help with song selection."

"That'd be great."

They walked up the aisle toward the back of the auditorium where her classmate Franny was waiting for them.

"Did you need to see me?" Hunter asked.

"I always need to see you, Professor Hunter," Franny said, batting her eyelashes at him.

Reese would trade her vocal cords for the ability to flirt like Franny.

Hunter laughed out loud. "I could get fired for having this discussion with you."

"Fine," Franny said, sticking her lower lip out in a pout. "I was waiting for Reese, anyway."

"In that case, I'll leave you ladies to enjoy your weekend," Hunter said and disappeared down the hall toward his office.

"Girl, you were amazing in there," Franny said, taking Reese by the arm and leading her in the opposite direction toward the building's exit.

Reese's face grew warm. "Thanks. So were you." Franny had strutted her petite body across the stage with her mess of reddish-blonde corkscrews bouncing around her pretty face as she'd performed Pink's *What About Us.*

"Meh." Franny waggled her hand in a so-so gesture. "My performance was mediocre. You, on the other hand, hit it out of the park. How do you manage to stay so calm?"

"I don't honestly know," Reese said. "It's just like that for me." Pretending to be someone else on stage was so much easier than being herself. Especially when she didn't know who herself really was.

They burst through the exit doors at the end of the hallway into a glorious early fall afternoon.

"Do you want to go with me to a party tonight?" Franny asked.

"I have to study. I have a lot of homework."

"On a Friday night? You're joking, right?" Franny's mouth formed an O. "I get it. You're rushing a sorority."

"Not hardly," Reese said with a humph. "Much to my mother's disappointment."

Franny burst out laughing. "I feel your pain. My mother is all over me about joining a sorority."

They compared notes about their overbearing mothers as they walked across the green to the flagpole. "So, we'll meet here at nine," Franny said, more a statement than a question.

"I guess," Reese mumbled.

As she headed toward the library, Franny called after her, "And don't forget to bring your guitar."

My guitar? Reese wondered. When she turned back around to ask why she needed it, Franny was already out of earshot.

Only a few students were in the library that afternoon, and even fewer in the cafeteria that evening for dinner. As she picked at her lasagna, she imagined her classmates going in groups for dinner to one of the trendy restaurants and pubs on Main Street in the small college town of Mapleton, Ohio.

When Reese returned to the room, Mary Beth had already gone out for the evening, the scent of her Chance perfume lingering in the air. Her roommate spent very little time in the room. And when she was there, she hogged the bathroom, which irritated their suite mates more than it did Reese.

She showered and was brushing her teeth when she noticed Mary Beth's makeup bag on the window ledge. Helping herself to a swipe of designer mascara, she practiced batting her eyelashes in the mirror the way she'd seen Franny do with Professor Hunter.

She spent two hours trying on every outfit in her closet before settling on an ochre-colored dress, washed-out denim jacket, and tattered Frye boots. A few minutes before nine, with one last glance in the mirror, she swung her guitar over her arm and set out to meet Franny.

"Whoa, girl! You look hot," Franny said as Reese approached the flagpole.

Reese thanked her. "You look pretty fab yourself." Franny wore a wine-colored, bell-sleeved top with skinny jeans tucked into black cowboy boots. She'd straightened her hair, which now flowed in a thick mane down her back. "I like your hair that way."

"It took, like, *forever* to blow it out," she said, emphasizing her frustration with expressive hand gestures.

As they started off toward town, Reese asked, "Who did you say is having this party?"

"Friends of mine. Of my brother's, actually. Well two of them. The third is from DC. They're upperclassmen, two juniors and a senior. I guess you can say they've adopted me. As a favor to my brother, they asked me to hang out with them one night the first week of classes. When they began playing, I started singing along. I guess they like my sound, because they've kept me around."

The smell of wood smoke filled the brisk autumn air as they strolled several blocks to Sycamore Street. For the first time since arriving on campus a month ago, Reese felt like a real college student.

Franny stopped in front of a two-story, white-framed house. Students swarmed the yard and front porch, and the Black Eyed Peas boomed through open windows. "Do you have a fake?"

Reese showed Franny the ID she'd purchased online over the summer. "I've never used it, though. Going to bars isn't my thing."

"This is a good one," Franny said, studying the Georgia

driver's license. "You don't want to lose it." She gave the card back to Reese. "This house gets raided at least once a week. Don't freak out if the police come. Just stick with me. I know the back way to campus."

Reese gulped. Her parents would be mad as hell if she got in trouble with the police.

"Come on. Follow me." Taking her by the hand, Franny led her up the porch steps. The house smelled of weed and stale beer as they made their way through the living room to the kitchen. When they exited the back door, Reese heard the band's muffled thumping coming from inside a nearby detached garage.

Franny pounded on the garage's side door, and a muscular mountain of a black man answered. When he saw Franny, he stepped out of the way to let them in.

"Noah, meet my friend Reese," Franny said in a voice loud enough to be heard over the band.

Noah waved at Reese and she waved back.

Franny whispered loudly in her ear, "The guys don't like to be disturbed while they're practicing. They pay Noah to keep everyone out."

Reese signified she understood with a thumbs-up. Franny grabbed two beers from a nearby cooler, handing one to Reese, and they went to stand in front of the band. Three guys with surfer-boy good looks—shoulder-length hair bleached and skin still golden from the summer sun—were jamming out to a Led Zeppelin song Reese recognized, but couldn't recall the title.

Franny yelled, "That's Pete on guitar with the baby face. Benny on bass with the bright-blue eyes. And Trey's the drop-dead gorgeous one on the drums. His real name is Walker Preston McDaniel the third, but they call him Trey, as in the French pronunciation of the number three but spelled T-r-e-y. He's the one from DC."

When the song ended, Pete moved to the edge of the

makeshift stage. "What say, Franny?" he asked with a gentle smile. "Is this the friend you were telling me about?"

Franny nodded and provided introductions.

Pete said, "Sing for us, Reese. Anything you're in the mood for?"

Reese thought about what Professor Hunter had said earlier. *I'd like to see you try some music from contemporary artists like Mariah Carey.* "How about *"Hello"* by Adele?" She'd won the talent competition her junior year in high school with this selection, but the disappointed faces on the band members told her she'd made the wrong choice.

To his credit and her relief, Pete did not complain. "Adele it is," he said, and offered her a hand onto the stage.

She found her way to the microphone and had only sung three lines of lyrics when Benny interrupted her. "No offense, babe, but I'm not feeling it. Do you have anything else for us?"

Panic gripped her chest, and her gaze shifted to Franny.

"Repeat your performance from class," Franny said with an encouraging nod.

Strumming a few chords, Reese turned around to face the band, saying Tina Turner's *"Proud Mary" opener,* "Every now and then, I kind of like to do something nice and easy."

The three guys hooped, and Benny hollered, "Now we're talking!"

Relaxing, she settled into her groove with the band. Near the end of her song, Franny jumped up on stage, and for the next hour, they rocked out.

Trey approached her afterward with an ice-cold beer. "That was fun," he said, clinking her bottle.

"A lot of fun," she agreed, taking a tentative sip of beer. Reese had never cared much for beer, but it tasted better coming from him.

He pointed his beer bottle at her. "You have a large voice for a little girl. Do you mind if I ask why you picked Adele to start?"

"I don't know. Doesn't everyone love Adele?"

His smile was both teasing and condescending. "No, Reese. Not everyone loves Adele. What's the real reason you picked it?"

"Professor Hunter suggested I try more contemporary music."

He slapped his thigh. "I was right. We've all heard the same thing from Hunter. Did he give you the Step-Outside-Your-Box speech?"

Reese laughed. "Pretty much, yeah."

"Don't get me wrong. I have great respect for Professor Hunter. And you should totally experiment in other genres. But, first and foremost, you should always remain true to yourself. Especially when you have an opportunity to sing to a new audience. You killed it up there tonight."

Except that I wasn't myself. I was impersonating Tina Turner.

He stood so close, the heat from his body made Reese feel lightheaded. Trey wasn't like the good-looking boys she'd known in high school. He was handsome in a manly way with a square face and eyes the color of the brandy her father liked to drink after meals on special occasions.

"I have higher aspirations than being a wedding singer," Reese said.

"Trust me, Reese. You have more soul than any wedding singer I've ever heard."

"My goal is to one day perform my own music." She'd never told anyone that before. Something about him made her feel she could trust him.

"Cool! Have you written any songs?"

"A whole notebook full of them," Reese said, holding her head a little higher.

"I'd like to hear them. Why don't you bring them with you the next time you come?"

Reese's heart skipped a beat at the thought of *next time*. More than anything, she wanted there to be a next time.

MAGGIE

*M*aggie spends her first three days in Richmond settling into her new home and familiarizing herself with the neighborhood. In the frigid predawn hours before the streets become congested with morning traffic, Maggie, dressed in layers of sports apparel with her hair in a single braid down her back and a pink fleece beanie on her head, jogs over to Franklin Street, down to the state capitol, and back up Main Street through Monroe Park.

After showering and dressing, she walks three blocks to the neighboring campus of VCU—Virginia Commonwealth University. Maggie has tried a few of the many coffee shops and quaint restaurants, but she prefers the no-frills homey feel of the Village Cafe. She spends her mornings and early afternoons in a window booth, sipping steaming mugs of coffee while researching local news stories on her laptop in preparation for her job interview with the local ABC affiliate at the end of the week.

Eric comes home late most nights. The scope of the outdoor shopping center project he's working on has grown, demanding more of his time than he originally anticipated. Maggie is proud of him for working so hard and has dinner waiting for him when he gets home, which sometimes isn't until nearly nine o'clock. He tells her about his day, and she talks on about her upcoming interview. They have multiple discussions about the types of cars she wants to test drive when they go shopping on Saturday.

By the time Friday rolls around, Maggie feels as ready as she'll ever be for her interview. She's confident she can at least improvise her way through any question asked of her. Because this job is important to her, she's still nervous and her hands shake as she fastens her hair into a low bun. Maggie prefers timeless clothing tailored from fine fabrics, which she purchases on sale at upscale designer boutiques. For her interview of a lifetime, she chooses a traditionally cut, charcoal-gray Armani pants suit and a cream-colored silk blouse with low-heeled black pumps. Seeing her professionally elegant reflection in the full-length mirror gives her a boost of confidence.

You've got this, she says, giving herself a thumbs-up.

Maggie has reminded Eric at least a dozen times that she needs a ride to the TV station. But when she comes downstairs for breakfast, instead of finding him at the breakfast table, she discovers a note in his tidy print beside the Keurig machine. `Sorry, Mags. Last minute trip to North Carolina. Uber to your interview, and I'll make it up to you when I get home tomorrow.`

Last minute? Eric warned her he would be making frequent trips to Charlotte to meet with his team of architects, but when exactly did he find out about it? He didn't mention the trip at dinner yesterday. Did he get a text message or email during the night?

She leans against the counter while she waits for her coffee to brew. *Focus, Maggie. You can't let this interfere with your performance. So what? He had to go to Charlotte on business. It's no big deal. Or is it?*

Removing her phone from her purse, she requests an Uber, connecting with one only five minutes away.

Al, a retired high school chemistry teacher, wants to chat.

Maggie thinks maybe he's had too much caffeine. She politely tells him she has an important job interview and buries her face in her notes.

Arriving at the station without a minute to spare, she gives her name to the receptionist, an attractive woman wearing a headset and tortoiseshell reading glasses. "I have an appointment with Raymond Clarke."

The receptionist's fingers dance across the keyboard. "Hmm. Your name is not on his calendar for today. Are you sure you have the right date?"

This interview is Maggie's big chance. There's no way she got the date wrong. "I'm positive. I have a job interview with him at nine o'clock. Maybe he forgot to put it on his calendar. We've been emailing back and forth for weeks about the news reporter position."

A sympathetic expression crossing her face, the woman shakes her head. "I'm sorry, ma'am, but that position has been filled."

Maggie's body temperature rises, and she imagines sweat soaking the armpits of her silk blouse. "There must be some mistake." She points at the phone on the woman's desk. "Call Mr. Clarke. He'll verify our appointment." Her voice is raised, but she doesn't care. The waiting room is empty.

Punching four numbers on her phone's keypad, the receptionist swivels around in her chair and carries on a conversation with her mouthpiece in a volume too low for Maggie to hear. When she finally spins back around, she gestures at the waiting room. "Mr. Clarke is in a meeting. If you don't mind waiting, he'll be free in a few minutes."

"I'll wait all day if necessary," Maggie says and takes the seat nearest the receptionist's desk.

Twenty-five minutes pass before the receptionist tells Maggie that Mr. Clarke is ready for her. Gesturing toward the elevator, she says, "Second floor. Take a left off the elevator. His office is at the end of the hall on the right."

"Thank you." Standing, Maggie smooths the wrinkles from her slacks and approaches the elevator.

When she enters his office, Raymond Clarke rises from his chair, but he doesn't come forward to greet her. He's in his fifties, fit and handsome, dark hair graying at the temples.

Maggie marches across the room and extends her hand to him. "It's nice to finally meet you, Mr. Clarke."

Clarke gives her hand a firm shake. "And you as well, Mrs. Jones. Although, I'm confused as to why you're here when you canceled our meeting for today."

The bottom falls out of her stomach, and she has to work hard to retain her composure. "I'm confused as well, Mr. Clarke. I never canceled our meeting. I've been looking forward to this interview."

Without offering her a seat, he sits down at his computer and begins typing. Seconds later, the printer beside him spits out a single sheet of paper. Back on his feet, he hands the paper to her. "This is a copy of the email you sent me at 11:07 Eastern Standard Time on Monday morning, withdrawing your application for the job."

Her mind races as she scans the email. At 11:07 Eastern Standard Time on Monday morning, she was on a plane traveling across the country. She spent much of that time studying the Richmond city and Virginia state travel guides she'd purchased. She may have dozed off for a while. But at no point during her flight did she sign into the airline's Wi-Fi and send an email to Raymond Clarke.

She smells a rat. *Eric! How does he even know my email password?*

She considers what to say. She can't very well tell him her husband canceled the interview because he doesn't want his wife to have a job that might put her life in danger. "I know what must have happened," she says, as though an explanation for the confusion has suddenly come to her. "You see, I was traveling on Monday, from Oregon to Virginia. I asked my husband to send several emails for me, one of them to you confirming our meeting for today. He must have somehow gotten confused. Believe me, Mr. Clarke, I'm extremely interested in this job."

Clarke doesn't miss a beat. "Unfortunately, the position has been filled. Too bad, too. With your professional good looks and impressive resume, you would've been the ideal candidate. I'll keep you in mind if anything else becomes available."

She sees through his lie, just as he'd seen through hers. He has no intention of keeping her in mind for anything. Her resume is headed for his shredder.

"Good day, Mrs. Jones." He sweeps his hand in the direction of the door, dismissing her.

She stares at the floor, avoiding eye contact with everyone she encounters in the hallway, the elevator, and the lobby. Despite the biting wind and subfreezing temperature, Maggie waits for her Uber outside the building. She isn't wearing a coat—she doesn't own one that complements her suit—and she's shivering, her teeth chattering, by the time Rebecca arrives twenty minutes later. If the stains on the upholstered seats and crumbs littering the floorboard of her minivan are any indication, Rebecca is a mother moonlighting as an Uber driver while her children are in school. She must sense Maggie's ill mood because she says nothing during the fifteen-minute drive back to Stork Alley. Maggie grips her phone as she taps on Eric's number. When he doesn't answer, she tries again. Over and over and over again.

At home, she takes her laptop to her bedroom and locks the door. She signs into her Gmail account where she finds the email in her trash folder, sent at 11:07 Eastern Standard Time on Monday morning, canceling the interview and Clarke's disappointed response to her.

She changes her password, signs out of Gmail, and accesses her online bank account. After their wedding, Maggie and Eric agreed to combine their separate accounts into one, and she's shocked to see the balance in that joint account is only $343.52. Why is the balance so low when Eric has plenty of money? Or so he says.

Eric also convinced Maggie to put her meager savings in his brokerage account for his wealth manager to invest.

"You'll get more return on your money than you would in your standard savings account," he said.

She readily agreed, trusting him with every dime she'd scrimped and saved after paying off her student loans. But she neglected to ask him how to access that money if she should ever need it. Stupid.

She taps her bank's customer service toll-free number into her phone and is informed by an automated voice that the current wait time for a representative is ten minutes. Putting the phone on speaker, she sets it on the bureau while she changes out of her suit into jeans and a turtleneck. The automated voice interrupts the elevator music to announce she has six more minutes to wait. Snatching up the phone, she goes to the window. The street below is deserted. It's too cold for anyone to be out on a day like today.

Maggie had such high hopes for the job. And now she has nothing. Not a single employment opportunity. At least not in the news industry. Not in Richmond. She now knows with absolute certainty, she can't trust her husband. If she turns to her family, she risks losing every ounce of respect she has for herself. She's an adult now. She created this mess, and she will have to find a way to get herself out of it.

When the customer service rep finally comes on the line, Maggie asks for confirmation of the balance in the account.

"Three hundred forty-three dollars and fifty-two cents," the woman says.

"That's what I thought," Maggie says. "Can you give me the balance on the other accounts listed in my husband's name?"

The representative says, "I'll need to speak with your husband before I can provide that information. Is he nearby?"

"No," Maggie snaps. "I can give you his social security number."

"I'm sorry, ma'am. I'll need his permission first."

Maggie ends the call without saying thank you or goodbye and hurls the phone across the room. It bounces off the wall onto the floor. She dives onto the bed, shimmies over the mattress, and snatches up the phone, relieved to see her screen protector prevented it from shattering.

She stuffs the phone in her back pocket, and for the rest of the morning and most of the afternoon, she slowly and methodically searches not only Eric's clothes but every drawer and cabinet in every room in the house. She finds not a single clue as to where Eric has stashed the money from the sale of her car.

When she finishes and Eric still hasn't returned her calls, she debates whether to leave him a message or send him a text. Deciding against either, she goes to the Village Cafe for happy hour and stays through dinner.

She already knows most of the breakfast and lunch staff by name. She's seen the freckle-faced ginger bartender, but she hasn't yet met him. He's distracted, filling a mug with draft beer for another customer, when he asks Maggie, "What's it gonna be?"

"A shot of tequila," Maggie says. "Please."

He comes to stand in front of her as he pours her tequila into a shot glass.

She kicks it back and slams the glass on the bar. "Another one, please."

The bartender replenishes her glass. "Bad day?"

Maggie can't even go there. "You have no idea."

She learns a lot about Greg. He's older than she originally thought, thirty-five in October, happily married with his first child on the way. But she tells him little about herself, only that she's originally from Oregon and recently moved to Richmond for her husband's new job.

Eric calls twice while she's at the bar, but she ignores both. By the time she leaves the cafe three hours, two glasses of pinot noir, and one bacon cheeseburger later, she has calmed down. On the walk home, she convinces herself that she's blowing everything out of proportion. *This kind of stuff only happens to women in movies.*

EVA

*F*ew customers venture into Claudia's Closet during Eva's first cold and lonely weeks without Annette. The shop's dingy interior depresses her. The white paint on the walls has long since yellowed and the oak floorboards are caked with grime. And she can't, for the life of her, comprehend Annette's method of organizational madness.

Why not do a complete overhaul? she says to herself while eating a container of yogurt for lunch one day in late January. And winter is the perfect time when the majority of her customers are either hibernating or vacationing in their second homes.

She pores herself into the project with more gusto than she's experienced for anything in a very long time. Pushing the circular racks of clothes to the center of the showroom, she paints the long side walls a soft french blue and covers the back one in a lattice wallpaper that's the same shade of blue and white. She waxes and buffs her hardwood floors, and then scatters about several Orientals from her attic at home—rugs Stuart inherited from his grandparents that don't fit any of the rooms in their house. She sorts her clothing inventory by weeding out items no one will ever buy and hanging the rest according to size on metal bars she mounts on the walls. On high-gloss white shelves above the hanging clothes, she displays hats on faceless wicker mannequin heads along with miscellaneous knickknacks for the home. Tiered racks housing their collection of shoes and boots line the baseboard, and metal stands showcasing belts and scarves occupy the back corners of the store. From the West End Antiques Mall, she purchases a pine armoire for folded clothes and an oak-and-glass display case for jewelry.

Getting rid of the clutter clears the cobwebs from her brain and the fresh interior lifts her spirits. Is it possible that, after ten years, she's finally ready to move on with her life?

During the evening hours, Eva continues her cleaning and purging spree at home. She starts in the living room by throwing out the artificial Christmas tree, ornaments and all. She reorganizes the books on the shelves, rearranges the furniture, and paints the dark wood paneling a soft cream color—a bold move Stuart would never have approved of.

On the fourth Saturday in February, Eva receives a surprise visit from her best childhood friend.

"It's so wonderful to see you," she says as she presses her cheek against Helena's. She's often wondered if their friendship would have survived if they hadn't grown apart in college. "How are Roger and the children?"

"Everyone's doing well. For the moment, anyway." Helena raises her hands, fingers crossed. "The girls are both living and working in Charlotte, and Roger retired last year from his job as corporate litigator. We just returned from a month in Italy. How about you?" She lowers her voice, even though they are alone in the shop. "Have you received any word about . . . um . . ."

"Reese? No. Nothing." Eva takes a step back to inspect her friend, thinking how the girl she once loved like a sister has transitioned into a stunning woman, a platinum blonde with wide blue eyes who carries herself with grace. "Look at you, Helena! You're positively elegant in faded denim and a navy pea coat.

Seeing you brings back so many memories of your mother. You're the spitting image of Claudia."

"The coat's Burberry, and it belonged to Mom," Helena says, and they both laugh.

"My fondest childhood memories are the times we spent playing dress-up in her closet. I owe her a lot."

"She was flattered you named your store after her. She loved you, you know?" Helena chuckles. "There were times when I thought she even loved you more than me."

Eva's heart swells. "Claudia was a source of strength for me when Mom was sick. I'll never forget her kindness. And I would never have gotten through my teenage years without her support. I was saddened by her death. I'm sorry I didn't get a chance to speak to you at the funeral. You were surrounded by your family and friends."

"I understand." Helena stares past her into the showroom. "I'm embarrassed I've never taken the time to stop in. Do you mind if I look around?"

Eva steps aside. "Please! Make yourself at home. Let me know if you have any questions."

She busies herself with rearranging stacks of jeans and sweaters in the armoire while keeping one eye on Helena. Circling the room, Helena fingers the fabric of a Hermès scarf, flips through a row of hanging clothes, and slips her right foot into a pair of Lucchese ostrich skin boots.

She looks up at Eva, her expression a mixture of awe and disbelief. "These are fabulous."

Eva grins. "Right? I wish they were my size."

Helena tugs on the left boot and admires the pair in the antique cheval mirror. "They fit perfectly. And they're in mint condition. I'll take them. In fact, I'm going to wear them home." She stuffs her driving shoes in her oversized black leather bag and walks to the front of the store to the new jewelry display case, which now doubles as a checkout counter. She hands her credit card to Eva. "I'm impressed with your business, Eva. Mom would be proud. Did she ever come in the shop?"

"A few times. Years ago. Before she got sick." Eva processes the sale and slides the credit card reader across the counter to Helena.

"Do you have any interest in buying some of the pieces in her wardrobe?"

Even though she'd buy every last piece if she had the money, Eva manages to appear only mildly interested as they discuss the details of Claudia's wardrobe. She recalls how Helena's mother traveled to Paris on shopping sprees at least once a year. She had impeccable style and the bank account that afforded her the best. The quality of her wardrobe has the potential to attract a whole new level of clientele to Claudia's Closet.

Helena enters her PIN number in the credit card reader. "Make me an offer, and I'll sell you the whole caboodle. Except for the pea coat. I've grown attached to it."

"Would you consider consignment? Claudia's wardrobe is extensive." Eva spreads her arms wide. "As you can see, my space is limited. I can't incorporate the entire *caboodle* at once. I would have to do it piecemeal."

"Maybe." Helena stares up at the ceiling as she considers her proposal. "My issue then becomes where to store the rest. I'm hoping to put Mom's house on the market in the coming weeks."

Eva's master bedroom springs to her mind. She'll have to clean out the closet, of course. But is she ready to get rid of Stuart's clothes? She thinks about it for a split second. For an opportunity like this, hell yes, she can get rid of Stuart's wardrobe.

Eva hands Helena her receipt for the boots. "I have an idea that might work. But it's been a long time since I last visited your mother's closet. It would help to see the scope of her collection." While she knows Claudia took meticulous care of her wardrobe,

Eva wants to make certain the pieces are in good condition before moving forward.

This appears to satisfy Helena, and as they walk together to the door, they discuss days and times to meet at Claudia's house to inspect the wardrobe. The women part with a hug, and Eva watches Helena make a dash to her white Range Rover. She turns away from the door and stands in front of the full-length mirror. She feels dowdy compared to Helena. Her pixie haircut has long since lost its shape and her black cashmere sweater has dime-size moth holes. Even though she has a closet full of timeless apparel, she can't remember the last time she wore anything but jeans. Long before Reese disappeared.

Eva has never been able to pinpoint the source of the profound sadness that has plagued her for the past twenty years. It started as postpartum depression after Reese was born and morphed into deep sorrow when her parents died in quick succession shortly thereafter. Then the housing market declined with the recession, and her husband, a residential contractor, began working long hours. Which left Eva alone much of the time with first a toddler and then an adolescent child. Eva hid her emotions from Stuart. He had enough on his plate with trying to make ends meet. With no one to turn to and no money for professional therapy, she began to take her anger and frustration out on her daughter. By that time, Reese had entered middle school. As if middle school wasn't already difficult enough for kids, Eva constantly criticized her daughter—imploring her to get better grades, be more athletic, make friends with the popular girls. Reese tried for a while, but when she couldn't please Eva— even a perfect child would not have pleased Eva in those days— she gave up. And that's when the battles began to rage.

Heavy snow flakes are falling when Eva leaves the shop at six o'clock that evening. The weather forecast is calling for snow, six to eight inches on Saturday night and into the day on Sunday. When she arrives home, with Claudia's wardrobe at the forefront of her mind, she climbs the stairs to the master bedroom. She opens the door but she doesn't cross the threshold. Stale air greets her and dust assaults her nose, bringing on a fit of sneezing. When the sneezing ends, she swipes her hand under her nose and ventures into the room.

In the days following the accident, Stuart's presence in their bedroom had been more than she could handle, and she'd moved down the hall to the guest room. But now, she experiences only pleasant memories of the years they'd spent here together. Eva tying Stuart's tuxedo tie before a New Year's Eve party. Nursing her newborn with Stuart curled up next to her. Reading the paper in bed on lazy Sunday mornings with Reese snuggled between them.

Standing at the foot of the bed, she considers the task at hand. Although the room isn't large, there appears to be ample room for her purposes. After she gives the room a thorough cleaning, she'll install two or three clothing racks to house the residual of Claudia's wardrobe. Opening the closet door, she grabs armfuls of Stuart's clothes—suits and slacks and dress shirts—and dumps them on the bed. Tomorrow, she will begin sorting them and loading them into the trunk of her car for Goodwill.

As best she can tell from her vantage point, the top shelf in the closet appears to be empty, but when she feels to make certain, her hand comes into contact with a hard rectangular object. Pulling the box off the shelf, she recognizes it as the safe for the handgun Stuart had purchased during the days following 9/11. Eva had always been scared of guns, but Stuart, convinced another terrorist attack was imminent, had insisted they needed to protect themselves.

She fingers the combination. "Something easy to remember," Stuart had suggested.

Setting the numbers to her birth date and month, she opens the box and removes the pistol. Stuart had enrolled them in a gun safety course. Not only had they enjoyed the classes, they became pretty good shots.

While she doesn't have much use for the gun now, she decides to keep it just in case. She returns the gun to its safe and slides it back onto the shelf.

MAGGIE

*T*he argument over the canceled interview marks the beginning of the downhill spiral in Maggie and Eric's relationship. After days of arguing, he finally admits to sending the email, canceling Maggie's interview with her potential employer.

"Why would you do that?" Maggie asks, balled fists at her side, face blood red with anger. She's standing in front of the fireplace, the school of fish above her head. She feels like the yellow fish, as though she's swimming backward against a strong current. Moving to Virginia was a mistake. She has no car. No job. No friends. Only a controlling bastard for a husband.

"You already know why, Maggie. I don't want my wife chasing after two-bit news stories."

"And what about my car? You sold it without my permission, and now I have nothing to drive."

"We'll buy you a car when the time is right."

She snorts. "When *you* deem the time is right."

His hand shoots up, silencing her. "The interview is canceled, the car sold. This discussion is closed. Let's move on."

And move on, they do, in silence. For the next five days, they speak not one word to each other. On Friday of the following week, he brings home an expensive bottle of red wine and a bouquet of white orchids. "I hate fighting with you."

"I don't like it either." More than the fighting, she hates living in a hostile environment. Taking the orchids and wine from him, she says, "I brought home some Brunswick stew from the grocery. Let's build a fire and eat in the living room."

"I like the sound of that," he says, nodding his approval.

She waits until after dinner to broach the other subject he's never adequately addressed despite her constant hounding. "You keep saying for me not to worry about money. But, how can I do that when there's never more than three hundred dollars in our joint account?"

They are camped out on the sofa, wine glasses in hand and blankets covering their legs, a warm fire crackling in front of them.

"That account is for household expenses," he says, sipping his wine. "You should never need more than three hundred dollars for groceries unless we're hosting an elaborate dinner party."

"What if I want to buy something?" Maggie asks. "Like an airline ticket to see my family?"

His nostrils flare but his voice remains even when he says, "Why would you do that when you've only been in Virginia six weeks? Use your credit card if you want to have your hair done or buy a pretty dress. But don't go crazy. I pay off the balance every month."

In other words, you're trying to keep me on a tight leash, she thinks. "What about our bills? Where does that money come from?"

"A totally separate account. I'm a partner in this development deal, honey. I'm not getting a regular paycheck. But once the shopping center is complete, the money will start rolling in. In the meantime, we're living off my portfolio. It's nothing for you to worry about. Many of the stocks in my portfolio pay dividends. I transfer funds from my portfolio to the account I use to pay bills on an as-needed basis."

Under the blanket, she runs her socked foot over the top of his bare one. "You're so busy, why don't you let me pay the bills?"

He casts her a suspicious sideways glance. "That's very thoughtful of you, sweetheart. But I've got it under control. Everything is set up on automatic withdrawal."

With no money of her own, and the *pocket change* from the sale of her car long gone, Maggie works harder to find a job. She applies for positions she's overqualified for at establishments within walking distance from her home. She's not surprised when she gets turned down for all of them.

She rides city buses whenever necessary, but she needs wheels in order to get the type of job she wants. It's futile to continue harassing Eric about buying her a car. Her lack of transportation is yet another way for him to keep her on a short leash.

She misses her family terribly, and they miss her equally as much. At least one of them calls nearly every day. When they pepper her with questions about her new life, she feeds them a string of lies.

"I've gotten plenty of job offers, Dad. I'm holding out for the right one."

"Sure, Mom! I'm making friends. In fact, Eric and I are having neighbors over for the Super Bowl on Sunday."

To each of her overprotective brothers, she says some version of, "You'd love it here. You should come for a visit." But she prays they don't. She already has enough male testosterone in her home.

On the last Thursday of February, Maggie's in the living room, sipping a glass of red wine and reading by the fire, when Eric arrives home from work around seven thirty—a bit early for him considering the late hours he typically keeps. He gives her a perfunctory kiss. "How was your day?"

A handful of unpleasant responses come to mind, but she decides it is best to say nothing. Earmarking the page, she closes the paperback and untucks her legs, sitting up straight in the chair.

"Look what I bought for the baby," he says, dropping a Target bag in her lap.

She sweeps the bag off her lap to the floor. "There isn't any baby, Eric."

"There will be soon." He takes off his coat and tosses it onto the sofa. "What's for dinner?" He raises his hand, palm out. "Don't tell me. We're having chicken tacos again."

"Bingo! How'd you guess?"

"It was easy considering your repertoire of dinners is limited to four," he says, holding up four fingers. "Spaghetti, although Ragu and noodles isn't my idea of an Italian dinner. Caesar salad with rotisserie chicken, although I'm not sure that falls into the home-cooked category since you buy the bagged salad and the already-cooked chicken at the grocery store. And chicken tacos, which counts as two separate dinners depending on whether we have the meat in shells or on top of lettuce. Which is it tonight, Mags? Tacos with shells or taco salads?"

"We could always go out, you know? I've been reading Yelp reviews. I made a list of some of the places we should try. And since you were away on another business trip to Charlotte on Valentine's Day, you still owe me a Valentine's dinner."

"I'm not in the mood tonight."

She looks away, staring into the fire. "You're never in the mood. We used to eat out all the time in Portland. But we haven't been out once since we moved here."

"We will soon. I promise." Exhaling, he lowers himself to the arm of her chair. "I'm under a lot of pressure right now. I have to think fast on my feet all day, and I look forward to spending a quiet evening with my wife in our new home."

She experiences a stab of guilt. She's needling him like a spoiled housewife. But she can't help herself. Nothing is as he promised it would be when he convinced her to move to Virginia. "I get that, Eric. And I'm busy with my job search. We could always order takeout."

"How about you cook a real meal for a change instead of reading a book and drinking wine?" His eyes travel to her glass. "That's bad for the baby. You really should be taking better care of yourself."

She jumps to her feet. "For the hundred millionth time, there is no baby." She picks up her glass, guzzles the rest of her wine, and leaves the room.

She's struggling to uncork another bottle when he enters the kitchen and takes the wine from her, setting it on the counter. "I hate arguing with you. This should be a happy time for us." He cups her cheek, running his thumb across her lower lip. "I realize there's no baby yet. I saw the tampon wrapper in the bathroom trash can this morning. What say you stop taking the pill, and we try to make one?"

"So, you're going through our trash now?" She has no intention of going off birth control until she's good and ready. "Never mind. Let's just eat, okay?"

She moves to the stove, heats up the taco meat, and places their plates on the table. When they're seated across from each other, pointing her fork at her plate, she says, "What problem do you have with this meal? I consider it healthy—ground chicken, lettuce, tomatoes, avocado, corn, and tri-colored tortilla strips."

"It's not that I mind chicken tacos, Mags. I just don't want to eat them every night."

The awkward silence that settles between them is broken only by the loud crunching of his tortilla chips. They're almost finished eating when he says, "By the way, I have to go to Charlotte again for the weekend. I'll be home late Sunday."

Maggie looks up from her plate. "Again? That's the third time this month."

Eric sets his fork down and wipes his mouth. "We're in the crucial planning stages of this project, babe. We're working nights and weekends to get this thing up and running."

Maggie gets up from the table and dumps her half-eaten salad in the trash. "I understand, Eric. It's just that I'm bored out of my mind without a job. I want to work. I *need* to work."

He balls up his napkin and tosses it in his plate. "You'll have plenty to do once the baby comes. But if you're determined to get a job, can't you do better than Starbucks?"

She spins around to face him. "How did you know about Starbucks? I only submitted my application this afternoon." It dawns on her that she never told him about the spa attendant job or the museum gift shop cashier position either, yet somehow he knew about both. *And you call yourself an investigative journalist? You're losing your touch, Maggie.* "Are you spying on me, Eric?"

"Do you know how paranoid you sound right now?" he says with a nervous chuckle.

Am I paranoid? Or has the bastard put monitoring software on my electronic devices?

He continues, "Regardless of how I knew, being a barista is beneath you."

"No, it's not, Eric. It's a way for me to earn money and meet new people while I search for a position that will further my career." She slams the dishwasher closed. "I'm going to bed."

She's quivering with anger as she climbs the stairs to her room. But it's fear she experiences when she opens the drawer of her bedside table and discovers her birth control pills are missing —the three-month supply she brought with her from Oregon to hold her over until she could establish herself with a new doctor. She's positive they were in that drawer yesterday. With the advent of her period, she'd double-checked to make certain of it.

She storms out of the room, but she makes it only halfway down the stairs before coming to an abrupt halt. Her husband has taken charge of every aspect of her life. The stakes in this cat and mouse game they're playing just got a lot higher. With shoulders slumped, she retraces her steps to her room. Since dragging her family into her problems isn't an option, for the time being and until she can figure a way out, she'll keep her wits about her and play her cards close to her chest.

Eric has already left for Charlotte by the time Maggie wakes on Friday morning.

Please, let me have imagined it. She kicks off the covers and swings her feet over the side of the bed. *Please let my pills be here.* She opens the nightstand drawer, but instead of her birth control pills, she finds a note from Eric. I'm sorry, Maggie. Taking the pills will make the decision to have a baby easier for you. You'll thank me once you're holding our newborn in your arms.

Her eyes dart around the room. How did he know she discovered the missing pills? Or is she jumping to conclusions? Maybe it's a coincidence that he left the note on the same night she found the pills missing. No. He's definitely watching her. She can feel his eyes on her. Is there a nanny cam hidden somewhere? In the lampshade? On the frame of the mirror hanging above the oak bureau? If he's spying on her with hidden cameras, there's a good chance he's having her followed as well.

Be cool. Act normal.

Changing out of her pajamas into running attire, she slips a twenty-dollar bill and her driver's license inside her sports bra, pulls a red cable-knit beanie over her head, and exits the house, purposefully leaving her phone on the bathroom counter.

She walks at a brisk pace down to the end of the street and over four blocks to the Village Cafe. The green leather upholstered barstools are all occupied with patrons enjoying breakfast while watching the morning news on the TVs mounted from the ceiling. Behind the bar, instead of pouring bourbon, Greg is moving from customer to customer, refilling their coffee mugs.

Maggie goes to the corner at the end of the black marble bar. "What're you doing here so early?"

"Angie called in sick. Coffee?" he asks, his pot hovering over a white ceramic mug on the counter.

"No, but thanks. Can I borrow your phone for a sec? I left mine at home by accident and I need to look up an address."

"Sure," he says, and slides his phone across the bar.

She conducts her internet search, deletes the browser tab, and hands him back the phone. "Thanks, Greg. I may see you later today."

Maggie heads toward the restrooms, but when she's sure no one is watching, she ducks into the kitchen and out the back door. She tugs the stocking cap off her head, zipping it in the pocket of her hoodie. Casting frequent glances behind her, she takes off toward Grove Avenue.

She jogs two miles to Planned Parenthood where, promising to come back in two weeks for a physical, she convinces a physician's assistant to give her a sample packet of pills. As she walks home, her fingers and her toes throbbing from the cold, she thinks about Liza, a friend at the news station in Oregon where Maggie had formerly worked. No one in the newsroom could comprehend why Liza refused to leave her abusive husband.

"You don't just walk out on a violent man," Liza had said to them.

Eric, although controlling and manipulative, has never given Maggie reason to think he's violent. She vows to be a model wife, to trick Eric into thinking she's on board with starting a family while she formulates an escape plan.

On Saturday, after lugging three bags of healthy food home from Kroger, under the guise of dusting and vacuuming, she identifies the hidden cameras in each of the rooms. The stuffed bear's eye in the nursery. The smoke detector in their bedroom. The black dot above the twelve on the wall clock in the kitchen. With cameras monitoring her every move, Eric will know if she tries to leave. Besides, the balance of $215.36 in their joint account as of yesterday wouldn't get her very far.

For the rest of the afternoon, she researches healthy recipes and makes an easy crock pot chicken and rice soup. She changes into her pajamas early and stands at her bedroom window as the first snowflakes fall to the ground and accumulate on grassy surfaces. Her neighbors are nestled inside their cozy homes with wood smoke billowing from their chimneys. She imagines them wrapped in blankets, eating popcorn and watching movies in front of roaring fires. Although she's waved at a few of them on the street, she hasn't met any of them yet. She hopes that will change when the days grow longer and the weather warmer.

Two houses down on the same side of the street lives a young family. Maggie feels for the harried-looking mother who's constantly shepherding her bundled-up four little children in and out of her Suburban.

Diagonally across to her left are the middle-aged gay cowboys. They wear boots and cowboy hats and throw rocking parties nearly every weekend night. Maggie wants to be on their guest list. Their house is quiet tonight, though, she notices with mild concern.

The neighbor who interests her the most resides in the house directly across the street. She leaves the house a few minutes before ten every morning and returns home just after six in the evenings. She never has any visitors, and even from afar, Maggie senses her aura of sadness. The woman is keeping a secret, and Maggie wants to know what it is.

EVA

*E*va takes a break from sorting Stuart's clothes to check on the progress of the snowstorm. Even though she hasn't been in the master bedroom in years, standing at the window and watching the world go by feels so familiar. She imagines Stuart lying in bed reading one of his legal thrillers.

From the window, she can see the snow has stopped and the sun has come out just as the local weather forecasters predicted. She watches her new neighbor across the street shovel her sidewalk. Every few feet, the young woman sheds a layer of clothing —hat, scarf, coat.

Why not invite the new neighbor in for hot chocolate?

Hurrying down the stairs, Eva steps into her Hunter boots and slips on her coat on the way out the door. As she's trudging across the street in the snow, she calls out, "You're wasting your time. We're supposed to get six more inches of snow this afternoon."

The young woman looks up from her work and a smile spreads across her rosy lips to her dimpled cheeks. As Eva gets closer, she can see that her new neighbor is more than pretty. She's movie-star gorgeous.

Tilting her head back, the woman stares up at the clear blue sky. "I heard that on the news, but I wasn't sure whether to believe it. Not with the sun out."

"The storm is redeveloping as a nor'easter, which is not uncommon around here. The forecasters are predicting we'll get dumped on this afternoon and evening."

"Oh well." She stabs her shovel into the snow. "I just wasted an hour of my not-so-valuable time." She extends her gloved hand. "I'm Maggie Jones."

Eva gives her a firm shake. "And I'm Eva Carpenter. I was just getting ready to have some hot chocolate. Would you care to join me?"

Uncertainty crosses Maggie's face and she glances back at her house. "I don't know. I have some chores I need to finish."

"Please. I'd love the company. I've been cleaning out closets, and I could use a little pick-me-up." When Maggie hesitates, Eva tempts her with the Godiva cocoa a customer gave her for Christmas.

Maggie's face lights up. "In that case, how can I say no?"

They cross the street and enter the house, leaving their snow-crusted boots and outerwear at the door. Eva leads her guest to the kitchen, and as she's measuring two cups of milk into a pan on the stove, Maggie says, "I'm grateful for the company, as well. My husband is in Charlotte on business this weekend."

"And what does he do?"

"He's in real estate. He's part of a group developing the outdoor shopping complex in Ashland."

Eva stirs the milk to keep it from burning. "I read about that in the newspaper. My husband was a residential builder."

Maggie's doe-brown eyes warm with concern. "Was?"

For the first time in a long time, Eva chokes up at the mention of her husband. She nods, and when she finds her voice again, she explains, "He was killed in a car accident."

"I'm so sorry," Maggie says, her tone genuine.

Eva stirs in two tablespoons of cocoa. When the cocoa dissolves, she fills two mugs, hands one to Maggie, and shows her to the living room. Maggie makes herself comfortable on the sofa in front of the window while Eva settles into her usual spot in Stuart's leather recliner.

Maggie blows on her hot chocolate before taking a tentative sip. "This is seriously good. Do you know where your customer bought the Godiva?"

"There's a chocolate shop up the street from my boutique. I don't know if that's where she got it, but I'm sure they probably sell it."

Maggie sips again. "What kind of boutique do you own?"

"Women's vintage clothing."

"Cool! I'd like to hear about it." Maggie relaxes against the cushions. "I prefer classically tailored clothes, but I've never shopped for vintage."

Clouds roll in while they talk about Claudia's Closet and Maggie's family in Oregon. By the time they've finished their cocoa, it's snowing heavily. Eva goes to the window, pressing her face against the glass. "This is typical for Virginia. We've had very little snow this winter, and now, when everyone's ready for spring, we get the worst storm of the year. Let's see if we can get an update." Aiming the remote at the TV, she enters the channel for the local network. Correspondents bundled in hats, coats, and scarves broadcast in nearly whiteout conditions from various locations in Richmond and along the I-95 corridor.

"Doesn't look like my husband will be coming home today," Maggie says.

Eva finds it strange for a newlywed to sound so happy about her husband's homecoming being delayed. "Maybe you should you try and call him."

"I'll call him later. I left my phone at home, anyway."

Eva clicks off the TV. "In that case, can I offer you some more cocoa? Or, how about a glass of wine? I have a nice bottle of red, another Christmas gift, this one from a neighbor. I know it's early for cocktails, but it seems festive with the storm."

Maggie jumps at the offer. "Let's have wine! I can't think of a nicer way to spend a snowy afternoon than getting better acquainted with a new friend."

Eva goes to the kitchen and comes back with a tray bearing a bottle of pinot noir, two stemless glasses, and a plate with a chunk of Gouda cheese and a bunch of red grapes. She sits down next to Maggie on the sofa and fills the glasses with wine.

"Do you mind if I ask how old you are?"

"I'll be twenty-nine in June," Maggie says.

"That's what I thought. You're the same age as my daughter."

Maggie clinks her glass against Eva's. "Awesome! As it happens, I'm in the market for new friends. Does she live in Richmond?"

"Not that I know of. I'm not sure where she lives. Or if she's even alive."

Covering her mouth with her hand, Maggie says between her fingers, "I'm so sorry."

"She's been missing for nearly a decade." Eva pops a grape into her mouth. "But it's a long story and there's no reason to get into all that."

Maggie taps her lightly on the arm. "No, really. I'd like to hear it. I'm an investigative journalist. I have an inquiring mind."

"Oh. I see." Eva isn't sure if this is good news or bad.

Maggie appears disappointed. "I understand if you don't want to talk about it."

"I don't mind." They sit in silence for a moment, sipping wine, while Eva collects her thoughts. "Nine years ago this past December, my husband drove to Ohio to pick my daughter up from her first semester at Erie State College. That was the year of the H1N1 flu epidemic, and Stuart was determined not to subject Reese to germs on an airplane."

"The swine flu," Maggie says. "I remember it well. When one

of my brothers caught it, my mother made the rest of the family wear masks."

"The epidemic was serious. Many people died." A faraway look settles on Eva's face. It's been a long time since she's talked about the accident with someone other than Annette. "I begged Stuart to take my car. But snow was in the forecast, and he thought his beat-up old Land Cruiser was a better choice. He left here on Friday, December eighteenth. Reese was one of the unfortunate students to have an exam scheduled for the last slot on the last day. He took her out to dinner that night and called me from his hotel afterward. He reported that they were on schedule to leave early the following morning in order to make it home in time for the Richmond Ballet's matinee performance of *The Nutcracker*. We hadn't seen her since drop-off day in August and had planned a big homecoming for her. I'd booked a reservation for an early dinner at Lemaire at the Jefferson Hotel for afterward. But Stuart was involved in an accident on the way home the next day and was killed on impact. Reese was nowhere in sight when first responders arrived. No one has seen or heard from her since."

Maggie closes her eyes, as if letting this information sink in. "Do you know for certain she was in the car with him at the time of the accident?"

"Footage from a surveillance camera shows him picking her up outside her door and them leaving campus together an hour earlier." Feeling the effects of the wine, Eva sets her glass on the coffee table. "I need some water. Would you like some?"

"No thanks. I'm fine with wine." Maggie raises her glass, showing she has plenty left.

At the sink in the kitchen, as she gulps down a large glass of tap water, Eva stares out the window at a pair of cardinals, male and female, seeking shelter from the storm in the cavity of a massive holly bush. Her gut aches with longing for Stuart. How would he have coped with their daughter's disappearance if he'd survived?

Eva refills her glass and rejoins her guest on the sofa. Maggie has one socked foot tucked under the opposite leg and she's sipping wine, seemingly lost in thought.

"Do you have any idea what caused the accident?" Maggie asks.

"The Land Cruiser, an early nineties model with no airbags, hit a patch of black ice, spun out of control, and crashed into the guardrail on the passenger side. Stuart wasn't wearing his seat belt. He was bad about that. And he was speeding, another bad habit. He was killed on impact. It happened less than an hour away from campus, near the Cuyahoga Valley National Park."

"Oh my God!" Maggie sips up straight, moving to the edge of her seat. "What about DNA evidence?"

"Traces of Reese's DNA was found on the seat, dashboard, and door. But that didn't mean anything. She rode with him to the restaurant the night before, and we know she left campus with him that morning. Every last drop of blood in the car belonged to Stuart."

Maggie leans over, propping her elbows on her knees, her wine glass cupped in her hands. Her eyes are bright, her face alive, as the questions fall from her lips. But Eva anticipates every one of them. She's answered them many times before.

"Were there any footprints?"

"Any footprints would've been covered in snow by the time the first responders arrived."

"Did your daughter have a cell phone?"

"Of course. But the police were unable to track it. Phone records showed the last text came in at 9:05 p.m. the previous night from her roommate asking Reese to check if she'd left her flat iron at school."

"Was there any luggage that didn't belong to your husband?"

Eva shakes her head. "Only his one duffle bag."

"And you've considered the possibility of amnesia?"

"Amnesia was a possibility, not a probability. Amnesia would've meant trauma to the head, which would've meant the likelihood of a concussion. At the bare minimum, she would've been confused and disoriented. The area was heavily wooded. When I got word of the accident, I drove to Ohio and helped organize search parties. We combed the area for days, but Reese had simply vanished. While the accident made national headline news, it got lost in the coverage of the blizzard that hit the East Coast that weekend. They called the storm Snowpocalypse."

Maggie pours more wine into her glass. "I can't even begin to imagine what you went through."

When a gust of wind shakes the house, they shift positions so they can see out of the window behind them. The world outside is white. "I'm sorry, Maggie. I've been going on about my husband's accident when your husband is caught in the middle of this storm."

"I'm sure he didn't leave Charlotte in this weather. He's probably working through the storm." Maggie's tone sounds more angry than sympathetic. "Tell me more about Reese."

Eva goes to the bookshelves and retrieves a leather-bound album. "As my only child, Reese's life was very well documented. This album is from her high school years." Eva hands Maggie the album, and they settle back against the cushions.

"She's so pretty," Maggie says thumbing through the pages.

Eva smiles. "Reese marched to her own beat. Correction—she marches to her own beat. I never know what verb tense to use when I'm talking about her. She's a musician—singer, songwriter, talented guitar player. But she's a loner. At least she was back then. She always wore headphones, whether to tune in the music or tune out everyone around her."

Maggie closes the album and hands it back to Eva. "This might seem strange to you, but I'd like to see her room. Would you mind showing it to me?"

"Not at all." They walk together up the stairs. Maggie pauses in the doorway of the master bedroom, gazing at the clothes piled high on the bed. "It's taken me ten years to get up the courage to go through Stuart's things."

They continue down the hall to Reese's room. Maggie marvels at the posters that cover nearly every square inch of wall space. Diana Ross. Stevie Wonder. Ray Charles. All the R&B greats.

"She has good taste in music," Maggie says.

"And those are the posters she left behind. She took twice as many with her to school. I haven't touched a thing in here. In case she ever comes home."

Maggie fingers the ribbon of one of the gifts stacked in the middle of Reese's Pottery Barn storage bed.

"I kept the Christmas tree decorated for her until a few weeks ago. It was artificial, of course. But I can't bring myself to give away her presents."

"How do you live with the not knowing? You must be on pins and needles all the time."

"Some days are easier than others."

They leave the room and head back downstairs. At the front door, Maggie says, "I should be going."

Eva doesn't argue with her. After talking about Reese, she needs some time to herself.

Maggie pulls on her boots, slips on her coat, and gives Eva a hug. "Your story has touched me deeply. I appreciate you sharing it with me. If there is ever anything I can do for you, please let me know."

"Talking about it isn't easy, but you're a good listener. Thank you for that."

REESE

Ten Years Ago

*C*ontrary to what her mother believed, Reese and Shannon were not best friends. They weren't even friends. Shannon's mother, who was divorced and hip and insisted Reese call her Paula, paid Reese to babysit Shannon's younger sister, Marie, while she worked as a bartender in an area of downtown Richmond known as Shockoe Slip. Why wasn't Shannon watching her little sister? Because she was always out partying, doing all the things Reese's mother accused Reese of—drinking, doing drugs, and having sex.

Reese had never been drunk or used drugs, and she'd arrived at college a virgin. She also didn't have many friends, certainly not one she considered a bestie. For that reason, she proceeded with caution into her new friendship with Franny. While Reese shared little about herself, Franny held nothing back. She told Reese in great detail about the boys she hooked up with at parties. And, while it was clear how much she worshiped her older brother, Will, she talked incessantly about her awful parents. Compared to her own, Reese didn't think her parents sounded awful at all.

As the days grew shorter, Reese's feelings for Trey intensified. Because she knew she didn't stand a chance with him—the prettiest girls on campus fell all over him, and he hooked up with a different one nearly every night—Reese resigned herself to being his protégé. After jam sessions, Trey offered feedback on the songs she was writing. His favorite was "True to Me," a song about a girl whose feelings for a guy take her on a journey of self-discovery. Ironically, she'd written the lyrics with him in mind, although she certainly didn't tell him that. Trey's faith in her talents as a musician increased her confidence every day.

Mid-October, when one of the fraternities booked their band for a Halloween party, Pete pulled Reese to the side one night after a jam session and asked her to take the lead.

"I'm flattered," Reese said. "But what about Franny? We've been splitting time at the microphone."

"Franny agrees you have the better vocals." Pete took a swig of his beer. "We need a name for our band. Do you have any suggestions?"

College State of Mind popped into her mind.

Pete repeated the name. "College State of Mind. I love it." He kissed her on the forehead. "You're a genius with words."

Reese's heart swelled with pride. She was more certain than ever that songwriting was her future.

That night, on the way back to campus, Reese apologized to Franny for having been chosen for the lead.

"Don't sweat it," Franny said, looping her arm through Reese's. "You're the better singer." A sheepish grin spread across her lips. "I can't be part of the band, anyway. I have a date to the party."

Most of the members of this particular fraternity were good-looking athletes from wealthy families.

Reese offered her a high five. "You go, girl. Who's the lucky guy?"

"His name is Rex. He's a junior." Franny let out a defeated sigh. "The problem is the costume. I hate dressing up."

"You're creative. I'm sure you'll come up with something."

Reese despised costume parties as well and was relieved when the band decided against dressing up for their performance.

The band room in the frat house, the largest of the brick mansion fraternity houses, was packed when College State of Mind took the stage at nine o'clock on Halloween night, which happened to fall on Saturday that year. Fighting off the jitters, Reese stood at the microphone and addressed the sea of vampires, Spidermen, and princesses. "Good evening, ghosts and goblins. Are you ready to party?"

The students responded with screams and shouts.

She spotted Franny near the front of the stage, looking hot in a pink Jeannie costume with bare toned midriff. Judging from the way her date was staring at her, he thought so as well. Cupping her hands around her mouth, Franny called out, "You got this, girl."

Reese had chosen a flowy black tunic to go with her faded jeans and boots. She'd strapped one of Pete's castoff electric guitars around her neck and wore a black felt fedora she'd snagged from her mother's shop over her honey-colored hair. The crowd went wild when she sang the first lyrics of "Witchy Woman," and for the next three sets, they rocked the house.

Students rushed the stage to congratulate them as they were breaking down their equipment. Keith Price—fraternity president, lacrosse team captain, and her roommate's boyfriend—wrapped his arms around Reese, lifting her off the stage. "You were sooo good," he said, setting her back down. "You've got real talent."

Out of the corner of her eye, she caught a glimpse of Mary Beth staring daggers at Reese with her emerald eyes.

"I hope that means you'll invite us back sometime," Reese said.

"We'd love for you to play for our formal," Keith said. "It's the first weekend in December."

Mary Beth stepped closer and tugged on his elbow. "You should talk to your social chairman first. He's probably already booked a more popular band. It's your *formal* after all."

Keith cut his eyes at his girlfriend. "I'm the president, Mary Beth. I know for a fact he hasn't booked a band yet. Besides, not everything's a popularity contest."

Amen to that, Reese thought.

As Mary Beth's popularity amongst the student body had grown, so had her ego, and she'd become increasingly bitchier toward Reese in recent weeks.

Reese angled her body away from Mary Beth. "I'm pretty sure we're free that weekend, Keith. But you should check with Pete to be certain."

Trey appeared at her side. "I'm leaving. Come back to the house with me." Taking her by the hand, he led her through the crowd to the french doors at the back of the band room. With hands still clasped and heads lowered against the cold, they darted across the green, stopping to catch their breath when they reached the flagpole. Removing her hand from his, he placed a round blue pill in her palm.

Reese stared down at the pill. "What's this?"

"Your bonus for a job well done."

"I'm not into drugs, Trey." Reese's newfound social life with the band had opened up a world of opportunity for partying. But Reese refrained from using drugs and limited her alcohol consumption to an occasional beer. She didn't consider herself a goody-goody. She just didn't want to turn out like her mother.

"But it's ecstasy. No one turns down ecstasy. Come on. Live a little. You'll love it. I promise you'll have fun." Pulling a can of beer from his coat pocket, he popped the top and handed it to her. "Be a good girl and take your medicine."

She would've said no to anyone else. But Trey's sexy smile and golden eyes melted her resolve. The night was magical. Her stellar performance and a chance to be with the boy of her dreams. Besides, it was Halloween, a time to take risks if ever there was one. She popped the pill into her mouth and chased it down with a swig of beer.

"Thatta girl."

When she shivered, he took her hand again and they took off running. They heard the music from the party before they turned the corner onto Sycamore Street. The house was already crawling with the usual groupies, their Halloween costumes now in varying degrees of ruin. As Reese and Trey made their way through the fog of cigarette and weed smoke, they received back slaps and congratulations on the night's performance. In the living room, Trey jumped onto the coffee table, pulling Reese up with him, and for the remainder of the party, he never left her side.

It was nearly two in the morning when the police showed up. Trey shouted above the music. "Pete can handle this. Come with me."

She followed him through the house to the kitchen, out the back door, and across the small lawn. But instead of entering the garage, Trey went behind it. Withdrawing a set of keys from his pocket, he unlocked a door and led her up a flight of stairs to a room with a sofa, two chairs, and a small refrigerator.

Wrapping his arms around her, Trey pinned Reese against the wall. She'd had a boyfriend once, for about a week during her freshman year in high school. She remembered the unpleasant kisses, him crushing his mouth against hers and ramming his tongue down her throat. But Trey's lips were soft on hers, his tongue gentle and probing. His hands were all over her, peeling off her clothes and caressing her naked body. Her body ached for more. She was desperate to feel him inside her. They collapsed on the sofa together, and when he entered her, she felt no pain, only desire. To her disappointment, he came within seconds, and when it was over, he lay on top of her with his face pressed into the folds of her neck. After a minute, his breathing deepened, and she realized he was passed out cold.

Rolling out from beneath him, she gathered her clothes and retreated to the tiny bathroom. She cleaned herself up as best she could with the few sheets of toilet paper left on the roll. Her makeup was smeared, and when she looked at her reflection in the mirror, she saw her mother. She'd done drugs and given away her virginity all in the same night. She was no better than Eva.

Reese didn't see Trey again for three excruciatingly long days. When they met for practice on Tuesday night, he gave her a buddy pat on her back, acting as though nothing had happened between them. "Great job on Saturday night. The crowd really loved you."

Did he not remember what happened in the room above the garage? Did he not realize he'd taken her virginity?

Word of their success at the Halloween party spread throughout the student body. Not only did Pete received requests for gigs for every weekend until Thanksgiving, Reese found herself the center of attention. She was invited to parties and asked out on dates. But Reese turned them all down. Their interest in her wasn't genuine. They didn't want her friendship. They merely wanted to share her moment in the spotlight.

On the flip side, her friendship with Franny deepened. Franny was heartbroken when Rex dumped her. Not that they were ever officially dating. "I thought we had something special," Franny cried to Reese one night. "I even had sex with him. I never have sex with a guy on the first date."

Reese knew that to be untrue. Franny had often confessed to having sex with guys she'd met for the first time at a party. While she listened to Franny's endless blabber about Rex, Reese never once mentioned what had happened with Trey.

The third week in November, Pete received an invitation for College State of Mind to play at a friend's deb party in Philadelphia the Saturday after Thanksgiving.

"Sounds sketchy to me, dude," Benny said. "Isn't it a little late to be looking for a band for a debutante party?"

"Yeah!" Pete crumpled up a beer can and threw it at him. "Kate got screwed. She just found out her original band is double-booked for the same date. But her loss is our gain. This could be our big chance. We'll get to play in front of an audience of well-connected parents. One of them may very well have a friend in the entertainment business. We need to make this happen. Franny and Benny, are you guys in town for Thanksgiving?"

Franny and Benny nodded in unison.

When Trey volunteered to drive up from DC on Friday, Franny begged Reese to go home with her for Thanksgiving. "We'll have a blast. I can't wait for you to meet Will. You're gonna love him."

Pete's eyes glimmered with hope. "What say, Reese? Are you in?"

Reese grinned. "I'm in." She'd go anywhere if it meant avoiding Thanksgiving with her parents.

When she broke the news to her mother the next night, Eva sounded relieved. Happy, even. "That's fine, honey. We'll see you soon enough. Christmas is only a few weeks away. Tell me about Franny. Does she come from a nice family?"

"She's just a friend, Mom." Over the past months, the few phone calls she'd exchanged with her parents had been forced conversations with little information exchanged. To avoid having to answer their endless questions, Reese didn't tell her parents about the band or her new friends.

"I'm glad you're making friends. Your father and I have been talking about going to one of the resorts for Thanksgiving. To the Homestead, or maybe the Greenbrier."

Her parents had never taken Reese to the Homestead or the Greenbrier. She'd never rated more than a takeout turkey dinner eaten at the kitchen table. Except that one year when their neighbor Ian had invited them for Thanksgiving. He'd been living with Richard, the Italian chef, at the time. The food had been incredible.

Franny's parents lived in a palatial home in the prestigious Bryn Mawr suburb of Philadelphia. Despite all the negative things Franny had said about them, Reese found Mr. and Mrs. Oliver welcoming and easy to be around. On Thanksgiving Day, the extended family of grandparents, cousins, aunts, and uncles sat down in their formal dining room to an elaborate feast at a table set with linens, china, and flowers. Afterward, while their waitstaff took care of the dishes, everyone gathered in the paneled den by a roaring fire to watch football.

Reese had a difficult time warming up to Will. Physically, Franny and Will could've been twins. But his personality was way more reserved. More than once, Reese caught him watching her with a skeptical look on his face.

On Friday afternoon, Pete arranged an impromptu practice session in his parents' garage and invited Will to attend. During a break, Will pulled Pete aside for a private conversation. Even though they spoke in hushed tones, Reese could tell that Will was furious about something.

Fifteen minutes before the band's first set on Saturday night, Pete approached Reese and told her that Franny would be singing the lead. "Not only is she a hometown girl, I feel she's deserving of the opportunity."

Reese thought, *You mean, Will feels she's deserving of the opportunity.*

Even though she knew many of the kids and parents at the party, Franny failed to connect with her audience. At least not in the special way Reese had of connecting with her audience. The rest of the band tried to make up for it by playing harder and louder, but the overall result was lackluster.

The debutantes invited the band to an after-party in a home even more impressive than the Olivers'. They'd been at the party thirty minutes when Pete sought Reese out.

"There you are. I've been looking for you." She was standing alone at the edge of a crowd gathered around a fire pit on the brick terrace. "Where's Franny?"

"In the game room playing pool with the others."

He offered her a can of beer.

"No thanks," she said, avoiding his gaze.

"Tonight was not our best performance," he said, sticking the extra beer in his Barbour coat pocket.

Reese lifted a shoulder as if to say, It's no big deal. "Franny should have the opportunity."

"Will's a friend of mine. I felt like I owed her a shot."

"It's *your* band, Pete. Not Will's. You have a responsibility to the rest of your members."

Pete hung his head. "I know, and I blew it for all of us."

"You'll have other opportunities."

Pete's brow shot up. "You're not leaving us, are you?"

"You can't have two lead singers, Pete. You'll eventually have to pick one of us. And Franny is my friend. I won't risk having her get mad at me over this. It'll be easier for everyone if I quit."

When she started to walk away, he grabbed her by the arm. "Give me a couple of days. Let me talk to Franny, to see if I can work something out."

"Don't waste your time." She tugged her arm free and went back inside.

Reese needed to pee. When she discovered the long line waiting to use the powder room on the main floor, she ventured downstairs to the game room. A new foursome was at the pool table, and Franny and the other band members were nowhere in sight. She cracked open what she thought was the door to the bathroom. Light from the fixture above the pool table spilled into the darkened room. As her eyes adjusted, Reese realized she was looking into a bedroom. A mound on top of the bed was moving, and sex sounds came from within. As Reese was backing out of the room, the couple rolled over, revealing their faces.

REESE

Ten years ago

*R*eese dreaded the trip back to school on Sunday. She would have to suffer through six hours of sickening details about Franny's hookup with Trey. She had no right to be angry at Franny. Her friend didn't know about her crush on Trey, because Reese had never confided her feelings for him. But she couldn't help herself. She was mad as hell.

But Reese worried for nothing. In the rearview mirror, as they left Philadelphia heading for Ohio, Franny kept her eyes on the road and her lips sealed. Her silence and dreamy expression hinted that she had much on her mind. Reese rested her head against the seat and closed her eyes, cocooning herself in her own misery.

The next few days were difficult for Reese. She missed hanging out with Franny and the jam sessions, the music and the camaraderie, that had been the highlight of her days. She didn't doubt her decision to quit the band. She sucked at relationships.

She'd always been a loner. Would always be a loner. Being alone was safe. It meant not having to count on others who inevitably let her down. Being alone meant protecting herself from the kind of hurt that was eating her up inside.

She managed to avoid Franny—her calls and texts and attempts to corner her in the hallways between classes—until she finally caught up with her in the cafeteria at lunch on Thursday. By that time rumors had begun to circulate that Trey and Franny were officially dating.

Franny plopped down in the empty seat opposite Reese at their table by the window where they'd eaten all their meals together for the past two months. "You can't ignore me forever, you know. Are you mad about the deb party? Because, I swear, Reese, I didn't know Pete was going to make me sing the lead. I sucked. We all know it. And I'm fine with that. I don't want to sing the lead. I get too nervous."

Reese considered faking like she'd finished eating, but she'd barely touched her salad. To leave Franny sitting at the table alone would be downright rude, and the last thing she wanted to do was hurt Franny's feelings. She would back out of their friendship gracefully. "You'll get used to it."

Franny stuffed a potato chip in her mouth. "I'm pretty sure that's never going to happen. We have a gig on Saturday night. You booked it yourself. The fraternity formal, remember? I can't handle this kinda pressure. Pete wants you, anyway. Please say you'll do it."

"I can't. I have to study this weekend." Franny's face fell, and she added, "I'm sorry, Franny. My grades are bad. If I do well on my exams, I might be able to pull them up. Otherwise my parents are going to kill me."

"Forget about practice, and just come for the gig," Franny suggested. "We're talking three hours max."

"I really can't. I don't have much time left until exams start."

"Just think about it, okay. Even if you change your mind at the last minute."

A girl from Franny's math class stopped by the table to ask her a question about an assignment. Once she was gone, Franny said, "So, I guess you've heard. Trey and I are together now. I've never felt this way about anyone. He's so amazing."

"Good for you," Reese said with more sarcasm in her tone than she'd intended.

Franny squinted her eyes as she studied Reese's face. "Wait a minute. What am I missing here? Do you have a thing for Trey?"

Reese panicked. She couldn't hold back the tears for much longer. She choked out, "Don't be ridiculous," and abruptly left the table.

Reese spent the weekend in the library. On Sunday afternoon, she was seated at her carrel, taking a break from studying with her head resting on the desk, when she overheard a whispered conversation on the other side of the partition.

"College State of Mind rocked the formal last night," a female voice said. "Franny is just as good if not better than that other girl."

"I wish I had Franny's hair," a second voice said.

"I wish I had her boyfriend," the first voice said. "She and Trey make such a cute couple."

That other girl? Reese had already been forgotten.

Reese was heartsick over Trey, over Franny, over being left out of her own life. And, as the days wore on, she began to feel physically sick as well. The following Friday, she was walking back to her dorm after her first exam when it dawned on her. The nausea. Sore breasts. Missed period. It all made sense. She made her way to a nearby bench and sat down. It was only one night. Her first time. How had this happened? There'd been so much fumbling around. And they'd both been so drunk. She'd just assumed Trey had used protection.

Blinded by tears, she ran back to her dorm room, grateful to find Mary Beth gone. For over an hour, she cried softly into her pillow. She would never tell Trey, not after the way he'd used her. And she couldn't confide in Franny, now that she was in a relationship with Trey. She'd never felt so alone.

When she'd pulled herself together, she put her coat on and walked two miles to a pharmacy far enough away from campus to avoid being recognized. A short time later, the pregnancy test confirmed what she feared. She was pregnant with Trey's baby. Seven weeks along according to her calculations.

Reese was too distracted to study, although she managed to show up for exams. Bundled up against the light snow that fell every day that weekend and early the following week, she paced back and forth in the commons as she contemplated her dilemma. Her mother's words from their last argument the morning she left for college echoed in her ears. *If you get pregnant, don't come crying to me. I'm done raising children.* Even in a worst-case scenario, Reese would never allow her mother to ruin her child's life like she'd ruined Reese's.

A mass exodus of students took place on Thursday leaving Reese among the few remaining for the last exam period on Friday. She'd barely slept that week, and had experienced at least one panic attack every day, but by the time her father arrived late Friday afternoon, she'd decided to tell him about the baby.

When she saw him waiting for her in front of her dorm, she ran to him and he engulfed her in his arms.

"Sweetheart, I've missed you so much," he said kissing the top of her head. "What was I thinking, letting you go to school so far away?"

She was his little girl. He would make it all better. He took her mother's side in most big issues. But this was serious. Maybe, for once, he would help her find a solution that didn't involve telling her mother. She burrowed her face deeper into his chest, inhaling his Grey Flannel cologne.

"Hey now." He pushed her away, holding her at arm's length so he could see her face. "Is something wrong?"

She bit down on trembling lower lip. "I'm just happy to see you."

She would wait until dinner to tell him.

They went for burgers at the town pub, a cozy restaurant with leather booths and a stone fireplace with roaring fire. They placed their order, and the waitress brought her father a vodka and soda.

"We need to leave before dawn to make it home in time for *The Nutcracker*," he said, taking a sip of his drink. "Your mom has made reservations for an early dinner afterward. We're celebrating your homecoming, and we have something important to talk to you about."

Now was her chance. "I have something to talk to you about as well."

"Really? By all means, tell me."

Her stomach lurched, sending bile to her throat, and she chickened out. "It can wait until later."

He patted her hand. "We have a long drive tomorrow. Plenty of time to talk."

Agreed! She would wait and tell her father about the pregnancy in the morning.

"Your mom is so excited to see you," he said. "She even bought a new Christmas tree this year. A thousand little white lights. It's all I've heard about for weeks. She has it decorated, pretty as you please."

Whoopee. Reese had never understood why they couldn't have a live Christmas tree like everyone else. When her mother found out about the pregnancy, her Norman Rockwell Christmas would go up in a mushroom cloud of smoke.

"Do you have plans for the break?" her father asked. "I'm sure you'll want to get together with some of your high school friends to compare notes about college."

What friends? "I don't have any plans. Except for shopping."

He tugged his wallet out of his back pocket and removed five crisp twenty-dollar bills. "Here. Buy your mom something nice."

Wow! What's been going on at home in my absence? She stared across the lacquered oak table at him. Since she'd last seen him in August, more gray had mixed in with the dark hair at his temples and the lines around his eyes had become more etched, but his smile was that of a contented man.

She took the money from him. In addition to the meager amount in her savings accounts, she might have enough to terminate the pregnancy. Was that what she wanted, though? One minute, yes. The next, no. Even if she wasn't ready to be a parent, could she do that to an unborn baby?

Later that night, back in her dorm room, she debated over how much to pack for the break. There was a chance she wouldn't be returning to school in January, depending on what she decided about the baby. Even if she terminated the pregnancy, based on her poor academic performance that semester, there was a possibility she'd flunk out. One way or another, she would have to make a trip back to campus to clean out her dorm room. Zipping her laptop into a front pocket of her backpack, she stuffed the main compartment full of jeans, sweats, and T-shirts, leaving enough room to add her toiletries bag on top in the morning.

Nightmares of telling her father about the baby plagued her sleep, and she woke feeling more exhausted than she had the night before.

She was leaving to meet her father in front of the dorm when she spotted her guitar in the corner of the room. She hadn't touched it since returning from Thanksgiving in Philadelphia.

Music had always been the one thing she could count on. But her fingers no longer itched to strum the chords and the lyrics no longer lingered on her lips. The melodies that had played inside her head since her early days of singing her ABCs had gone silent.

She closed and locked the door, leaving the guitar behind.

Her father was waiting by the Land Cruiser under the portico, shivering in his navy parka with a disposable coffee in hand.

Eyeing her backpack, he asked, "Where's your suitcase? Do I need to run up to your room and get it?"

She lifted her backpack. "This is it. I have clothes I can wear at home."

He chuckled. "You should give your mother lessons on traveling light."

He opened the passenger door for her, and she climbed in. Warm air blew from the vents inside the Land Cruiser. She dropped her backpack on the floorboard and buckled her seat belt. As they departed campus via the long tree-lined driveway, she reclined her seat a little and closed her eyes, pretending to be asleep while she mentally rehearsed what to say to her father about the baby. When she opened her eyes forty-five minutes later, they were driving through the Cuyahoga National Park.

When she righted her seat, her father asked, "Did you have a nice nap?"

"I wasn't asleep, Dad. I have some disturbing news, and I was trying to figure out how to tell you."

"Uh-oh. Bad grades?" He chuckled. "Too much partying? Everyone's grades suffer their first semester of college."

"I wish it were just my grades," she said in a soft voice. She drew in a deep breath. "I'm pregnant, Dad."

His jaw dropped and neck snapped as he turned to look at her. "Did you just say what I think you said?"

She sunk lower in her seat. "Unfortunately."

He continued to stare at her, the color draining from his face.

"Dad! Watch the road."

He returned his eyes to the highway, and neither of them spoke for a couple of miles. Van Morrison sang on low volume from the stereo and the windshield wipers beat back and forth, wiping away flurries of snow.

"You realized you've screwed up your life, don't you?" His tone was one of controlled anger. "I don't understand how this happened, Reese. We talked to you about the importance of practicing safe sex. Your school taught you about the importance of safe sex. Did you not use protection?"

"Obviously not, Dad."

He let out a loud sigh. "Who's the father?"

"Just some random boy. We're not in a relationship or anything like that." She turned away from him, staring out the window at the bare trees as they passed by. "I know what you're thinking, but I'm not a slut. It was my first time. I wasn't planning to have sex. We'd both been drinking that night. I'm not even sure he remembers it."

"Damn it!" he said, pounding the steering wheel. "I can't believe you lost your virginity to a *random boy* in a moment of drunken lust."

Tears welled in her eyes and streamed down her face.

"You're planning to tell him, right? Regardless of whether he remembers it or not, he's equally responsible, if not *more* responsible, for creating this mess."

"I'm not telling him, Dad. I'd rather handle it myself."

"You're not handling it yourself, though, are you? You're dragging us into it." His face flushed with anger. "You've disgraced not only yourself but your family. This will destroy your mother."

"Then don't tell her," Reese muttered. "I was hoping we could keep this between us."

"How can I not tell her? Your mother and I don't keep secrets from one another."

Oh really? Reese thought. *If only you knew.*

84

"Damn it! You've really done it this time." White-knuckling the steering wheel, her father stomped on the gas pedal. The speedometer reached seventy and eighty and then eighty-five miles an hour. At the ninety mark, the Land Cruiser began to vibrate.

"Dad! Slow down! You're driving too fast." From the left, a doe leapt out of nowhere onto the highway. "Watch out!" she screamed, grabbing hold of the steering wheel and jerking it toward her. The Land Cruiser missed the deer but spun out of control, crashing into the guardrail on the opposite side of the road with the ear-splitting sounds of shattering glass and crunching metal. The impact propelled her body forward, but the seat belt tightened around her midsection, holding her in place.

She raised her head, rubbing her neck. Her eyes darted about the car. Blood was everywhere. Then she saw him, her father's bloody form slumped over the steering wheel. She realized with a gasp that he wasn't wearing his seat belt. He never remembered to buckle up. And Reese had been too distracted with her own problems that morning to remind him.

"Dad! Dad, wake up." She shook him, but his body remained limp against the steering wheel. "Oh my God, Dad. You've gotta get up. Please, Dad, don't die. Please, don't die."

His blue eyes stared back at her. Blank. Unseeing. Dead.

MAGGIE

*D*espite the late-season snowstorm, Spring comes early to West Avenue. Blooming tulips, blossoming cherry trees, and her budding friendship with Eva brighten Maggie's otherwise disheartened spirits. She's grateful her husband works late most nights and travels to Charlotte most weekends.

The manager at Starbucks, a beastly woman who terrifies Maggie, turns her down for the job. "I don't need your kind of trouble, honey," she says to Maggie.

"What kind of trouble is that?" Maggie asks, even though she suspects the woman is talking about Eric.

"Your husband kind of trouble. He came here threatening to call the health department on me if I hired you." The manager places a beefy hand on Maggie's shoulder as she shows her to the door. "Do yourself a favor and leave that man while you still can."

Maggie takes her advice to heart. She's working on a plan.

Deciding it's pointless to continue searching for full-time employment, she agrees to help Greg during peak hours at the cafe. Because it's part-time and temporary, he pays her in cash from his own tips. Every few days, she stops in at one of the area banks and exchanges the smaller bills for fifties and hundreds, which she keeps in the inside zippered pocket of her small cross-body bag along with her birth control pills. She wears the bag all the time, and at night, she sleeps with it under her pillow.

Maggie learns to manipulate Eric's surveillance devices and tracking software to her advantage. She plays the role of dutiful wife for the cameras—cooking and cleaning and putzing around the nursery. She leaves her phone at home unless she's running legitimate errands. And she uses her computer for the sole purposes of shopping for baby gear and reading articles about pregnancy and childbirth. Her efforts appear to satisfy Eric, who is too busy at work to monitor her every move.

Maggie chooses not to tell him about her friendship with Eva for fear he'll try to sabotage it like her job applications. Eva offers to pay Maggie to help organize an extensive consignment wardrobe, but Maggie insists on doing it for free. She likes hanging out at Claudia's Closet and the clothes are elegant, fashioned by celebrated designers like Dior, Chanel, and von Fürstenberg. She convinces Eva to plan a Girls' Night Out, a cheese and wine reception to lure customers into the shop to view the clothes.

"I love this idea," Eva says. "Would you be willing to model the clothes during the event?"

Maggie clasps her hands together. "Yes! Please! That'll be so much fun."

They set the date for the second Wednesday in April.

Eva doesn't mention her daughter again, and Maggie is afraid to broach the subject for fear of upsetting her. But she can't get Reese out of her mind—the curse of being an investigative journalist. She has so many questions about her disappearance. About her friends. Her grades. Her professors. It seems too farfetched that some lunatic happened upon the accident and kidnapped her. Either she got out of the car before the accident, or she ran away afterward. But why? What reason would she have to run away? What was Reese's frame of mind when she had dinner with her father the night before the accident?

When curiosity finally gets the best of Maggie on the second Monday in April, she visits the downtown branch of the Richmond Public Library where she uses free-to-the-public computers to research reports of Reese's disappearance. Interviews with students and faculty offer some insight into Reese's personality and campus life. Most are consistent in their description.

One of her professors, a Mr. Hunter, said, "Miss Carpenter is the quiet sort. She always wears those big headphones over her ears, signaling to those around her she doesn't want to be disturbed. But when she opens her mouth to sing, she really comes alive. It's an incredible thing to behold. It's like a switch flipping somewhere deep inside of her, letting the light shine through."

Her roommate, Mary Beth Lawrence, reported that Reese mostly kept to herself. "I don't know who her friends are. I don't think she has many. Other than the freaks in that band." When asked what band, Mary Beth answered, "They call themselves College State of Mind. Reese was the lead singer for a while. Another girl, Franny, took over the position after Thanksgiving."

Deep in her Google search, Maggie discovers an interview by a campus reporter with the bass player in Reese's band. "I was blown away the first time I heard her sing," Benny, the bass player, said. "But it wasn't just her voice. Man, she could really play the guitar."

Maggie falls back in her chair. *The guitar! Of course.* That's what's been bugging her since Eva showed her Reese's room.

She needs to talk to Eva. She's no longer Maggie the curious neighbor. She's a reporter obsessed with solving the case.

She's race-walking back up Franklin Street toward West Avenue when she remembers she promised to help Greg during happy hour. Beginning at four, the Village Cafe is offering a prolonged happy hour, with special prices on food and drinks, in advance of the NCAA basketball championship game. The University of Virginia Cavaliers from the neighboring city of Charlottesville are playing the Texas Tech Red Raiders for the title. Many of the cafe's nonstudent customers are Virginia fans who are beyond themselves with excitement over their team's first opportunity to play for the championship since 1984.

Instead of going left at North Harrison Street, she detours to the right. Eva will have to wait.

The cafe is already mobbed when she arrives a few minutes before four. Greg is behind the bar, filling several pitchers at once with draft beer. "Thank God you're here," he says when he sees her. "Kristin's kid is sick. She can't come in until after her husband gets home. Can you stay until then?"

"Depends," she says, tying on an apron. "Do you know what time that'll be?"

He places the pitchers on a tray for one of the waitresses. "She's not sure. She hopes around seven thirty."

"Okay. But I'll have to leave if she's not here by then." Maggie will be in big trouble if Eric beats her home.

He slides an order pad across the bar. "Good luck. This crowd is fired up about the game."

Greg is right. Their patrons are in an exceptionally good mood. A generous mood. And Maggie's apron pocket is soon bulging with tip money. Kristin arrives at seven thirty, but it's going on eight o'clock before Maggie finishes with a large table of customers. She removes her apron, and when she's stuffing her tip money in the zippered pocket of her bag, her fingers graze her packet of birth control pills. She checks the packet to make certain she took her pill that morning and then drops the packet back in her bag as she hurries out the door.

As she heads for home, she bows her head against the drizzle that lingers from an earlier rain shower. By the time she rounds the corner onto West Avenue, her hair is dripping and her cotton blouse is soaked through. Her heart skips a beat when she approaches her house and sees Eric's car parked on the curb out front.

Before she can insert her key into the lock, the door swings open and a hand jerks her inside. "Where the hell have you been?" Eric demands.

She's been preparing for this moment for weeks, and the lie is on the tip of her tongue. "Shopping for the baby at Target."

He lifts a strand of damp hair off her shoulder. "You're soaking wet. Why aren't you wearing your raincoat?"

"It wasn't raining when I left." Her gaze travels to the hall table where she left her phone when she went out. Her phone is gone.

He flashes her cell phone at her. "Looking for this?"

She straightens, chin up. "Yes, as a matter of fact. I left it here by accident. I couldn't call an Uber without it, so I had to walk home."

"From now on, I want you to take your phone with you wherever you go," he said in a threatening tone of voice.

She stares him down. She's sick of living like this. "Or what, Eric?"

"Or the same thing will happen to your phone that happened to your computer." He steps out of the way so she can see the shattered remains of her laptop on the hall floor.

Her eyes grow wide. "How dare you? That's my computer! I paid for it with my own money."

"As the saying goes, what's mine is mine and what's yours is ours. What else are you hiding that belongs to me?" He yanks her bag from around her neck, zips it open, and dumps out the contents. Her packet of birth control pills tumbles to the floor along with her cardholder, lip gloss, and two tampons. But her money remains safely inside the side pocket.

Her heart beats in her throat. The packet of pills infuriates him and he slams the bag to the ground. Her money, her only means of escape, is safe. For now.

"What the heck, Maggie? Where'd you get the pills?" He picks up the packet, examines it, and throws it at her. It bounces off her chest onto the floor.

Be brave, Maggie. "From my new gynecologist."

"So, all this time you've been pretending. Shopping for baby gear. Reading parenting articles. You got my hopes up. I was optimistic we'd gotten pregnant this month."

She thinks of all the excuses she's invented to avoid sex with him—headaches and allergies and any other excuse she can make up. But when he's sullen or angry, she finds it easier to simply endure the few minutes of perfunctory intercourse.

Maggie can see he's wounded, and she almost feels sorry for him. Almost. "I won't stop taking the pills, Eric. I'm not ready to have a baby."

He moves so close she can smell whiskey on his breath. "We'll see about that."

The manic glint in his eyes sends a ripple of fear through her body. She doesn't see it coming. It happens so fast. But she feels the sting of his hand on her cheek. The force of the blow jerks her head, and she stumbles backward into the wall, sinking to the floor. He looms over her, kicking her thigh with his leather sole dress shoe. "I picked you out of the crowd the night we met at O'Brian's. You sparkled like a diamond among all the other rubies. You possess all the qualities I want for my offspring—beauty, solid instincts, engaging personality. And you have an innocence about you I find endearing." Grabbing her by the neck, he lifts her off her feet. "But, I've misjudged you. I thought you'd be easier to manipulate. I'm finding your disobedience tiresome. From now on, you will do as I say." His grip on her neck tightens as he pins her to the wall. Particles of his spit cover her face. "Do you understand me?"

She nods, her eyes bulging. He removes his hand from her

neck, and she sucks in big gulps of air. Flattening his body against hers, he grabs a fistful of fabric and tears open her blouse, the buttons pinging as they scatter about the hall. Fumbling with her zipper, he pulls her jeans down around her ankles and wrestles her to the floor. He kicks off her jeans and knees her legs apart. Turning her head away from him, she squeezes her eyes shut, the tears streaming down the side of her face, while he forces himself on her.

When he's finished, he rolls off, and she scrambles on all fours to the corner, shivering uncontrollably as she tucks herself into a ball. He gets to his feet, fastens his pants, and goes into the living room. Seconds later, he returns with the lambswool throw from the back of the sofa, which he tosses at her on his way to the stairs.

Maggie stays in the corner until long after she hears the door of the master bedroom click shut. She crawls to the living room and curls up on the sofa, clenching one of his decorator's pillows to her chest.

While she knew this day would eventually come, she never expected it would be this bad.

She's still awake when he comes downstairs early the next morning. He sits down on the edge of the sofa, resting his hand on her blanketed hip. "I don't want to hurt you, baby. All marriages experience growing pains. We just have to work through our issues. I'll try to come home early tonight so we can spend some time together, maybe watch a movie."

She waits until he leaves to close her eyes. She falls asleep and doesn't wake up until lunchtime. *Show time,* she thinks as she musters the energy to drag her battered body off the sofa. She staggers into the kitchen for three Advil and then up the stairs to her room. The house is in total disarray—chair cushions askew, drawers open with contents spilling out, clothes torn from hangers and lying in a heap on the floor. He must have gone on a rampage the night before when he arrived home to find her missing.

In the bathroom, for the benefit of the nanny cam, she says to her reflection in the mirror, "You can't blame him for being angry, Maggie. You betrayed him. You just need to try harder. You can start by fixing him a nice dinner."

Twenty minutes later, dressed in a black turtleneck and jeans with her hair pulled back in a ponytail and her bag around her neck, she leaves the house on foot with cell phone in hand. She walks half a mile to the nearest Kroger, drops her phone in the trash can out front, and leaves without entering the store.

EVA

*E*va is surprised to see Maggie standing in the open doorway of Claudia's Closet. She can't remember if Maggie mentioned coming to the shop today.

She leaves the checkout counter to greet her. "This is a surprise." Up close, she can see that her young friend's face is pale. "Are you feeling okay? You don't look so good." She presses the back of her hand to Maggie's forehead. "You're burning up."

"Because I'm wearing a turtleneck," Maggie explains. "I neglected to check the forecast before dressing this morning. I haven't yet adapted to Virginia weather. I never expected eighty degrees in April."

Eva narrows her eyes as she studies Maggie more closely. "Are you sure?"

"I'm fine. I just need to ask you something."

"In that case, ask away."

"It's about Reese."

Eva's face falls. "Oh." Her gaze shifts to some college students in the back of the shop who are giggling and cutting up in front of the mirror as they try on some of Claudia's outlandish hats. She calls out to them, "Holler if you need anything, girls."

A petite blonde waves at her. "Yes, ma'am."

Eva and Maggie move away from the door and stand in front of the window near the checkout counter. "What is it you want to know about my daughter?"

"It's about the guitar I saw in her bedroom," Maggie says. "Is that the one she took with her to college or did she have another one?"

"That's the only guitar she ever owned. The police discovered it in her dorm room when they went through her things. She bought it herself with money she earned babysitting. She never went anywhere without that guitar." Eva can almost see the wheels turning in Maggie's head. "I know what you're thinking. If she loved it so much, why didn't she have it with her in the car? Especially when she was coming home for a month."

Maggie taps her lip as she considers this. "Or, if she planned to go missing, wouldn't she have taken the guitar with her?"

"Unless she didn't *plan* to go missing. Unless it was a spur of the moment decision. We can sit here all day pondering the what-ifs." Eva notices beads of sweat on Maggie's forehead. "For goodness' sake, Maggie, before you die of heat stroke, get yourself a short-sleeve blouse or T-shirt off the rack. You can wash it and bring it back later."

"I'm fine," Maggie says, but when she tugs at the neck of her sweater, Eva can see angry purple bruises on her skin.

"You're definitely not fine." She takes hold of Maggie's arm, pulling her closer. "How did those bruises get on your neck?"

Maggie stares down at her black, quilted Steve Madden sneakers. "My husband attacked me last night. But he'll never hurt me again," she says with both anger and determination in her voice. "I'm leaving him."

"I'm so sorry, sweetheart." Eva tucks a strand of Maggie's hair behind her ear. "Have you called your family? Where will you go?"

"I haven't told my family yet. There's something I need to do first." Maggie looks up from her shoes. "I want to go to Ohio, to see what I can find out about your daughter's disappearance. I've been researching the interviews and newspaper articles. I have a lot of questions. I'm hopeful I can find some answers."

Finding it difficult to breathe, Eva falls back against the display case.

Maggie's hand grazes her arm. "I didn't mean to upset you. I won't go to Ohio without your blessing."

The college students file past them and out of the store. Through the window, Eva and Maggie watch them saunter down the sidewalk, arms wrapped around one another's waists.

"You'd be wasting your time, Maggie. It's been ten years The trails have gone cold, not that there were many to begin with." Eva moves to the back of the store and begins cleaning up the mess the girls left behind.

Maggie follows her. "I need to try, Eva. I can't explain it. I just have this feeling." She picks up a denim jacket one of the students left on the floor, fingering the sewn-on patches from heavy metal rock bands. "Although I have never met Reese, from what I know of her, I imagine she would've loved this jacket."

Eva takes the jacket from her. "It's exactly the kind of thing Reese loves," she says, and returns the coat to its hanger.

"I can't stop thinking about Reese. And about you, Eva. If nothing else, you should have closure."

Eva cringes. As much as she despises the word, she wants closure so bad she can taste it. But at what cost? Maggie is an intelligent young woman. If she goes digging around in her past, she's likely to find out about her troubled relationship with her daughter. That Eva is the reason Reese ran away. That Eva has a secret. And if Maggie learns what she is hiding, what will she think of Eva then? "I appreciate your offer, Maggie, more than you'll ever know. But I'm more concerned about you right now. Have you reported your husband to the police?"

"No, and I'm not going to." Maggie places a black wool beret on her head and spins around to face Eva. "What'd you think?"

"Very Parisian. Now stop changing the subject." She snatches the hat off Maggie's head and returns it to the mannequin. "Are you in danger, Maggie?"

Maggie drops down to a tufted ottoman. "Not anymore. I walked out of the house this morning with only these clothes I'm wearing. Eric has surveillance cameras hidden all over the house. And he put spyware on my phone and computer. He smashed the computer last night, and I tossed the phone in the trash can at Kroger before coming here."

A chill slides down Eva's back. "You are one gutsy gal."

"Not gutsy. Desperate. And stupid. After last night, I'm sure Eric is monitoring my GPS. Right about now he's freaking out, thinking I've been grocery shopping for a long time. I never told him about our friendship. He won't know to look for me here."

"What if Eric calls your family? I know what it's like to have a missing daughter. You don't want to put them through that. What's the harm in letting them know you're okay?"

"I will. When I'm ready." Maggie picks at a thread in the hole of her jeans. "He won't call them, anyway. He knows they don't like him. My brothers and my parents all warned me not to marry him. But I didn't listen, and I'm too proud to go crawling home with my tail between my legs. I don't even know if I want to live in Portland, anyway. Being away from my family these past months has forced me to grow up. My journey is just beginning. I stumbled into some quicksand with Eric, but I'm strong enough and smart enough to find my way out. I just need a little time, Eva, to decide what I want to do with my life."

Eva sits down beside her on the ottoman. "And you think that chasing after my missing daughter will give you that time?"

"I do. My husband will never think to look for me in Ohio."

"Have you given any thought to how you'll get there?"

"I guess I'll take the bus."

Eva admires this young woman's spunk and determination. If Maggie can risk her life to find out more about Reese's disappearance, then Eva can surely summon the courage to face the past. "Money's tight for me, but I can spare a few hundred dollars."

"And I have some money of my own. I'll be frugal."

Eva fingers Maggie's cheek. "Promise me you'll be safe. If you run out of money, you call me. I'll get more, even if I have to borrow it from friends."

Maggie smiles. "I promise."

"Okay, then. We need to hurry." Eva jumps up. "There's a suitcase around here somewhere. It came in with Claudia's wardrobe."

Maggie's expression is pained. "Oh, Eva! Your Girls' Night Out is tomorrow. I promised I'd model for you."

"That's the least of our worries right now. But I'm sure I can convince Helena to model." Eva locates the vintage suitcase, and the two women scurry about the showroom, gathering jeans and tops and sweaters in Maggie's size.

"And you're sure your husband doesn't know about our friendship?" Eva asks. "I need to know what to say if he comes looking for you."

"As far as he's concerned, we've never even met," Maggie says as she tries on a down vest. "But don't mess around with him, Eva. If he threatens you for any reason, you call the police."

Eva remembers the handgun on the top shelf of her closet. "Don't worry about me. I can take care of myself."

Maggie folds the down vest into the suitcase. "Tell me everything I should know about Reese. Does she have any birthmarks or identifying features?"

"She has *rock 'n' roll* tattooed behind her right ear." Eva smiles. "She hid it for months by wearing her hair down. I spotted it one morning when she was coming out of the bathroom with her hair wrapped up in a towel. I pretended to be mad, but I actually thought it was pretty cool. Reese has a rare talent, a unique voice that brings tears to the eyes of her audiences."

Maggie nods. "In the articles I read, some of the kids and professors mentioned that in their interviews."

Eva closes the suitcase and retrieves her purse from under the front counter. She removes a wallet-size duplicate of Reese's senior photograph and hands it to Maggie. "Take this with you. I have more at home. I bought the deluxe package with twenty wallet-size photos thinking Reese would want to exchange them with her girlfriends." Her throat swells. "Wishful thinking on my part. She didn't have many girlfriends."

Maggie stares at the photo. "If it's any consolation, from what I read online, it sounds like she made friends in college."

"I wouldn't know anything about that." Eva turns her back on Maggie's curious face. She goes to the door and locks it. "You're going to need a car. We'll rent it in my name. It'll have to be economy-size."

Maggie slips the photo in her bag. "Economy-size is perfect." She can get out of town and away from her husband faster than she would on the bus.

A sense of apprehension overwhelms Eva as she heads back to the shop after seeing Maggie off. She considers detouring toward home, to the bottle of vodka waiting for her there. What was she thinking turning an investigative journalist loose on her past? When she stops at a red light, she says to her reflection in the rearview mirror, "Be productive. Stay focused. You have your Girls' Night Out to prepare for."

She returns to Claudia's Closet, but for the rest of the afternoon, she's unable to stop thinking about her relationship with her daughter—what it had been like back then and what it would be like if Maggie performs a miracle and finds Reese. As the saying goes, *Time heals all wounds.* Eva wants nothing more than to have a second chance with her daughter. She'd so badly botched her first chance at motherhood.

She and Reese had been battling it out for years, but the real war began during Reese's sophomore year in high school.

Eva thinks back to that blustery day in late February of that same year when a man entered the store hoping to consign his recently deceased wife's best dresses.

She eyed the bundle of dresses in his arms. "From what I can tell, your wife had good taste. But Claudia's Closet is a vintage store. We sell goods that are at least a decade old, preferably older."

He gave Eva a once-over. "You're about her size. Why don't you keep them for yourself? I have no use for them. I'll give them to you for free. Here." He thrust the armful of dresses at her. "Try them on."

Eva was alone in the store when the man came in because Annette was out for a dental appointment. He wasn't particularly handsome or charming, but Eva recognized in him the same sadness that consumed her. Their intense attraction was undeniable, and before she knew what was happening, she'd locked the doors and they crammed into the tiny dressing room, stripping off each other's clothes.

After that, they met three or four times a week at his house during lunch. Eva didn't love Frank. She didn't even enjoy his company. But she couldn't get enough of the sex. It was frenzied, often bordering on kinky, and for the first time in her life, she was able to lose control of her body with complete abandonment.

The affair lasted for a month. That time was the closest thing resembling happiness Eva had experienced in the fifteen years prior. She even slowed way down on her drinking and was a more loving parent to Reese and wife to Stuart.

Then, one day at the end of March, Eva got careless. She'd never thought much about the close proximity of Frank's house to Reese's school. Her daughter wasn't allowed to leave campus without Eva's permission. On this day, however, the school nurse had called Stuart for permission to let Reese go home early with cramps. Frank had walked Eva to her car and was kissing her goodbye, a passionate embrace in broad daylight, tempting fate as though they wanted to get caught. And that was exactly what happened. When Frank and Eva pried themselves apart, Eva spotted Reese on the sidewalk across the road, watching them. Eva ran toward her, but Reese bolted down the street, disappearing around the corner.

Eva went back to work, pretending as though nothing had happened.

When Reese arrived home that evening, Eva was in the kitchen, stirring pasta in a pot on the stove. Stuart, as usual, was working late. Eva heard the front door slam shut and footsteps in the hallway followed by Reese's voice in the kitchen doorway.

"I saw you today. With that man. Don't try to tell me he's a friend or one of your clients, not that any of your clients are men, because that was no innocent peck on the cheek."

Removing the pot from the burner, Eva turned to face her. "Actually, he did start out as a client. He brought a bundle of his dead wife's clothes in to sell."

"Let's be real, Mom. You're totally having an affair with him."

Eva realized there was no sense in lying. "He doesn't mean anything to me, sweetheart. I'm going through some stuff, personally, that has nothing to do with you or your father. I made a mistake, but I promise I'll never see him again."

Reese's face was set in stone and her gray eyes glinted with hatred. "Sorry, Mom. But I'm not letting you off that easy. You cheated on Dad. You have to tell him."

Eva shook her head. "I can't do that, honey. I'm not going to destroy our marriage because of an affair with a man I care nothing about."

"You should've thought about that before you slept with him.

I'm warning you, Mom. If you don't tell him, I will." Reese spun on her heel and stalked out of the kitchen.

Eva was already in bed when Stuart got home around eleven. She listened intently, expecting to hear Stuart and Reese talking downstairs. But the house remained quiet. Stuart soon crawled in beside her and began snoring within minutes. Every second of every day after that, for the rest of the week and month and then years, Eva lived on pins and needles, waiting for her life to come crashing down around her.

REESE

Ten Years Ago

*R*eese was wedged between rows of stacked boxes in the back of a Costco tractor trailer, on her way to who-knew-where, before she had a chance to question why she'd fled the scene of the accident instead of calling for help. There was nothing anyone could do for her father. She didn't need medical expertise to know he was dead.

There was no turning back once she'd left the mangled Land Cruiser on the deserted stretch of highway. She'd encountered no one while navigating the paths of the national park on foot. She'd chucked her phone and computer into the water as she crossed over the Cuyahoga River, and not long after emerging from the park, she'd come to a small town where she'd spotted a team of employees unloading a tractor trailer at a Costco Wholesale warehouse. When no one was looking, she'd snuck into the cargo hold.

She rode in the inky darkness for hours, shivering from the

cold but grateful she'd thought to pack her stocking cap and gloves. She had plenty of time to think. And to pray. *Please, God, let someone find my Daddy. Please let him know how sorry I am. For everything.*

Reese was on her own from now on. She could never go home again. Her mother would blame her for her father's death. And with good reason. The accident was her fault. She'd forgotten to remind him to buckle his seat belt. And what had she been thinking, breaking the news about the pregnancy while he was driving?

Then there was the issue of the baby. *If you get pregnant, don't you dare come crying to me.* Her father had been right. She had to tell Trey she was pregnant.

When the truck finally stopped, Reese waited another twenty minutes for an opportunity to slip out of the cargo hold. Hurrying away from the truck, she rounded the building to the front of Costco and race-walked a block to a restaurant. Harrisburg Diner was painted on the window beneath a red-and-white striped awning. She was either in Harrisburg, Pennsylvania, or Harrisburg, Virginia. She prayed it wasn't Virginia.

The restaurant's interior was too cheery for Reese's mood, with black-and-white tile floor, sunshine-yellow walls, and a bright-blue Formica countertop. All the booths and tables were taken, so she snagged the only vacant seat at the counter.

Reese flagged down the waitress, an older lady with bleached-blonde hair piled on top of her head. "Can you tell me what state I'm in?"

"Pennsylvania." The waitress slid a laminated menu across the counter to her. "Today's special is eggs Benedict." She removed her order pad and pen from her apron pocket. "Do you need a few minutes to look at the menu or do you already know what you want?"

With the image of her father's bloody face so vivid in her mind, food was the last thing Reese wanted. But dry foods like saltines, cheerios, and pretzels were the only thing that settled her stomach from the ever-present morning sickness. Although she admitted the cheeseburger she'd eaten at the tavern with her father the previous evening had hit the spot. Tears blurred her vision as she studied the menu. "I'll have an order of toast and a ginger ale," she choked out without looking up.

She was waiting for her order when a breaking news report interrupted *The View* on the TV mounted in the corner. The newscaster, a clean-cut man in his thirties with wire-rimmed glasses, reported on a tragic car accident near the Cuyahoga National Park in Ohio involving the death of a Virginia man. "The man has been identified as Stuart Carpenter of Richmond, Virginia. His daughter, a student at Erie State College, is missing. If you've seen this young woman"—Reese's yearbook picture from her senior year in high school flashed on the screen—"call 9-1-1 immediately. Authorities are concerned she may have suffered a severe head injury and may be in need of immediate medical attention."

He followed up with a warning about a blizzard predicted to bring massive snowfall amounts to the Eastern Seaboard. "This one's gonna be a doozy, folks. They're calling it Snowpocalypse. A storm of this magnitude has the potential to cripple transportation, stranding holiday travelers during this weekend before Christmas."

Reese tugged her gray stocking cap lower on her head, covering her hair and part of her face. Once again, she waved the waitress over. "How far is the nearest Greyhound bus station?"

"From here? Oh . . ." She smacked her gum as she considered her answer. "Fifteen, maybe twenty minutes."

Reese's heart sank. "So, it's too far to walk."

"In this weather, yes. But there's a bus stop a block away. Take a right out of the front door, and it's a straight shot down Jonestown Road."

Reese handed the waitress one of the twenties her father had given her the night before. "Can I pay for my order? I just heard about the storm. I need to get to the bus station as soon as possible."

The waitress waved away her money. "Don't worry about it. Your order's not even up yet. Where ya headed?"

The first of many lies rolled off her tongue. "To visit my sister in New York for the holiday."

As she emerged from the diner, she spotted the bus waiting at a stoplight a block away. Ignoring the sleet stinging her face, she sprinted to the corner and boarded the bus seconds before the doors closed. She stuffed two dollars in the fare box and took the first available seat four rows back. Keeping her eyes glued to her lap, she avoided the gaze of the person sitting next to her.

She made it to the Greyhound station as the bus to Washington was boarding. "You're in luck," the ticket agent said. "This is the last bus out today. We're canceling service ahead of the storm."

There were only a dozen or so passengers on the bus. Making her way to the very last row, Reese pressed her forehead to the window, closed her eyes, and cried softly for the duration of the two-hour trip.

Union station was a mob scene with stranded passengers camped out on benches, stretched out on the floor, and standing in long lines at the food court. All departing trains and buses had been canceled until further notice. Holiday plans for the weekend were ruined. Even the elaborate decorations—a model train set and ginormous Christmas tree stretching toward the vaulted ceiling—did little to lighten moods. With over a foot of snow predicted for the area, they were in for a long wait.

Reese located a gift shop where she spent six dollars on a map of DC, and then found a bank of pay phones where she looked up the address for Walker Preston McDaniel, Junior—father of Walker Preston McDaniel III, aka Trey–in the white pages of the thick phone book. After studying her map for some time, she ascertained that Trey's parents lived near the National Cathedral, the nearest Metro stop being Cleveland Park.

The snow continued to fall throughout the night and all during the day on Sunday. Sanitary conditions in Union Station declined. Trash cans overflowed and toilets in restrooms backed up. Even though she ate very little, it quickly became obvious that the exorbitant DC prices would deplete her money within a few days.

When news channels on televisions positioned in key spots around the train station weren't broadcasting coverage of Snowpocalypse and the H1N1 flu, they were discussing the strange disappearance of the Erie State coed.

CNN reported that search parties were working around the clock to locate the missing college student from Virginia.

Charlie Gibson, the ABC *World News* anchor, said, "Even though surveillance tapes show Miss Carpenter leaving the Erie State campus with her father earlier on Saturday morning, authorities can't say for certain that she was in the car at the time of the accident."

Matt Lauer, NBC *Today* host, said, "While Ohio has been spared the brunt of the storm, several inches of snow has fallen in the area near the accident, making for a dangerous situation for someone with potential head trauma."

A reporter from Fox News interviewed Eva Carpenter. "We're reporting to you live from Cuyahoga National Park. We're here with Eva Carpenter, who is helping authorities lead a search party to find her missing daughter." The cameras zoomed in on Reese's mother who spoke into a bank of microphones. "Please, I beg of you, if you know anything about my daughter's whereabouts, call 9-1-1 immediately."

"What choice did I have, Mom?" Reese whispered to the television. "You made the decision for me." *If you get pregnant, don't come crying to me.*

It stopped snowing late in the day on Sunday, and by nine that night, trains and buses were once again on the move. Reese waited until the following morning before taking the Red Metro Line to Cleveland Park and traipsing fifteen minutes in the snow.

When she arrived at Trey's house, there were no cars in the driveway or by the curb out front, and no one answered the doorbell when she rang. She waited for over two hours on the swing set at the elementary school playground across the street. With only her leather boots protecting her feet, her toes were numb and her teeth chattering when Trey finally pulled his red BMW into the driveway. He looked the part of the preppy college student in his L.L.Bean boots, faded jeans, and a Barbour coat. Watching him remove two armloads of shopping bags from his trunk, she ran after him when he headed up the sidewalk toward his front door.

"Trey! Wait up. I need to talk to you."

He spun around, confusion crossing his face when he saw her. "Reese? What're you doing here? Everyone's looking for you. Don't you know? Your father was killed in a car accident. Your mother's worried sick about you."

"I know all that. I was in the car with my father when the accident happened. But I can't be at home right now. I have some things to sort out."

He shook his head, as if trying to understand. "I'm so confused. You were in the car with him? Why'd you run away? What could possibly be more important than your father's death?"

"I'm pregnant, Trey. And the baby's yours."

The color drained from his face. "Bullshit. How is that even possible?"

"Really, Trey? Do I need to explain the birds and the bees to you? Remember Halloween? In the room above the garage after the Sigma Epsilon party?"

The sun peeked from behind the clouds turning his amber eyes into gold coins. "You're making that up."

A wave of nausea hit her that had nothing to do with morning sickness. What had she ever seen in him? "You're pathetic. You took my virginity that night. And you were too drunk to even know it. I've never been with anyone else. A simple paternity test will prove you're the father."

"Look, Reese. I'm studying to take the LSAT. I'm hoping to go to law school in the fall. There's no way I can have a kid right now."

"Then I suggest you stop having unprotected sex with virgins."

He blew out a lungful of air. "Look, I just spent my savings on Christmas presents," he said, gesturing at the abandoned shopping bags on the sidewalk. "But my grandparents always give me money for Christmas. Figure out how much it will cost to get rid of it, and I'll pay for it. Text me the amount, and I'll meet you the day after Christmas with the money."

She felt a pang of envy. Both sets of her grandparents had died before she was born. "I ditched my cell phone."

Beads of perspiration dotted his forehead. "Okay, then. I'll figure out how much the abortion costs and get you the money. Meet me Saturday at eleven o'clock at the Starbucks on Connecticut Avenue, across from the entrance to the zoo."

"Fine." She walked backward down the sidewalk away from him. "The spotlight's on me, Trey. And you know how the media loves drama. If you tell anyone you saw me, I'll tell the whole world I'm pregnant, and you're the baby daddy."

Reese retraced her steps, but instead of getting on the Metro, she walked back to her home base at Union Station. For the next seventy-two hours, she wandered the city streets by day and slept curled up using her backpack as a pillow in a corner of the train station at night. With her eyes glued to the ground, she kept the hood of her sweatshirt pulled tight over her head. No one paid her any attention. She was just one of many kids living on the streets. She didn't know what the future held for her, only that she wouldn't be meeting Trey on Saturday. He'd made it abundantly clear he wanted nothing to do with the baby growing inside of her. *If* she decided to get an abortion—and that was a gigantic *if*—she'd figure out a way to pay for it herself.

Late in the day on Christmas Eve, she spent her last ten dollars on a hamburger at a dive bar around the corner from the station. Going forward, she would have to get her meals from homeless shelters.

Upon her return from dinner, when she saw police officers surrounding Union Station and overheard an onlooker say they were in pursuit of a missing girl, Reese hightailed it out of there, traveling on foot until her legs wore out. She ducked into the alcove of a trendy looking restaurant, tucking herself into a ball out of sight in a dark corner. As the hour grew late, the traffic on Eighteenth Street slowed and the flow of customers entering and leaving the restaurant dwindled. It was Christmas Eve, and everyone had someplace to be. Everyone but Reese.

She was dozing with her head resting on her knees when someone nudged her awake with the toe of a shoe. The deep voice belonging to the shoe, said, "Move along now. You can't sleep here." Grabbing her by the arm, he lifted her to her feet. "It's Christmas Eve. Go find yourself a shelter."

Reese estimated him to be in his upper twenties, with dreadlocks, caramel skin, and eyes the color of Spanish olives.

When she tried to hide her face from him, he pulled her hoodie off her head. "Hey, aren't you that missing college student?"

MAGGIE

*E*arly on Wednesday morning, upon arrival on the Erie State College campus, Maggie meets with the president, Dr. Moody, an academic sort with gray hair and horn-rimmed glasses.

"I remember the case well," Dr. Moody says. "It was the strangest thing the way that young girl just disappeared into thin air." He rests his hands, one on top of the other, on the desk. "I don't know what good will come from probing into this mystery again after all this time, but my office will assist you in any way. I can't discuss her academics, but I'll have my assistant check to see which of her professors are still on staff."

"That would be helpful. Thank you." Maggie makes a mental note to ask Eva about Reese's grades that first semester. "Would it be possible to speak with your security team?"

"Of course. My current head of security, Grady Palmer, was on patrol the morning of the disappearance." Moody rises from behind his desk and walks Maggie to the door, pointing her down the hall and out the front of the building to the security office under the portico. "Stop back by when you're finished. I'll have my assistant draw up that list of professors."

Maggie thanks him again as she heads off to meet with security.

"Well I'll be damned," Grady Palmer says when Maggie explains her mission. "I've often wondered what happened to that girl. I saw them that morning. The girl's father waved at me as he passed by in his Land Cruiser, the early nineties model I'd always dreamed of owning."

"Do you remember what time it was?"

"Not off the top of my head. It was early. I know that much." He motions her to a table with four folding chairs. "Have a seat, and I'll get the file."

He returns several minutes later, dropping a thick manila folder on the table in front of her. "Here it is—all the correspondence I have relating to the case." He thumbs through the file until he finds a stack of black-and-white photographs. He places two photographs side by side on the table in front of her. "Two images are pertinent, time-stamped 5:08 and 5:10 a.m., respectively." He jabs a nicotine-stained finger at the photo on her left. "In this image, father and daughter meet in front of her dorm." His finger moves to the second photograph. "And here, the two are leaving campus together."

One at a time, Maggie brings the photographs close to her face to study them. The images are grainy, taken from too far away for much detail, but the subject matter is apparent.

"I have copies of the tapes," Palmer says. "You're welcome to look at them, but you won't find anything."

"In that case, I'll pass on them for now." She eyed the open file on the table. "If you don't mind, I'll skim through this. Maybe I'll learn something I don't already know."

"Of course. Take your time." He offers her water or coffee, which she declines, before leaving her alone in the room.

She spends an hour with the file but learns nothing new. She feels discouraged but reminds herself she can't expect to do in an hour what a team of professionals hasn't been able to do in ten years.

After retrieving the list of professors from Moody's assistant, Maggie heads outside to the commons. The sight of students stretched out on blankets, studying and picnicking and enjoying the warm spring rays of sunshine, evokes fond memories of her college days. Colorful tulips and daffodils border sidewalks and pathways as she makes her way to the academic buildings.

She pays visits to the professors on staff who taught Reese her required courses during her one and only semester of college— English, biology, French, religion. The professors all tell her the same thing—that Reese put forth little effort and missed classes regularly. Lauren Burton, who taught Music Fundamentals, claims Reese had natural talent but didn't apply herself. Professor Hunter, whose interview Reese read online and whom she really wants to speak with, is teaching a class, which doesn't end for thirty minutes.

Maggie goes next door to the library and asks the librarian where she might find the old college yearbooks. She locates the volume from 2009 to 2010, but Reese's name is listed as *not pictured*. She purchases a coffee from a Starbucks kiosk and takes it outside to a vacant table on the terrace. Exhausted from the long drive from Virginia and a sleepless night in a cheap motel, she questions her motives for being in Ohio looking for a girl she's never met who's been missing for ten years. *Because you're an investigative journalist who needs answers. And the trip provided a convenient escape from your abusive husband.* As she finishes her coffee, she makes a promise to herself. If her search for Reese leads to a dead end, she'll confess her marital problems to her parents and ask them to fly East to be with her when she asks Eric for a divorce. Maybe one day, after she's established her career, she'll return to Portland. But not now.

Maggie catches Professor Hunter as he's exiting his classroom. He is younger than she expected—mid to late thirties—and handsome in a studious way. She increases her pace to keep up with him as he heads down the hall. "Professor Hunter, if I may have a word with you."

He casts a sideways glance at her and smiles but doesn't slow down. "If you can make it quick. I have another class in ten minutes."

"I'll talk fast. I'm Maggie Wade. I'm an investigative journalist hired by Eva Carpenter to reopen the case of her missing daughter, Reese. I realize it was a long time ago, but if there's anything you remember about Reese that might be helpful, I'd like to hear it."

He stops walking and rubs his scruffy beard while he thinks about it. "I remember the voice better than the personality. She had more raw talent than any student I've ever taught. She was a quiet girl. That's about all I remember. As far as I know, she only had one friend, a girl with a mess of strawberry-blonde curls whose name escapes me."

Maggie scrawls `friend with curly strawberry-blonde hair` on the notepad she took from her motel room. "Anything else?"

He shakes his head. "Sorry I couldn't be of more help."

"You've given me a place to start. I appreciate your time, Professor."

Hunter takes a few steps and turns back around. "You may want to talk to Pete Lambert. He's a music professor now, but he was a student here at the time. He might be able to tell you more. His office is on the third floor at the end of the hall."

"Awesome. Thanks," she says and hurries toward the stairwell.

Pete Lambert is locking his office door when she arrives. If not for the leather messenger bag slung over his shoulder, she might've mistaken him for a student with his thick blond hair and young-looking face.

When she asks him about Reese, he says, "We weren't best

friends or anything like that, but I knew Reese well enough. She was one of the lead singers in my band."

Maggie's heart skips a beat. "I read about College State of Mind. I'd like to hear more about it, if you can spare a few minutes."

Pete shakes his head. "I'm pressed for time. I have back-to-back classes all afternoon. But I can meet you afterward, around five."

"Five works. Should I come back here?"

"Why don't we meet somewhere off campus for a coffee or glass of wine?"

"Name the place," Maggie says.

"Bogart's on Main Street. They have an outdoor patio. Might as well take advantage of this incredible weather."

"Good idea. I'll arrive early and get us a table."

She spends much of the afternoon roaming the campus, speaking with a variety of people on the college's staff—professors and administrators and janitors—who remember Reese. She discovers nothing new.

Around three o'clock, she gives in to her exhaustion and returns to her motel for a nap. She feels refreshed when she wakes an hour later. As promised, she gets to Bogart's early enough to secure an outdoor table in the far corner of the patio. She's sipping a glass of the house chardonnay when Pete joins her twenty minutes later.

He notices her wine glass. "Good! I was worried you'd want coffee. I need a drink," he says and orders a Rolling Rock from the waitress when she passes by.

"Tough day?" she asks.

"The usual." They talk for a moment about the trials and tribulations of being a college professor.

She waits until the waitress delivers his beer and he's taken several swallows before broaching the subject. "You mentioned earlier that you knew Reese well enough. What exactly did you mean by that? Can you be more specific?"

"Reese was aloof. I'm not sure anyone knew her well. Not even her best friend, Franny."

"Franny?" Maggie pats the top of her head. "Strawberry-blonde curly hair."

"That's Franny. I take it you've already spoken with her."

"No, but I'd like to. Professor Hunter mentioned Reese's best friend, but he couldn't remember her name."

"Franny Oliver. She's a fashion designer in New York. I can give you her contact information."

"That'd be great." Maggie hands him her notepad. He jots down a number and slides the notepad back across the table.

"I actually met Reese through Franny."

Maggie plants her elbows on the table, chin cupped in hands. "Tell me everything you remember."

Pete settles back in his chair, legs crossed and beer mug in hand. "College State of Mind started out as a jam band, a bunch of us guys playing music for relaxation. Franny's older brother is a close buddy from childhood. When Franny chose Erie State for college, I asked her to come hang out with us. You know, to introduce her to some people. Not that she needed help making friends. She's super hip. And a pretty good singer. Anyway, one night she asked if she could bring a friend along."

"And she brought Reese?"

"Right. I've never heard anyone sing like Reese. She has a big voice, deep and soulful." Uncrossing his legs, Pete sets his empty mug on the table. "One of the fraternities asked us to play at their Halloween party. They didn't have any money for a band, and I agreed to do it for free just for the sheer fun of it. The crowd loved Reese. Because of her, we became an overnight success. By Monday morning, we'd booked gigs for every weekend night until Thanksgiving. With Reese as lead singer, we had something special. And then I blew it."

This is getting good, Maggie thinks, signaling the waitress for another round of drinks. She's on a tight budget, but the information he's providing is well worth the splurge. "How'd you blow it?"

He lets out a sigh. "At the last minute, we received an invitation to play at a debutante party in Philadelphia the Saturday night after Thanksgiving. Reese came home with Franny for Thanksgiving, and our drummer, Trey, drove up the day after. When I invited Will, Franny's brother, to our practice on Friday afternoon, he was pissed that Franny was singing backup and pressured me into letting her take the lead. I should never have given in to him. It was my band. Not his decision to make."

"I'm guessing this made Reese mad?"

"Who would blame her?" Tilting his head back, he stares up at the sky, and for a moment, he's deep in thought. "You know, though, at the time, I felt there was something more going on with Reese. She wasn't the vindictive type, and Franny was her best friend."

The waitress arrives with their second round of drinks, and Maggie waits until she leaves again to ask, "Any idea what might have been troubling her?"

He takes a sip of his beer, licking the foam from his upper lip. "This is my speculation, and I may be totally off base, but I got the impression Reese had a thing for Trey. I asked Trey about it once, but he laughed at me and told me she wasn't his type. The week after the band party, Trey and Franny started dating."

"Uh-oh. Love triangles rarely have happy endings." This could be the break Maggie is looking for. "Where is Trey now? Have you kept in touch with him?"

"Last I heard, he was in DC practicing law. I can give you his cell number, but I haven't talked to him in years." He accesses Trey's contact information on his phone and recites the number to Maggie. He thumbs the screen some more. "I'll give you

Benny's number as well—he was also in the band—but I doubt he can add much."

Maggie scribbles both numbers on her pad and slips it in her purse. "Did you tell all this to the police when you talked to them after the accident?"

"I never talked to the police. My parents took my sister and me to Hawaii for two weeks over Christmas and New Year's. We flew out the day before Reese went missing. By the time we got back, the second week of January, the hype had died down. Honestly, I never thought much about her disappearance. I assumed Reese needed some time to sort out whatever was bothering her and would go home when she was ready."

"But she never went home. What do you make of that?"

Pete takes a long time to answer. "That maybe her problem had nothing to do with Trey or Franny. Maybe her problem was at home."

REESE

Ten Years Ago

*R*eese spent fifteen minutes and all of her energy convincing Raimi not to turn her into the police.

He finally, reluctantly agreed. "But only because it's Christmas Eve. If you don't call your mother in the morning, I'm calling the police. In the meantime, you can stay at my place. I'm sure you could use a hot shower."

She'd been wearing the same clothes since the day of the accident, and the thought of a shower and clean clothes won her over. What choice did she have, anyway? If she tried to bolt, he would come after her. He appeared in good physical shape. She had no doubt he would catch her.

They walked north on Eighteenth Street for about a half mile, rounded the corner onto a tree-lined street, and entered a row house, climbing the stairs to the second floor. Raimi's apartment was cozy, decorated in masculine shades of brown with accents in red, blues, and greens. The main room featured a kitchen and sitting area with a single bedroom and bath off to the side. A bay of windows overlooked the street and a landscape of a boathouse on a mountain lake occupied the space above the fireplace.

Dropping her backpack on the floor, Reese crossed the room to the fireplace and studied the painting.

"My grandmother painted that scene," Raimi said, coming to stand beside her. "It's the lake where she lived in Tennessee. I visited there once when I was six, right after she was diagnosed with cancer. That was the only time I met her. She died the next year."

"All my grandparents are dead. And now my father." Reese choked back a sob.

A moment of comfortable silence passed between them as they admired the painting.

He turned away from the fireplace. "I'm sure you'd like to get cleaned up," he said, and led her through the bedroom to an outdated but immaculate bathroom. He gave her a clean towel and a fresh bar of soap. "Let me know if you need anything. I'll be in the other room."

She stayed in the shower until her fingers were shriveled, relishing the warm water beating against her aching body as it washed away six days of dirt, grime, and sweat. When she emerged from the bathroom in sweatpants and a Widespread Panic T-shirt, Raimi was stirring boiling water into two mugs of cocoa.

He handed her a mug, and she took it to the window, gazing down on the street below. Christmas lights twinkled from windows and plumes of smoke drifted up from chimneys. The setting reminded her of West Avenue, and she was suddenly homesick for Christmases past. Every year on Christmas Eve, her father would read to her in front of the fire—first from the Bible and then *The Night Before Christmas*. She remembered the feel of his arms around her, the sound of his voice echoing in his chest, the scent of his woodsy cologne.

Raimi joined her at the window. "You're a million miles away."

"Maybe not a million miles but at least a dozen years." She wrapped her hands around the steaming mug, bringing it to her lips and taking a tentative sip. "Have you ever disappointed your parents, Raimi?"

"It's just my mama and me. I never knew my dad. But yes, of course, everyone makes mistakes when they're growing up."

"I'm not talking about making mistakes. I'm talking about your mom being disappointed in you as a person."

His olive eyes peered at her over the rim of his mug. "My mama is proud of me. As I'm sure yours is proud of you."

Reese shook her head "She's not, though. She wishes I was someone else."

His eyebrows squished together. "I have a hard time believing that."

"It's true, though. All my life, she's wanted me to be smarter and prettier, more popular and more athletic."

"I'm not much of an athlete myself," Raimi admitted. "Which defies the myth that all black men are athletic studs. I was a nerd growing up. I read all the time, every novel I could get my hands on—mysteries, sci-fi, fantasy. I wasn't half bad with computers either. Everyone is special in their own way. What's your gift, Reese?" He dug his elbow into her rib cage. "I know you've got one."

"I'm a musician. Although I haven't felt much like singing or playing the guitar or writing songs since . . . "

He cocked his head to the side. "Since when?"

Her eyes welled with tears. "Since the night I saw my best friend in bed with the guy who got me pregnant."

"Oh boy." He took her by the arm. "Let's go sit down." He walked her to one end of the emerald-green velvet sofa and sat down beside her in a chestnut-colored leather swivel chair. "My friends tell me I'm a good listener. Whatever you say, I promise not to judge you."

Feet tucked beneath her, she told him everything that had happened since arriving on the Erie State campus in August. He listened without asking questions, his expression one of genuine interest and concern.

When she'd finished talking, he said, "I say good riddance to Trey. And you can't blame Franny since you never told her about your feelings for Trey. But you can totally work through your problems with your mom. You're both mourning the loss of your father. You need each other right now. And she can help you figure out what to do about the pregnancy."

"You're wrong about that. On the morning I left for college, mom's parting words to me were, and I quote, 'If you get pregnant, don't come crying to me. I'm done raising children.' That's why I ran away from the accident. Why I can't go home."

He shifted in his seat, leaning in closer to her. "Come on, Reese. Everyone says things they don't mean in the heat of an argument."

"You don't know my mama. She meant it." Reese pressed her palms together. "I'm begging you, Raimi, please don't turn me in to the police. I need time to figure out what's best for me and the baby. I won't involve you. I'll leave first thing in the morning. No one will ever know I was here."

"Where will you go?"

She shrugged. "I haven't figured that out yet."

"Homeless and pregnant is not a good look, Reese. Especially not in DC."

She stared into her empty mug. She had no argument for him.

"We're not going to solve anything tonight," he said. "And you've had an exhausting few days. Why don't you take the bed, and I'll sleep out here on the couch."

"That wouldn't be right," she said. "I'll be fine out here."

"Then I'll get you some blankets and a pillow." He left the room and returned a minute later, tucking her in and turning out the lights.

She felt safe for the first time since the accident, and she slept better than she had in a month. Although she'd only just met Raimi, his calm and caring personality instilled trust in her.

When she woke on Christmas morning, she was alone in the apartment, and he still had not returned by the time she'd folded her bedding into a neat pile and dressed in jeans and pink crewneck sweater. She'd decided to take off, to escape before he turned her in to the police, but when she opened the door to leave, he was standing in the hallway with a bag of warm-from-the-oven bite-size muffins from Sal's Bakery around the corner.

"Merry Christmas," he said, holding the bag open for her.

She took a cranberry and orange muffin and popped it into her mouth. "I'm surprised the bakery is open today."

"Sal never closes. Poor guy's wife died several years ago, and he never had any children. His customers are his family." Raimi set the bag on the counter and powered on his Keurig. "No caffeine for you. I have decaf, tea, or orange juice."

"I'll have juice, please."

He filled a glass from the container of orange juice in the refrigerator and handed it to her. "I called my mama while I was out. She insists I bring you to dinner."

She raised an eyebrow. "Does that mean you've changed your mind about turning me in?"

"For now. I want you to meet Mama first. I think she can help you."

Reese cast an uncertain glance at the door. "I really should be heading on."

"To where? Unless something's changed since last night, you have nowhere to go." He stood in front of the door. "You have nothing to worry about, Reese. My mama is sympathetic to your situation. The two of you have something in common."

"What?" Reese asked, her curiosity piqued.

"I'll let her explain."

She hesitated. "I wouldn't want to intrude on your family time."

"Trust me, you won't be intruding. My mama loves to entertain. We normally have a full table for holiday celebrations, but it's just the two of us for Christmas this year. We'd appreciate your company."

"Are you sure she's not gonna call the police on me?"

He drew an imaginary *X* across his heart. "I made her promise. She's not like that, anyway. You'll see. She has a special way with people. Everyone comes to her when they have problems."

Reese felt immediately at ease when Raimi's mother welcomed her with a warm embrace. "Call me Mama Clara. Everyone does." She was tall and lean with the same olive eyes as her son. She smelled of rosemary and cinnamon, and her arms were comforting. Reese felt as though she'd come home.

Clara dropped her arms but held tight to Reese's hands. "I'm so terribly sorry about your father. This has been a tough few days for you, but you can relax here. You're among friends."

Reese's throat swelled. "Thank you for having me."

"Everything's ready to come out of the oven," Clara said. "Let's put the food on the table, and we'll get acquainted while we eat."

Raimi and Reese followed Clara through the parlor into the kitchen. Every surface in her modest home was decorated for the holiday with collections of angels, Santa Clauses, and Christmas trees. Reese's stomach rumbled at the aromas of baking bread and roasted turkey that greeted them in the kitchen. Clara gave them aprons and they worked together to transfer casserole dishes of mashed potatoes, green beans, and cornbread dressing to the dining room.

An enormous red poinsettia occupied the center of the rectangular table, which had been set with lace placemats, crystal goblets, and china patterned with red ribbons and holly. Raimi, seated at the head of the table, offered the blessing and carved the turkey.

They made small talk while they ate. The food was the best she'd ever tasted, and she wasn't shy in helping herself to seconds. They took a break from eating long enough to clear the table and clean up the kitchen before retiring to the parlor for dessert—warmed pecan pie with a scoop of vanilla ice cream. A white Christmas tree, decorated with white lights and pink ornaments, occupied one corner, and a wood fire crackled in the small fireplace.

Clara forked off a bite of pie. "You know, Reese, I was once in a situation not unlike yours."

Reese looked up from her pie. "Really? How so?"

"I, too, was an unwed pregnant teenager. My mother kicked me out of the house."

Reese remembered what Raimi had said about the grandmother who'd painted the landscape of the boathouse above his mantel. *I visited there once when I was six, right after she was diagnosed with cancer. That was the only time I met her.*

"Were you pregnant with Raimi?" Reese asked.

"He's my only child." Clara looked over at her son, her eyes full of love. "That was twenty-eight years ago. His father made the decision not to be a part of his life."

Reese set her fork on her plate and wiped her mouth with her linen napkin. "What'd you do?"

"I came to DC to live with my Aunt Sally. I don't know what I would've done if not for her." Clara sipped coffee from a dainty china cup. "How far along are you?"

"About eight weeks."

"You still have time to decide," Clara said. "Do you have any idea what you want to do?"

Reese shook her head. "Not really. I'm too young to be a parent, but I'm not sure how I feel about having an abortion."

"I've seen your mama on TV. She's obviously torn up about your father's death and losing you. You can put an end to her suffering with one phone call."

Raimi added, "You don't have to tell her where you are. Just let her know you're safe."

Her appetite suddenly gone, Reese placed her half-eaten pie on the coffee table in front of her. "She's better off thinking I'm dead."

"Oh, honey," Clara said. "Surely, you don't mean that."

"Actually, I do." Reese locked eyes with Raimi. "I didn't tell you everything last night. My mom has a lot of problems. She's an alcoholic, and when she drinks, she becomes irrational. And I'm the spark that lights her fuse. We're better off not living in the same house."

"Even so, tragedy has a way of mending relationships," Clara said.

"If you give her a chance, she might surprise you," Raimi said.

Reese's head throbbed above her left eye. "I know my mother. She'll try to make this about her. And it's not. It's my body. My baby. My future."

Clara and Raimi exchanged a look, and Clara let out a sigh. "All right, then. I'm willing to let you stay here with me for a while. I'm a midwife. Whichever way you decide about the baby, I can help you through it."

Reese's eyes grew wide. *Wait, what? A midwife? Is this the Christmas miracle she's been praying for?* "But I don't have any money. I can't afford to pay you."

"Are you any good with computers?" Clara asked.

Reese thought about her laptop at the bottom of the Cuyahoga River. "Good enough. I'm not a computer science major or anything like that. Why do you ask?"

"I'm looking for a new assistant," Clara said. "Mine quit on me last week. The job involves booking appointments and sending out invoices. I can show you how to do both. You'll get the hang of it in no time. I'll pay you a salary, minus a small portion for your food. You can live here for free as long as you help out with the chores. That'll give you a chance to save some money for later, when you go out on your own."

Reese felt a flutter of hope in her belly. "Are you serious?"

Clara smiled. "As long as you understand that I'm going to continue to pester you about calling your mother."

"Understood," Reese said, nodding. "Why are you doing this for me?"

"Because, like I said, I know what it feels like to be in your shoes. Aunt Sally saved me once. It's time for me to pay it forward."

Reese moved to the edge of her chair. "You won't regret this. I'm good at being invisible. I'll be so quiet, you won't even know I'm here."

Clara laughed. "That's not at all what I want. My home is now your home. This is a safe place. You can be yourself here."

Reese smiled so wide her cheeks hurt. "I don't know how to thank you."

"Thanks are not necessary," Clara said. "Most folks around here don't have much. We're not just neighbors and friends. We're one big family. We help each other out. That's just what we do."

EVA

he last guest leaves Eva's Girls' Night Out at twenty minutes past nine. She's beaming when she turns to Helena. "We sold nearly every stitch of your mother's wardrobe."

Helena's blue eyes sparkle. "I can hardly believe it."

Eva spreads her arms wide at the empty racks. "I'll have to bring another load over tomorrow. We made a lot of new fans tonight. We want to keep them satisfied."

"I'll help you, if you tell me what time and text me your address."

"That's an offer I can't refuse. With both our cars, we can make the transfer in one trip. We'll bring the rest of the spring and summer things now and save the fall and winter clothes for later."

"Sounds like a plan," Helena says. "Do you have any idea how much we made tonight?"

Eva moves to her point-of-sale terminal. "I can tell you in a minute."

While Eva crunches numbers, Helena gathers plastic cups and screws caps on wine bottles. "I had such a good time tonight. I felt like a little girl again playing dress-up in Mom's clothes, like I was watching her get ready for an evening at the ballet or a dinner dance at the Commonwealth Club. I'm available, if you need a part-time worker. You don't have to pay me. I think it would be fun and I'll do it for free."

Eva looks up from tallying the sales receipts. "Another offer I can't refuse."

"I'm serious. I'm bored with my life, Eva. Aside from traveling, I have nothing to occupy my time. Except for Roger. I can't seem to get rid of him since he retired." Helena laughs. "He's really cramping my style, if you know what I mean."

Eva tries to imagine what it would be like if Stuart were still alive. Retirement had seemed so far off, they'd never really talked about it. "Actually, I don't know what you mean."

Helena covers her mouth. "I'm so sorry, Eva. That was insensitive of me."

"No worries," Eva says as she comes to stand beside Helena, handing her a slip of paper with the tally of sales from the party.

Helena eyes grow wide at the number. "Wow! That's incredible."

"I'm not surprised," Eva says. "Claudia's wardrobe is high quality."

As they exit the shop and walk to the parking lot together, they discuss the hours and days Helena is available to work. After bidding each other goodnight, Eva is getting into her car when her phone rings with a number she doesn't recognize but prays that it's Maggie calling from the prepaid phone she promised to buy. When she hears her friend's voice she says, "Thank goodness. I've been so worried."

"I didn't want to call until I had something to report."

Eva squeezes her eyes shut. "And do you? Have something to report?"

"I'm not sure. But I think it's a lead worth tracking."

Eva puts the key in the ignition, but she doesn't start the car. Her heart pounds against her rib cage as Maggie tells her about the young college professor she met, whose band Reese sang for, and the debutante party they played in over Thanksgiving of that year. "What do you know about College State of Mind?"

"Not much," Eva says. "A couple of kids mentioned the band during questioning, but Reese had never said anything about it to me, and I didn't think it was any big deal. This is certainly the first I've heard of the deb party in Philadelphia."

"None of the professors I spoke with were willing to discuss her grades," Maggie says. "Did you ever get an official report card?"

"Typically, the grades are sent to the students. But, considering the situation, the dean of students provided me with a copy. I wasn't surprised at her grades, it being her freshman year in college. But Reese was definitely capable of much better."

"Was Reese capable of violence? Is there any chance she might have caused the accident?"

Even though she's not driving the car, Eva tightens her grip on the steering wheel. "That's crazy, Maggie. My daughter was not violent. Misguided at times, perhaps. And determined to do things her own way. But she would never have hurt anyone on purpose. Least of all her father."

"You and I have talked about a number of possibilities, but what do you really think happened to your daughter?"

"I think she walked away from the accident and is hiding out somewhere, possibly living under an assumed name. Maybe she had some personal problems she didn't trust me to help her with."

"Tell me about your relationship with Reese. Were the two of you close?"

The agony of those last tormented years with her daughter comes rushing back, landing like a kick in the gut and taking her breath away. When she doesn't respond, Maggie says, "I'm not judging you, Eva. I have to ask these questions in order to understand what was going through your daughter's mind at the time."

"We had our differences," Eva manages in a weak voice.

"And your husband? Did he and Reese get along?"

Eva swallows past the lump in her throat. "Suffice it to say, our house was extremely tense during Reese's high school years."

A long moment of silence fills the line before Maggie says, "I don't have unlimited minutes on this prepaid phone. I need to know how you'd like me to proceed. I'm meeting with the chief of police first thing in the morning to go over the case file. After that, I've done all I can do here. I've left voice messages for several of Reese's friends. So far, none of them have called me back. I have a hunch about one of them who lives in DC. If he doesn't call me back, I'm considering tracking him down in person. Are you okay with that?"

Eva inhales an unsteady breath, collecting herself. "Yes, of course. Do whatever you think best. How is your money holding up? I can wire you more if you need it."

"I'm fine for now. I'll call you tomorrow," Maggie says and hangs up.

On the drive home, Eva's mind is preoccupied with thoughts of Maggie's investigation. When she turns onto her street, she notices a police officer getting into a patrol car in front of Maggie's house. Eva parks her Volvo on the curb, collects her belongings, and gets out. She's climbing her porch steps when the officer calls out to her. "Excuse me, ma'am. I know it's late, but do you have a moment to spare?"

Eva turns to face him. "Oh. Officer, I didn't see you there. Yes, of course. Is something wrong?"

The policeman wears his head shaved and a scowl on his ruddy face. "I'm afraid the woman across the street is missing."

Eva brings her fingers to her throat. "Can you be more specific? What do you mean by missing?"

"She vanished. Yesterday morning, as best we can tell. We discovered her cell phone in the trash can at Kroger on Lombardy."

"That's terrible. Her husband must be worried sick." Eva applauds her acting job. She'll do whatever is necessary, including lying to a police officer, to protect Maggie from her sick bastard husband.

"He's concerned, to say the least. By any chance, do you know anything about her whereabouts?"

She feigns surprise. "Me? No. I'm sorry. I don't."

"How well do you know Maggie Jones?"

"Not well at all. She and her husband are new to the neighborhood. We've only exchanged pleasantries once or twice in the street."

"Have you noticed any suspicious-looking people lurking around?"

Eva pretends to think about it. "Can't say that I have."

"I'm Officer Castillo." He hands her a business card. "Here's my contact information. If anything comes to mind, don't hesitate to call me."

"Will do." She watches him retreat across the street to his squad car and drive off. When she looks up, she sees Maggie's husband standing in his upstairs bedroom window staring down at her. She hurries inside and pours herself a vodka and soda.

Grabbing a sweater, she takes her drink outside into the cool night air and stretches out on one of the wrought iron chaise lounges on her bluestone terrace.

Her conversation with Maggie is at the forefront of her mind. *I'm not judging you, Eva. I have to ask these questions in order to understand what was going through your daughter's mind at the time.*

Suffice it to say, our house was extremely tense during Reese's high school years.

Once Reese left for college, that tension shifted. With their daughter out of the way, the problems in their marriage became glaringly obvious. Instead of the second honeymoon Eva had hoped for, she found herself firing shots at a different opponent in a brand-new war. For years, their daughter had been the sole focus of their conversations. Without Reese, Stuart and Eva found they had nothing to talk about. They tiptoed around, avoiding each other more and more with each passing day. Eva's drinking intensified. The more she drank, the longer hours her husband worked.

On the Wednesday of the third week in September, Stuart arrived home to find Eva passed out on the sofa and the house filled with smoke from the charred brick that had once been a meatloaf in the oven.

"I can't take it anymore, Eva," Stuart said, throwing open the front door and fanning the smoke out of the living room. "Either you quit drinking, or this marriage is over."

So, she quit. Cold turkey. And she found it surprisingly easy. They invented new ways to spend time together. Evening walks in parks. Dinners out with old friends. Saturday movie matinees. She went with him to a Redskins football game, and he humored her by going to see David Copperfield perform at the Carpenter Theatre. Slowly, they began opening up about their feelings. She told him about her depression, and he described how lonely he'd felt in recent years.

On a rainy Saturday morning in mid-October, they were lounging in bed when Stuart said, "You've been consumed by this thing between you and Reese, and I'm nothing more than a referee. Whatever is going on between the two of you is about way more than her staying out late."

Guilt took up residence in Eva's gut and began to fester, eating away at her like a malignant cancer. She started drinking again to numb the pain, and a new round of arguments commenced. When she could take it no more, she told him about her affair with Frank.

That night, no matter that it was well past midnight, he packed his bags and left her.

But two weeks later, as abruptly as he'd left, he returned. "I have to share some of the blame," he said. "If I hadn't been working those crazy hours, been so obsessed with my business, I might've realized how unhappy you were. I want to give our marriage another try. I've scheduled an appointment with Dr. Simpson, a highly recommended marriage counselor, for first thing in the morning."

Unburdened of her guilt, Eva was free to be the doting wife she'd been in the early years of their marriage, and Stuart made an effort to spend more time at home. They rented a cabin in the mountains for Thanksgiving and cooked a traditional meal with all the fixings. While they ate, they planned a special home-coming for Reese.

"Once she finds out I told you about the affair, she'll forgive me, and we can start being a family again."

"I applaud your optimism, sweetheart." Stuart drew her to him, kissing her forehead. "But I wouldn't count on it being that easy."

"I don't expect it to be easy. But I'm willing to do whatever it takes to save my family."

Now, as she stares up at the starry night sky, she can't help but wonder how things might have turned out differently if she'd gotten the chance to talk to her daughter. If only she'd told her over the phone. If only Reese had come home for Thanksgiving instead of going with Franny to Philadelphia.

Ten years is a long time. Is it possible I will finally get a second chance?

MAGGIE

$\mathcal{M}$aggie is waiting in front of the Mapleton Police Station at eight the following morning when Chief Marshall arrives. In his forties now, Marshall had been a rookie detective assigned to Reese's case at the time. He's a big man, tall and beefy with a crew cut and kind face. He reminds Maggie of a giant teddy bear, and she feels an immediate bond with him.

He escorts her to his office, which is cramped, windowless, and cluttered. Maggie sits across from him at his desk with the case file spread out between them. "Give me your best guess on what caused the accident," she says.

"It's not rocket science, Miss Wade. Stuart Carpenter swerved to miss a deer and spun out on black ice."

"And you think it's possible Reese walked away when her father was killed on impact?"

"Possible and probable. The driver's side took the full brunt of the impact. Mr. Carpenter wasn't wearing a seat belt. Old Land Cruiser with no airbags. Guy didn't stand a chance."

"I realize they left campus together, but the accident

happened an hour away. Is there any chance he dropped her somewhere?"

"Even if she wasn't in the car with him, the outcome is the same. She's still missing."

"True." Maggie rifles through the file until she locates the statements of the people who were closest to Reese. "I've left messages for some of her friends. So far, none of them have responded. I see here that her roommate returned to campus to help with the search. What do you remember about Mary Beth Lawrence?"

Maggie hands Marshall the statement, and he scans the page. "She's from Cleveland. The forty-minute drive wasn't a hardship for her. Mary Beth spent a lot of time talking to reporters and shedding dainty tears for the cameras. She and Reese weren't close. At least that was my impression. Mary Beth was not interested in finding her roommate. She was only in it for the fame."

"What about Franny Oliver? According to your notes, you spoke with her on the phone."

"Briefly. She reported that there'd been a disagreement between some of the members of the band, driving Reese to quit. I can't recall the details. I'd have to study my notes. I investigated the lead, and it turned out to be nothing more than a simple squabble."

"What was your take on Reese's disappearance?"

"For me, the case is open-and-shut. Reese used the accident as an opportunity to disappear. No one has seen or heard from her since, because she doesn't want to be found."

"Did the other authorities involved feel the same way?"

"Oh yeah. It was general consensus. I think even Mrs. Carpenter agreed, even though she never admitted it. She did everything she could to find her daughter. She was distraught. She'd just lost her husband, and her daughter had vanished."

Maggie closes the file. "I guess that's it, then."

"What's your next move?" Marshall asks.

"I'm going to DC to track down Trey McDaniel."

"I might be able to give you a head start." Marshall angles his chair toward his computer on the credenza to the right of his desk, his fingers flying across the keyboard as he types.

Maggie gets up and goes to stand behind him, looking down at Trey's profile on the law firm's website where he's employed as a young associate. Trey is a study in contrasts. His sharp facial features hint at arrogance while his amber eyes are sensual. "Nice-looking guy. Can you print that picture for me?"

Marshall cranes his neck to look up at her. "Don't you have a smart phone?"

Why lie? She trusts Marshall. "Nope."

"Laptop?"

"Nope."

Marshall furrows his brow. "And you call yourself an investigative journalist?"

"Let's just say I had to leave home in a hurry."

Marshall clicks his mouse, commanding the computer to print the photograph, and stands to face her. "Abusive husband?"

Maggie nods, biting her lower lip.

His gaze is intense. "Are you in danger?"

"Only if he finds me."

"You seem confident he won't."

"I'm not confident about anything, Chief. He raped me. The man is pure evil."

"Where'd you come from, and how'd you get to Ohio?"

"Eva . . . Mrs. Carpenter rented a car in her name. I live in Richmond, Virginia. Across the street from Eva. That's how we know each other. I'm going by my maiden name. I never changed it on my Oregon driver's license after I got married. I used it for identification at the motel where I'm staying. They believed me when I told them someone stole my wallet, and I needed to pay cash for my room."

Marshall offers a gentle smile. "Did you report your husband to the police in Richmond?"

"Not yet. Maybe I will eventually. I'll see how things go. It's his word against mine. I don't have any evidence aside from these." She tugs off the pink geometric scarf to reveal the still-angry bruises on her neck.

"I'll photograph those and sit on the pics until you're ready for them." He doesn't give her a chance to argue. He lifts the phone receiver from the cradle on his desk and barks an order to the person on the other end. "Have Brown bring the camera to my office."

A rookie officer appears with a professional Canon camera and snaps images of Maggie's neck from multiple angles.

Marshall waits until Brown leaves the office before asking, "Have you ever run a background check on him?"

Her face turns pale. "I did, before we got married. My family was somewhat suspicious of him. They thought him sketchy because he didn't appear to have many friends and he rarely spoke of his past or his family. My mother claims I was in denial, that I was afraid to find out he wasn't the man I wanted him to be. Perhaps she's right. Because, honestly, I didn't dig too deep."

"Give me his name and social security number?" Marshall asks and jots down both as Maggie recites them to him. "Do you have a current photograph of him?"

Her mind races. "I ditched my phone, along with all my photos, so my husband couldn't track the GPS." She gestures at his computer. "May I?"

"Of course," he says stepping out of her way.

She accesses their engagement announcement in the *Oregonian*, Portland's premier daily newspaper, and the photograph of Eric and Maggie, smiling at each other like lovebirds, appears on the screen. She steps away from the computer. "This was taken six months ago."

"Perfect." Marshall clicks his mouse, and his printer spits out a copy of the photograph. "I'll do some digging, see what I can find out. Is there any way for me to call you?"

"I have a prepaid phone," she says and tells him the number.

He clicks another button, printing out another sheet with Trey's addresses—the law firm where he works and the brownstone where he lives near Dupont Circle. "In the meantime, this might help with your investigation," he says, handing Maggie the page.

She folds the paper into her purse. "Thank you, Chief, for all your help."

"It's my pleasure." Marshall walks Maggie to the front of the police station. "You be careful now, you hear? I'll call you as soon as I learn more about your husband."

Maggie gets into her rental car and is heading out of town when she receives a call from Franny. "I can't believe Reese is still missing," Franny says. "That's just crazy. Maybe something bad really did happen to her."

Turning on her blinker, Maggie pulls into the parking lot of a nearby dry cleaners. She parks the car and removes her notepad from her bag. "Did you not think something bad had happened to her ten years ago, after the accident?"

"Never even crossed my mind. Reese was very private, not one to talk about her problems with anyone. Including me. And I was her best friend. I know she didn't get along with her parents. I assumed something was bothering her, and she needed some time to herself."

"Do you think she was upset about Pete giving you the lead?" Maggie asks.

"That's not it. I talked to Reese. I begged her to come back to the band. I told her I was out of my league, which was true, and that singing in front of big crowds made me nervous. Also, true. She was worried about her grades, said she needed to focus on exams in the hopes of pulling them up." Franny goes silent, and when she speaks again, her tone is remorseful. "For ten years, I've regretted never telling the police this. Don't ask me why I didn't. I guess I felt guilty about what happened. You gotta believe me. I would never have started dating Trey if I'd known. The last time Reese and I talked, although she never admitted it, I could tell she had feelings for him."

"Pete mentioned something about that," Maggie says. "He, too, thought Reese was into Trey. Do you think anything ever happened between them?"

"I talked to Trey about it. He said no. But then, he had a reputation for getting around. I broke up with him before Christmas break. What a douche he turned out to be."

"I'm beginning to get that picture," Maggie says. She thanks Franny for the information and asks her to please call back if she thinks of anything else.

Maggie makes the six-hour drive in five and a half, stopping once at a Wawa near Pittsburgh for gas and lunch—a protein bar and cup of black coffee. Although she arrives in DC in the thick of rush hour traffic, she finds a parking place on the street near Trey's downtown office. Positioning herself at the main entrance of the building, she calls the law office and asks to speak to him.

The operator says "Mr. McDaniel is in a meeting at the moment. May I take a message and have him return your call?"

"I'll try back later," Maggie says and hangs up. Trey is still in the building, which means he'll have to emerge at some point. She's prepared to wait all night if necessary.

She's no sooner ended the call when another one comes in from Chief Marshall.

"Brace yourself, Maggie. I have some disturbing news."

Maggie takes a deep breath. "Go ahead."

"Your husband's real name is Robert Charles Wheeler, originally from Salt Lake City, Utah. Father unknown. Mother abandoned him as a young child. He grew up in the foster care system. He graduated from high school but never went to college."

Her knees go weak, and she falls back against the building's windowed exterior. "Go on."

"In November of 2014, Robert Wheeler married Kara Chapman, a young woman from a wealthy family in Phoenix, Arizona. Kara fell to her death from the balcony of their tenth-floor apartment in April of 2016. Her family claims Robert abused her, and accused him of pushing her, but there was not enough evidence to bring charges against him."

Heart hammering against rib cage, she chokes out, "Did he inherit money from her?"

"Quite a lot of it, as a matter of fact."

Maggie slides down the glass façade to her bottom. "Then who is Eric Jones?"

"We found several Eric Joneses born in 1986 in Topeka, Kansas. Eric was a popular name that year. We're only concerned with two of them. One bears a striking resemblance to your husband. Parents both dead. Graduated from Seaman High School and Kansas State University."

"Right. He's the one I investigated."

"And the one your husband wants you to believe he is. The social security number your husband is using belongs to the identity of the second Eric Jones who died in a motorcycle accident in February of 2016."

Maggie runs her fingers through her hair. "I don't understand how this can be true," she says, although she doesn't doubt that it is. "I mean . . . I don't even know what I mean."

"I understand. It'll take some time for all that information to sink in. Don't beat yourself up about this, Maggie. Robert was very thorough in his cover-up."

"I should've dug deeper."

"Not necessarily. At the time, you had no reason to suspect he was lying."

While that's true, it doesn't make her feel any better. "Maybe."

"I'm under obligation to contact the police in Richmond regarding this matter. But they're gonna need to talk to you. Are you okay with that?"

Silence fills the line. She needs time to think the situation through before deciding how to proceed. "Can we wait a few days? I need to find Reese Carpenter first, and then I'll sort through the mess of my marriage."

Marshall sighs into the phone. "Okay, then. I'll be waiting to hear from you, but let's not wait too long," he says, and the line goes dead.

Eric's words from the night of the attack rush back to her. *I picked you out of the crowd . . . You possess all the qualities I want for my offspring.* He didn't need money. He'd gotten plenty of that from his first wife, the woman Maggie is convinced, despite the lack of evidence, Eric, aka Robert, murdered.

Her eyes well with tears and her throat throbs, but she doesn't allow herself to cry. Not here on the sidewalk in front of Trey's building. Swiping at her eyes, she walks herself back up the window to her feet. She forces Eric . . . Robert from her mind. *Save it for Later Maggie. When you're alone and can process it.*

In a daze, she watches hordes of people pass by—commuters of every race, gender, size, and shape dressed in everything from custom tailored suits to shorts and T-shirts—until Trey finally emerges from the building a few minutes before seven. He starts off in the opposite direction and she has to hustle to catch up with him.

"Mr. McDaniel," she says, walking along beside him. "If I might have a moment of your time."

He casts a sideways glance at her. "I don't know you. What'd you want?"

"I'm Maggie Wade, investigative journalist. I'd like to talk to you about Reese Carpenter."

"I don't know who that is either," he says, but his jaw tightens as though he knows exactly who Reese is.

"That's funny. I've spoken with Pete Lambert and Franny Oliver. They both claim you not only knew Reese in college but were in the same band together and that you and she had a thing." *Nothing like a little exaggeration.*

Irritation crosses his face. "Right. Reese. College. That was a long time ago. And *we* didn't have a thing. *She* had a thing for me."

"But you were romantically involved?"

"We weren't in a relationship, if that's what you're asking." He checks the time on his Apple watch. "I'm in a hurry. I'm meeting my fiancée for dinner. I'm sorry I can't be of more help."

When the pedestrian crossing light changes, he takes off across the street like a racehorse out of the starting gate. She watches him go. If she goes after him now, she'll only make him angry. But she's far from being done with Walker Preston McDaniel the third.

Locating an Enterprise franchise a few blocks away, she turns in her rental car to a friendly clerk who suggests an inexpensive but clean Marriott Courtyard where the desk clerk, once again, buys her lie about a stolen wallet. Desperate to be alone with her thoughts, she ignores the hunger pangs in her belly and goes straight up to her room.

She tosses and turns for hours, trying to make sense of what she's learned from Chief Marshall about her husband. While she knew something was off about Eric, she never considered him capable of murdering his wife. Murder! Was he planning to kill her as well? What would be his motive? Certainly not money. Is it possible he's a psychopath who kills for sport?

All the heartache could've been avoided if only she'd done her job. Like her mother said, she'd been in denial.

Maggie dozes off but she's wide awake again at five. Emotions whirl inside her like a windstorm, and she needs fresh air to clear her head and make sense of them. Dressed in exercise attire, she ventures out in search of coffee, which she discovers in the lobby of her hotel. She hits the nearly empty sidewalks and race-walks for miles. She feels pity for Eric, because he's obviously mentally ill, but she's terrified of him as well, afraid for herself and others that he's still free to do them harm. Despite the early hour, she shoots off a text to Eva. I've learned disturbing information about my husband. Beware of him. He's more dangerous than I originally thought. If he threatens you in any way call the police immediately.

She's angry as hell at herself for being so naïve and tells herself the same things over and over until she believes them. *You're human, Maggie, and humans make mistakes. Learn from them. You've suffered a setback from which you can return stronger and smarter.*

Stopping in at Starbucks for a coffee refill, Maggie makes her way to Dupont Circle where she's camped out on the front steps of Trey's row house when the first rays of daylight turn the sky pink. Unlike yesterday, she doesn't have to wait long. Trey returns from a run ten minutes later.

"Ugh. You again," he says when he sees her.

"That's right, Trey." She smacks his sweaty back. "You can get rid of me for good by answering my questions."

"Come on in, then." He unlocks his red lacquered front door. "I need some coffee."

As she follows him through the house to the newly renovated kitchen in the back, she notices his tasteful furnishings, traditional and expensive.

In the kitchen, he pops a pod into his Keurig machine. "Can I offer you a refill?" he asks eyeing her Starbucks cup.

"I'm fine, but thanks."

Once his coffee has finished brewing, he adds a splash of almond creamer from the fridge and turns to face her. "Let's get this over with. I need to leave for work soon. What is it you want to know about Reese?"

"Anything you can tell me about her disappearance."

With a bored expression on his face, he leans back against the counter with hands wrapped around his black Yeti insulated mug. "Why now? This is ancient history."

She glares at him. "Maybe so, but Reese's mother hasn't given up hope of finding her. It's like that for a parent when their child goes missing."

His mouth falls open. "What're you talking about? Are you saying her mother still thinks she's missing?"

Little hairs on the back of her neck stand to attention. "That's what I'm saying. What're you not saying, Trey? Do you know where Reese is?"

"She's here." He points at the floor. "In DC."

Maggie sets her coffee on the granite-topped island and removes her pen and notepad from her bag. "Start at the beginning," she barks. "And don't leave anything out."

He glances at his watch. "This will have to wait. I'm gonna be late."

"This can't wait, Trey. I will hound you night and day until you tell me what I want to know. When and where have you seen Reese in DC?"

He rakes his fingers through his thick blonde hair. "I've seen her twice. Once, right after she went missing. She came to my house, asking to borrow money. I'd blown my savings on gifts for my family, but I told her I was anticipating getting money from my grandparents for Christmas. We made a plan to meet on Saturday, the day after Christmas, at the Starbucks near the entrance to the zoo."

Maggie purses her lips. "Why would she come to you for money?"

Trey shrugs. "Convenience, I guess. She was broke. And she knew my parents lived in Georgetown."

"Did you meet her at Starbucks? Was that the second time you saw her?"

He shakes his head. "She never showed up at Starbucks. Not

that I know of, anyway. I didn't wait around for long. I wasn't thrilled about parting with my Christmas money."

Maggie arches an eyebrow. "Then why'd you offer it to her in the first place?"

"Because I felt sorry for her. She seemed so desperate."

His story smells like five-day-old fish. Like Reese was bribing him for money. But why? "Did you ask her why she'd run away from the accident? Did she know the police were looking for her?"

"Yes and yes. She said she had some things to sort out before she went home."

"But she didn't say what?"

He shakes his head. "When she didn't show up at Starbucks, I assumed she'd figured out her problems." He drums his fingers on the island.

He's growing agitated. My time is running out. "Just a couple of more questions. When was the second time you saw Reese?"

"Several years ago. She was working as a bartender. The place was packed. I didn't get a chance to talk to her. But I'm certain it was her."

"What place?" Maggie asks, pen hovered over notepad.

Trey taps his chin, eyes on ceiling, "I can't remember. Somewhere in Georgetown, I think. I was out with my friends. We were celebrating the Redskins beating the Cowboys."

She scribbles down her number, rips the paper from the notepad, and hands it to him. "Call me if you think of anything else that might be useful." But she knows, as she shows herself out, that she'll never hear from him again.

REESE

Ten Years Ago

*R*eese was working in the office at the computer when she heard the front door slam and footsteps in the hallway. She was about to crawl under the desk and hide when Raimi appeared in the doorway.

She fell back in her chair, hand over pounding heart. "God, you scared me. You're supposed to call before you come."

He dropped a small manila envelope on the desk. "I'm sorry. I forgot. I was so excited to give you these. You're officially Anna McKenzie."

She snatched up the envelope and ripped it open, removing a birth certificate and social security card. She carefully studied the documents. "These look legit."

He sat down on the edge of the desk. "That's because they are legit. You are legally Anna McKenzie. We need to establish credit for you. Mom can start paying you by check, and you can apply for a credit card."

She fingered the raised seal on the birth certificate. "But how'd you get them?"

He examined his fingernails. "I cashed in a few favors. That's all you need to know."

"You're the best, Raimi." She jumped to her feet and hugged him around the neck.

Placing his hands on her hips, he held her at arm's length, staring down at her baby bump. "Wow! Look at you. You're starting to show."

When he tried to rub her belly, Reese swatted his hand away. "Duh. I'm four months pregnant."

"Are you happy living here? Do you have everything you need?"

"Are you kidding me? I love it here. I wanna stay here forever. I'm sorry, Raimi, but you've been replaced. Clara is *my* mama now."

He laughed out loud. "We can share. We're fam now."

Reese liked the sound of that. *Fam.* Even though they weren't blood related, Raimi and Clara were her people. In the couple of months she'd known them, they'd already supported her more than her real mother and father ever had. "Seriously, Raimi. I don't know what I would've done without you and Mama Clara. You've both been so good to me. You're the sibling I've always wanted, and she's . . . well, she's the best mother anyone could ever hope for. I hope you know how lucky you are to have her."

His expression softened. "She's pretty remarkable, isn't she?"

"She's awesome. I've been on patient visits with her and witnessed a few births. She's talented, but her bedside manner is the reason for her success. She's accepting of everyone regardless of their skin color or personality or any mistakes they may have made in the past."

"Everyone except Jana." His mood shifted, and he left the room.

Reese followed him into the kitchen. "Clara likes Jana fine.

She's just worried she's a little too self-absorbed. And she thinks she could be more supportive of you."

Raimi removed a box of peppermint tea bags from the cupboard beside the stove. "Want some?" he asked, opening the lid of the box.

"Sure." Reese reached for two mugs while Raimi filled the kettle with water. "So, this thing with you and Jana is serious?"

"Serious enough that I've asked her to marry me."

"Raimi! That's great." She gave his arm a slap. "Does Clara know?"

"Not yet." He set the kettle on the stove and turned on the gas burner. "I'm dreading telling her. She's gonna say it's too soon."

Reese placed a tea bag in each of the mugs. "Well, you *have* only been dating for nine months."

"True, but we're not getting any younger. And Jana wants to start a family right away. We're both eager to have children." His eyes traveled to her baby bump. "When is your ultrasound? Are you going to find out if it's a boy or a girl?"

"My ultrasound is scheduled for next week. I'd like to know the sex. But I've been talking to this couple, Nora and James, who are considering adopting the baby. They want it to be a surprise."

He poured water over the tea bags, and they took their mugs to the table.

"I knew you were thinking about giving the baby up for adoption, but I didn't realize you'd moved forward with the process."

"Clara introduced me to Nora and James last week. They've been trying to have a baby for a while. If it works out, they'll pay all my living and medical expenses, which is huge since I don't have health insurance. And since Clara is letting me live here for free, I'll have a nest egg when I move out on my own."

He stroked his chin, his thoughts elsewhere.

"What're you thinking, Raimi?"

"If the timing works out, you could take over my apartment when I move in with Jana."

Her hopes soared at the thought of having a job and a place of her own. Never mind that his apartment was fabulous. "Really, Raimi? That'd be awesome."

"You're welcome to stay here, though. Even after the baby comes."

"I know. Clara has made that clear. She even offered to help with the baby if I decide to keep it." She removed the tea bag and took a tentative sip. "Have you and Mama Clara always been so close?"

"Pretty much. I tested my limits when I was a teenager. Everybody does. But I never got into serious trouble." Raimi spooned sugar into his tea. "I know what you're thinking. And you'll be able to settle your differences with your mom one day."

The lines in Reese's brow deepened.

"You promised, Reese. You *will* call your mom after the baby comes."

Reese buried her face in her hands. "I can't go back to Richmond, Raimi. Living with her was hell."

He massaged her back. "Nobody said you had to go home. You're over eighteen. You're free to live how you want. But she's your mother. You owe her the courtesy of letting her know you're alive."

"You're right. I'm just worried I won't have the courage to stand up to her when the time comes." She smiled at Raimi. "But I have five months to worry about that. Thanks for the new identity."

"You're welcome. I dub you Anna McKenzie." He held his mug out to hers and they clink. "I'll have to call you Anna from now on, so I don't slip when we're in public. But I like the name. It suits you."

"Just as Raimi suits you. What does it mean, by the way? I've been meaning to ask you."

"That's a good question. Some say it's of African origin while others argue it's Hebrew. In both languages, Raimi means compassionate."

Reese rested her head on his arm. "In that case, the name suits you even more."

Depending on her patient's preferences, Clara delivered babies in hospitals as well as in their homes. James and Nora had insisted Reese's baby, their baby, be born in a hospital, which suited Reese fine. Although she'd never admit it to Clara, she found the hospital environment more sterile.

Reese went into labor on the hottest day of July. Clara had just gotten home from work when her water broke. Her contractions came on hard and fast, and by the time she got to the hospital, she was ready to push. The baby came within minutes—a seven-pound nine-ounce little girl. After Clara had stitched her up and the baby had passed her tests, Clara asked the other nurses to leave the room. She placed the swaddled baby in Reese's arms, and dragged a chair over close to the bed. "It's not too late, you know. You don't have to go through with the adoption. I will help you. As far as I'm concerned, the two of you can live with me until she goes away to college."

Reese planted kisses on the baby's downy head and scrunched-up face and sucked on her delicate fingers. "I can't back out now. Nora and James have given me money. They're paying my medical expenses."

"That's the least of my concerns. We'll figure something out."

"You're too good to me, Mama Clara. But, as tempted as I am, I've made up my mind. I've grown to love this baby and I'd love to keep her, but the timing is all wrong for me. I want to work while I put myself through school. I can't do that and raise a baby at the same time. She'll be better off with Nora and James. They can provide a loving home and a stable lifestyle." She gave Clara an apologetic look. "Do you mind if I have a few minutes alone with her?"

"Of course not," Clara said and quietly exited the room.

Reese spent the next half hour examining her baby from head to toe, taking mental images that would have to last her a lifetime. When Clara returned for her, Reese handed the baby over. "Take her away, please."

She'd prepared herself for this minute. She'd vowed to say goodbye to her baby and walk away forever. But as she watched Clara leave the room with her pink bundle, Reese had the strangest feeling that she would see her baby again.

REESE

Present Day

*R*eese stands on the sidewalk side of the fence behind a maple tree out of sight of teachers supervising the children on the playground. She feels like a stalker, even though she means no harm to the children. She's only interested in the well-being of one nine-year-old girl. Bella, who is leaning against the brick school building watching her classmates play kickball. Reese has been watching the child since she was old enough to amuse herself on the neighborhood playground near Nora and James's home. Bella has always seemed so happy and well-adjusted. Until recently.

Reese slings her guitar over her back and drags herself away from the schoolyard, back to the Metro station where she catches the next train to her job as bartender in the Dupont Circle corridor.

Even though it's not yet noon, Reveler's Tavern is already packed with patrons celebrating the glorious weather with a leisurely lunch. Reese would like to be outside and is disappointed when her manager assigns her to the downstairs bar instead of the roof-top patio. But her spirits lift when she sees Raimi is working the downstairs bar as well. Dropping her guitar and backpack in the break room, she joins him behind the bar.

He shoots her a look as he pours straight whiskey into two glasses. "You've been to the school again."

She gives him the death stare. "Are you having me followed now?"

"You can't hide anything from me." He slides the whiskey across the bar to his patrons. "You should know that by now."

"I can't explain it, Raimi. I just have this need to see her, to make sure she's okay."

"As long as that's all it is." He chucks her under the chin. "Whatever you do, don't mention it to Mom at dinner tonight. She worries enough about you as it is."

Reese ties her light-brown hair back with an elastic band. "Why's she worried about me?"

"You know Mama Clara. She thinks you should be doing something with your life other than bartending."

"I'm doing fine. I can take care of myself," Reese mumbles and moves to the other end of the bar to take an order.

The next few hours fly by as she hustles behind the bar, filling drink and food orders. The restaurant offers nearly every brand of bourbon whiskey on the market in addition to a wide range of signature cocktails and typical tavern food—chicken tenders, nachos, burgers.

Sammy Baker, a fun-loving guy who seems to know everyone in town, enters the bar at five o'clock for happy hour. Reese knows the crowd is about to get rowdy. Sure enough, two Absolut Citron on the rocks later, Sammy hollers, "Hey, Anna! Sing us a song. Serenade us with your lovely vocals."

Reese doesn't look up from processing a sales transaction. "Not now, Sammy. I'm busy."

He two-finger whistles to get the room's attention. "Who wants to hear Anna sing?"

Cheers erupt and the chanting starts. "Sing, Anna, sing. Sing, Anna, sing."

Reese knows from experience. The only way to appease them is to give them what they want. "All right, already. But just one song."

One of the waitresses brings Reese her guitar from the break room, and Sammy gives her his barstool. She sits, crossing her legs, and strums the first chords to the song they love the most, "True to Me," the one she wrote ten years ago as a freshman at Erie State College.

When the song ends, the crowd begs for more and she sings four of her other titles before finally putting her guitar away.

"Why don't you put poor Sammy out of his misery and go out with him?" Raimi says.

"I will, when you go out with Brenda. She's sweet on you."

"No thanks. I've been married and divorced and have a six-year-old son whom I only get to see on Tuesday nights and every other weekend. Bottom line—been there, done that!"

"Come on, Raimi. I know you want more children. You're not getting any younger, you know."

He grunts. "And neither are you."

They drop the subject. Reese wants to get married and have children of her own. Not ones she sneaks peeks of at the playground every few weeks.

She's tired of hiding, tired of not recognizing herself in the mirror. After years of changing her hairstyle and color every few months, she recently let it go back to its natural honey color. A step in the right direction, she thinks. Every now and then, someone she recognizes from home or college comes into the bar. She turns her back on them when they look at her as if trying to place her. Trey came in once, on a Sunday evening during football season. They locked eyes and held each other's gazes, a million unsaid things hanging in the air between them. But when Reese looked away to tend to a customer he disappeared.

Reese was depressed for months after giving her baby up for adoption. Mama Clara and Raimi tried everything to perk her up. They even dragged Reese with them to Sunday services and bible study at their church—Columbia Heights Baptist. Fascinated by the choir, she asked the director, Otis Blake, if she could become a member. She has sung with them every Sunday since then. No one in the congregation seems to care that hers is the only white face in a sea of dark ones. She enjoys gospel singing as much as, if not more than, rhythm and blues. The choir members praise her talent and encourage her to reach her full potential. Otis is the one who convinced Reese to apply for a scholarship to study music theory at Catholic University. It's taken her twice as long as students on a normal track, but in a month, she will graduate.

After church on Sundays, Reese and Raimi have a standing date with Mama Clara for brunch. But, since Clara had a bad cold this past Sunday, she's invited them for Wednesday night dinner. Reese and Raimi leave work together at seven and arrive as Clara is putting her macaroni and cheese casserole in the oven.

"How're you feeling, Mama?" Raimi asks, giving Clara a hug.

"Much better, thank you." Clara pours them each a glass of sweet tea. "Let's go sit on the porch while we wait for the casserole to heat."

The wide-screened porch is Reese's favorite feature of the house. A row of rocking chairs stretches out between a hammock at one end and a picnic table, set for dinner, at the other end. Raimi and Reese sit down in rocking chairs on either side of Clara. In the small yard off the porch, clumps of pink azaleas that grow along the wooden fence are just beginning to bloom.

Reese is silent while mother and son discuss the estimate for roof repairs Clara recently requested to replace missing shingles and damaged snow guards.

Clara strokes Reese's arm. "You're awfully quiet, sweetheart. Is something bothering you?"

Reese takes a deep breath as she summons the nerve to ask, "By any chance, have you seen or heard from Nora or James lately?"

Raimi groans. "I warned you not to bring this up."

"We've been through this a thousand times, honey," Clara says." When are you gonna let her go?"

"It's not about letting her go," Reese says. "I let her go when I put her up for adoption. I don't regret that decision. It was the right choice for the baby."

"Then why do you keep stalking her?" Raimi asks.

Clara's eyebrows draw together. "What do you mean by *stalking her?*"

Reese looks away from them, staring at the hammock end of the porch. "I'm not stalking her. I prefer to think of it as checking on her. About once a month, I walk past her school while Bella's class is on the playground. Just to make certain she's okay. Until now, she's seemed perfectly fine, like a happy little girl. But she's changed. I have this sense of unease that something's wrong in her life."

"Of course, she's changed," Clara says. "She's a growing child."

"Wait a minute." Raimi leans forward in his chair so he can see Reese on the other side of his mother. "You didn't tell me this earlier. What makes you think something's wrong?"

"Her clothes are often dirty and torn," Reese says. "And her hair is never brushed. She's always been aloof with the other kids. That doesn't bother me so much. I've always been a loner. But now, it's like she's afraid of something. I have this sick feeling in my gut that she's hurting in some way."

Clara says, "I know this is hard on you, but you relinquished your rights to that child nine years ago. Now, with graduation next month, is the perfect time for you to make a change. Go home to Richmond. Visit your mama. Put her out of her misery. Let her know you're alive. Show her what a lovely young woman you've become."

"I agree with Mom," Raimi says. "You need a change. Obsessing about this little girl is making you crazy. Your mom will be thrilled to see you."

Reese springs to her feet. "You don't know my mother," she says. "We didn't have the loving relationship like the two of you have. She's probably gotten remarried, anyway. I'll bet she has stepchildren and grandchildren."

Clara stands to face her. "So, what if she does? That doesn't mean she loves you any less. You spy on the child you put up for adoption because you love her, yet you don't even know her. Not really. Think about how your mama feels? She took care of you for eighteen years, and she doesn't even know whether you're alive or dead."

They've had this argument many times, but Reese has never seen Clara this angry.

Raimi is on his feet and the threesome stand in a circle. "You're an adult now. You have a college degree you paid for yourself. You don't have to move to Richmond. Just go for a visit. If you're not happy with the way things are going, you can always leave."

Clara reaches for her hand. "You won't be able to move on with your life until you settle the past. At least that's always been my experience."

Reese knows Clara is thinking about her own past—her mother and the trip to Tennessee to visit her when she was dying of cancer.

Clara squeezes her hand. "It's time for you to get out from behind that bar and go live your life. Pursue your song-writing career. God gave you a talent. Use it."

Reese smiles a sheepish smile. "I've actually been freelancing some songs. I'm not ready to quit my day job yet, but my reputation is starting to grow. I've attracted the attention of some big names in both pop and country music."

Raimi's eyebrows reach his receding hairline. "Country? Really?"

Reese sticks her tongue out at him. "I can write in other genres, you know. I'm a music major. Duh."

"Maybe you should consider moving to Nashville," he suggests.

Clara's face lights up. "Nashville would be an exciting place to live for someone in the music business."

Reese's lips turn down. "I know I've overstayed my welcome by nine years, but why are the two of you so eager to get rid of me?"

"We don't want to get rid of you, honey," Clara says. "We love you. You're one of us. This is your home. But we feel you need a fresh start."

Raimi pinches her chin. "Which you won't be able to get as long as you're in such close proximity to the Neilson child."

As much as she hates to admit it, Reese knows they're right. But can she leave DC? Can she leave Bella? "I'm not making any promises, but I'll think about what you've said."

"That's all I'm asking." Clara brushes a strand of hair out of Reese's face. "Regardless of where you live, I'm proud of you. You've worked so hard. You deserve success."

EVA

*E*va is a hot mess of nerves. Although they haven't spoken since Wednesday night, for the past two days, she and Maggie have been texting back and forth. Maggie is tracking down an important lead in Washington. When Eva offered to drive up to DC to help with the investigation, Maggie said she had everything under control and for her to sit tight. But Eva, after ten years, is tired of sitting tight. Reese is her daughter. If and when Maggie finds her, Eva has a right to be there.

Then, there's the matter of Eric, who hasn't left the house since his wife went missing. Maggie texted for Eva to beware of her husband, that she'd learned something disturbing about Eric and for Eva to call the police if he threatens her. Although he's made no verbal threats, he constantly watches her from his upstairs bedroom window. When she looks out one of her own windows or her storm door, he's there. When she's going to and coming from work, he's there. He's clearly suspicious of her. And she can't risk having him follow her to DC.

Heavy rain has been falling throughout the morning and is predicted to continue the rest of the day. Even though it's Friday, typically one of her busiest days, no one has ventured into the store since she opened at ten. Trying to calm herself, she rearranges the showroom and reorganizes her shelves to better showcase some of the new items—a Victorian beaded handbag, a straw hat with pastel straw flowers, and a sterling silver belt buckle.

She's preparing to close early, around three, when the front door swings open and in blows Helena on a gust of wind.

"Boy, it's nasty out there." She shrugs off her dripping coat, letting it drop to the floor inside the door. "I'm surprised you're still here."

Eva dangles her keys. "I was just getting ready to leave."

Helena snatches the keys from her. "You can't go until I tell you about the rental space I found for us." She shivers. "It's freezing in here. Do you have any fresh coffee?"

Eva resists a sarcastic remark. Why would she have made coffee when she's getting ready to leave?

She holds out her hand to Helena. "Give me back my keys, and I'll make you some."

Helena drops the keys in her palm and follows Eva to the stockroom.

"I wasn't aware we were looking to move," Eva says as she scoops ground coffee from the bag into the coffee maker's filter. Since the Girls' Night Out, Helena has been proposing various ways to make Claudia's Closet grow. When she hinted at a partnership, Eva didn't discourage her. Having a partner would solve a lot of her problems.

"The space is limited here," Helena says. "There's no room to expand."

"Since when are we expanding?"

Helena paces while she talks. "I've given this considerable thought, and I'm convinced we should try our hand in the home interiors market. In talking to my friends about cleaning out their closets and consigning their nicer pieces, nearly every one of them suggested we sell home goods as well. My friends, who are constantly redecorating, have good taste and plenty of money. The items they would consign would be stylish and of high quality."

As she fills the coffee maker with water and sets it to brew, Eva says, "Let me get this straight. You want us to move into a larger building so we can sell home goods, and transition from a vintage store to a consignment shop? You're talking about a lot of changes, Helena. I applaud your enthusiasm, but are you truly serious about a partnership?"

"I truly am," she says, her eyes bright and smile wide. "With your experience and my connections, we can make this work."

"Then we need to have a heart-to-heart about our expectations for the future to make certain we're on the same page."

Helena claps her hands like a delighted child. "I agree. I've arranged for the leasing agent to meet us at six fifteen. I can't wait to see the space. It's farther west, near the intersection of Patterson and Libbie, in a cluster of attractive boutiques. We'll go for drinks afterward to discuss our partnership."

Isn't she full of ideas this afternoon. Although perfectly charming, that area of town is off the beaten path for my usual customers. On the other hand, it will draw an entirely different clientele.

Eva pours coffee into two mugs and hands one to Helena. "Why don't we discuss it now, before we meet the leasing agent. If we decide to become partners and we like the building, we'll go for drinks to celebrate."

"Fine." Helena drops to one of the chairs at the small round table in the corner. "You need to lighten up, Eva. You're so serious."

Eva sits down in the other chair. "I take my business very seriously, Helena. I've been running Claudia's Closet for twenty years. I give careful consideration to every change I make."

"Duly noted." Helena sips her coffee. "Shall we discuss?"

Eva positions her chair in order to see the front door on the off chance a customer enters the store. "I'm going to be honest with you, because I want you to know what you're getting into. Business hasn't been great these past few years. Before you brought me Claudia's wardrobe, I was on the verge of having to close the shop. I'm all for making some changes, but money is tight for me, and I can't afford to make a mistake."

Helena nods. "Understood."

"With that being said, a partnership and the changes you've suggested might be just what Claudia's Closet needs to stay open. But I have several concerns and I need answers. What exactly is your level of commitment? Is this a fleeting fancy for you? The other day, you mentioned being bored with your life. Are you looking for a distraction until something better comes along? Or are you in this for the long haul? Are you willing to cosign on a five-year lease?"

Helena clasps her hands together on the table. "It's true. I am bored. But I'm not a bored housewife, Eva. I've volunteered untold hours for nonprofits around the city. I've chaired boards and organized elaborate events—receptions and auctions and black-tie galas. But I'm tired of giving away my time for free. I've been looking for an opportunity like this for years. If you agree to this partnership, I'll insist we do things by the book. I'll officially buy half of the business from you. The infusion of cash will allow us to expand. We'll have an agreement drawn up that gives each of us the first right of refusal should one of us decide to sell out in the future."

When Helena finishes talking, Eva stares at her coffee mug while she considers the offer. She'd underestimated the extent of Helena's involvement in nonprofit organizations. Her organizational skills would certainly come in handy, and she's genuinely interested for all the right reasons. It would be nice to have someone share the burden. She looks up at her old friend. "I say we give it a shot!"

They talk for another hour about expansion plans and market shares and profit sharing. When she walks Helena to the door around four thirty, the rain has slowed to a drizzle, but the gray clouds are heavy, and not a soul is roaming the sidewalks. Eva's rinsing out the coffee pot a few minutes later when the sound of someone clearing their throat drifts in from the showroom. Assuming it's Helena, she calls out, "Did you forget something?"

Her question meets with silence. She places the pot in the drying rack and wipes her hands on a tea towel. Emerging from the back room, she sees a man of average height with a lean frame and muscular shoulders standing in the middle of the showroom inspecting a pair of cat eye sunglasses, vintage Marilyn Monroe days.

"Can I help you, sir? Are you shopping for Mother's Day?"

When he looks up, she sees that it's Eric Jones.

At the sight of her, his face registers surprise, followed by confusion. "It's you."

His eyes are crystal clear and aqua blue like the Caribbean Ocean.

Be cool, Eva. Pretend you don't know who he is. "I'm sorry, but have we met?"

Returning the glasses to the shelf, he removes a business card from his raincoat pocket. Eva knows that pale-pink card stock. It's one of her business cards. "I'm Eric Jones, your neighbor. My wife, Maggie, is missing. But you already know that because the police told you. And you told them that you don't know Maggie, but I found this in the drawer of her nightstand."

Eva gulps back fear, but she manages to remain calm. Maggie's life depends on it. Something in his blue eyes makes her uncomfortable and she realizes it's evil.

"I don't know her. Not really. We're not friends or anything like that. We've spoken a few times in the street. Maybe I gave her my business card. I don't remember. I give lots of people my cards. I'm always trying to drum up new business."

"Did she ever come in your store?"

"Not that I know of. If she came in on a busy day, when the store was packed with customers, I may not have noticed her."

His lip curls in disgust. "I can't imagine why anyone would buy cast-off clothes." He slips the business card back in his pocket. "My wife and I have our share of differences, but I love her very much. I'll do whatever it takes to find her. Do you understand, Mrs. Carpenter?" He steps into Eva's personal space, sending a shiver down her spine.

"Yes, of course, you will."

"You know where to find me if you think of anything that might be helpful in locating Maggie." Turning, he strides to the front of the store like a panther after his prey.

She rushes to the door, locking it behind him and falling back against it. Squeezing her eyes shut, she prays to God he believed her, even though a feeling deep inside her gut warns her he'd seen straight through her lies. She considers calling the police, but then decides against it. He didn't exactly threaten her. At least, not in so many words. At least, not yet.

REESE

*N*o matter how hard Reese tries, she can't get Bella off her mind. During rehearsal for an end-of-year performance on Thursday morning, she misses song lyrics she's known all her life, and that afternoon at the bar, she repeatedly messes up drink and food orders. After work, Reese sneaks her boss's binoculars—the ones he uses for lady watching—from under the patio bar and slips them into her backpack. She knows the playground schedule by heart and is waiting beside her tree at ten o'clock the next morning when Bella's class emerges from the building for recess. Reese lifts the binoculars to her face, sharpening the focus and zooming in on the child. A teacher, a pleasant-looking woman in her forties, leans in close to speak to Bella, pointing at the other groups of children as though encouraging her to join them. Bella shakes her head and takes her position against the wall. She's dressed in dirty jeans and a sleeveless tank top, with no jacket despite the chilly weather, and she's clutching her left wrist to her chest like a bird with a wounded wing.

A gruff voice calls out, "Hey! What do you think you're doing?" When Reese sees one of the male teachers approaching her from the right, she takes off down the street in the opposite direction. She hears footsteps on the pavement behind her, but he's heavyset and out of shape, and she easily outruns him. She gains distance on him, and ducks into an alley three blocks away, then shimmies over a wooden privacy fence into someone's backyard. She hides behind a holly hedge, its thorns prickling her skin. Peeking through the branches, much to her relief, she sees neither a homeowner nor a large aggressive pet. After hearing the crunch of gravel in the alley, she waits a minute before climbing the fence and running back the way she came. She weaves through neighborhood streets to Connecticut Avenue and flags down a taxi, spitting out her work address to the driver as she collapses against the seat.

Once her breathing steadies and her mind clears, she realizes what a drastic mistake she's made. The school's surveillance cameras most likely captured her image. She'd neglected to cover her head with a baseball cap, and with a simple enlargement, they would be able to read the restaurant's logo on her black polo shirt. The police will undoubtedly show up at her workplace. She was stalking a child on a school playground. Identifying grounds for arrest will be easy. What if they question her fake credentials? Her true identity will be exposed, and they will call her mother.

At Reveler's Tavern, she returns the binoculars to the rooftop and joins Raimi behind the bar. She avoids eye contact, but he knows something's wrong.

"I can't be here right now," she says and flees the tavern.

"Wait! Anna!" Raimi calls after her, but she runs all the way home—home to the apartment she'd taken over from him after he married Jana.

Looking around, she feels safe. At least for the moment. With her landlord's permission, she'd painted three of the walls eggplant for a dramatic effect and the rest dove gray. Her furniture is an eclectic mix purchased piece by piece at consignment shops and on sale at high-end interior design stores. She's most proud of her collection of R&B vinyl, which she plays on the good-condition vintage turntable she bought several years ago at a yard sale.

Placing a Barry White album on to spin, she throws open the windows, the sheer curtains billowing in the April breeze. She curls up on the sofa and stuffs her cell phone under the cushion, ignoring Raimi's repeated texts and calls. She cries herself to sleep and wakes sometime later to loud pounding on her door. She's expecting the police and is relieved to see Raimi through the peephole. She opens the door and once again bursts into tears.

"What the heck, Reese?" He only uses her real name when he's angry or frustrated. "What happened? Why are you so upset?"

"I really screwed up this time, Raimi." She falls into his outstretched arms.

He strokes her hair while she cries. When she becomes quiet, he walks her to the sofa, and they sit down together. "Tell me everything."

"I was looking at Bella through a pair of binoculars at the playground and one of the teachers saw me."

Lines appear on his forehead. "What'd the teacher say?"

"I didn't wait around to find out. I ran."

Raimi grimaces. "Which makes you look guilty."

"As if I didn't already look guilty, staring with binoculars at a child who isn't mine?" She tugs on the hem of her shirt, and adds, "To make matters worse, I was wearing this."

He sighs. "So now the police know where to start looking for you if they decide to do that. I thought you were going to stay away from the playground."

"I can't ignore this, Raimi. I don't have any proof she's being abused, although I wouldn't be surprised. But I know for certain she's being neglected. Am I supposed to just stand by and watch it happen?"

A moment of silence passes between them. "You can turn this situation to your advantage," Raimi says. "It sounds like you have good reason to be worried about Bella. If the police question you, you'll tell them the truth—who you are and why you're so concerned. You have the documentation from the adoption to support your claim. Worst-case scenario, they slap a restraining order on you. The bright side is, they'll be forced to investigate the Neilsons."

"Which leads to my biggest fear—that they'll take her away from the Neilsons and put her in foster care."

"At least the abuse will stop."

"*If* she's lucky enough to be placed with a loving family." Reese chews on her lower lip. "That loving family should be me, Raimi. I should never have gone through with the adoption. Mama Clara warned me that I would regret giving her up. She offered to help me raise her. But I didn't listen to her. I was too selfish. Too worried about my own future."

Draping his arm around her neck, he draws her close. "You were young, Reese. Too young to have a baby, even with Clara's help. Of course, you were thinking of your future. You had no way to support that child. What you did wasn't selfish. It was selfless. You gave your child the opportunity for a better life."

"I gave the Neilsons the opportunity to raise my child, because they couldn't have one of their own. But they blew their chance, and now it's my responsibility to get her back, to make sure she's safe."

"It's not your responsibility. It's the law's responsibility." Raimi gets up and crosses the room, removing two Vitamin Waters from the refrigerator. "Let me ask you a question." He hands her one of the bottles but remains standing. "Do you think of yourself as Anna or Reese?"

She picks at a loose thread on her tapestry throw pillow as she considers his question. "I don't know. That's a stupid question, anyway. What does my name have to do with any of this?"

"Because, in the process of getting her back, you might risk having your true identity discovered. Are you willing to do that?"

She shrugs.

"Your past, present, and future are on a collision course. Your happiness depends on the successful merging of the three—the runaway college student from Virginia, birth mother concerned about the welfare of the child she put up for adoption, talented singer and songwriter with a brilliant future ahead. Whether you like it or not, a part of you resides with your mother in Virginia."

"The part of me from my much younger days." She misses that mother, the Eva of her early childhood years, the mother who once loved her no matter what. Before that woman turned into a control freak and tried to make Reese into something she was not. Before that woman became an alcoholic and a cheater.

Reese looks up at him. "I'm willing to do whatever it takes to get Bella in safe hands, whether those hands are mine or someone else's. Should I go to the police?"

"Not until you're ready. But you shouldn't hide out here, either. Come back to work with me. If the police show up, you have a logical explanation for being at the school and legitimate concerns about your biological daughter."

"I guess you're right," Reese says in a resigned tone.

He offers his hand, pulling her to her feet. "You won't be alone. I'll be with you every step of the way."

"I'm counting on it," she says with a weak smile.

She closes the windows and locks the door behind them as they leave the apartment. Looping her arm through his, she leans into him as they walk down Eighteenth Street. "I don't know what I would've done without you all these years. You've been so good to me, Raimi."

"You're my little sister. No matter what happens, I will always be here for you."

"And me for you. When this big collision happens, I hope all the people from my past and present can play nicely together in the future." Her thoughts shift to her mother as they walk the rest of the way in silence. Her mother won't be very accepting of Clara and Raimi when she finds out they've kept the secret of her whereabouts for all these years.

MAGGIE

Maggie, after talking to Trey that morning, spends the rest of the day and much of the evening in Georgetown, showing the staff in restaurants and bars Eva's black-and-white photograph of Reese. While a few appear to recognize her, no one can say for certain they know her.

Maggie's aching legs and blistered feet prevent her from walking the long distance to the Metro, and she spends a precious ten dollars to taxi back to the hotel. Her money is dwindling. She has enough for two more nights at the hotel, and then she'll have to ask Eva for more. Or she'll have to call her parents. Do they know she's missing? She doesn't want to worry them. Not the way Reese has worried her mother all these years. She doubts Eric has called them, anyway. Talking to them would put him in the vulnerable position of having to answer some very uncomfortable questions about why their daughter left home in the first place.

Instead of going to her hotel, she enters the bar next door. It's dark inside with only a few patrons occupying barstools. She orders a glass of pinot noir from the bartender, whose name she soon learns is Andrew. On a whim, she shows him Reese's photograph, but he claims he's never seen her.

Munching on a bowl of mixed nuts, which will be her dinner, she contemplates her next move. According to Trey, he'd been out partying the night he saw Reese. It's possible he's confused about the location. There are several hip neighborhoods in DC where millennials hang out. According to Andrew, Adams Morgan, where her hotel is located, and Shaw are the most popular.

She hits the sidewalk midmorning on Saturday. Most of the eating establishments are closed at that hour, but many boutiques open at ten. She enters Vinyl Sounds, an independent record store. As much as Reese is into music, Maggie should've thought of it before.

Bins of vinyl records are arranged by genre and displayed on shelves lining the walls and rows of tables in the center of the room. Circling the store, she thumbs through a section of Elvis Costello before moseying over to the checkout counter. A black man, younger than she, looks up from his iPhone.

"Can I help you?"

Maggie slides Reese's picture across the counter. "Do you by chance know this woman? Her name is Reese Carpenter, but she may be using an assumed name."

He glances at the photograph and back up at Maggie. "Who's asking?"

"Her mother. Well . . . obviously, I'm not her mother, but I'm here on her mother's behalf." Maggie jabs her finger at the photograph. "I really need your help. She's been missing for ten years. I have a source who claims Reese is living in DC and working as a bartender. She's a musician with a passion for R&B."

"Ten years, huh?" He places his phone on the counter and picks up the photograph, studying it carefully. "Oh yeah. I know her. She's that white girl with the crazy vocals who sings in the choir at my church."

Maggie's heart skips a beat, and she resists the urge to jump across the counter and hug him. "Is this church . . . um . . ."

"African-American? Yes, but we don't discriminate."

Maggie's face grows warm. "I'm not prejudiced. I'm just wondering how Reese ended up there."

"I'm not sure, but I think maybe she lives with one of our church families. I don't know the details."

Maggie removes her notebook from her purse. "If you don't mind me asking, what's the name of your church? Maybe I can catch her after services tomorrow."

"Columbia Heights Baptist Church. But you might be able to catch her at work today. She bartends at Reveler's Tavern."

Maggie can't believe her luck. She jots the names of the church and the tavern on her notepad. "Do you happen to know if she's using the name Reese?"

"Nah, she goes by Anna. I'm not sure of the last name."

"Is this tavern near here?"

He inclines his head in the opposite direction she'd come. "Straight down Eighteenth Street about a mile on your right. You can't miss it."

She smiles at him as she slips her notepad into her purse. "Thank you so much! You've been very helpful."

"Sure thing." He returns his attention to his phone, and Maggie is almost out of the door when he calls out to her, "By the way, you didn't hear any of this from me. It'd be bad for business."

"No worries," Maggie says. "I always protect my sources."

As she power-walks down Eighteenth Street, Maggie contemplates her approach. She doesn't want to scare Reese away by asking a bunch of questions. *You're getting ahead of yourself, Maggie. First, confirm that Anna is, in fact, Reese Carpenter.*

Reveler's Tavern is not open when she arrives. According to the sign painted on the window, their hours are from eleven thirty until closing at 3:00 a.m. She waits at a sidewalk table for forty-five minutes until a staff member, whom Maggie assumes is the manager, unlocks the door for the line of people that has begun to form.

A community table occupies the center of the dining room with round tables on one side and a long bar occupying the back wall. Taking a seat near the center of the row of leather barstools, she's disappointed when a man instead of a woman appears from the back to take her order.

Maggie cautions herself to be patient. There are too many ifs to start making assumptions.

The bartender's smile reaches his mesmerizing yellow-green eyes. "What can I get you?"

She splurges on a Bloody Mary. And why not? If things go as she hopes, her investigation will soon be nearing an end and she will be faced with sorting out her life. Who knows? Maybe she'll stay in DC. She likes the vibe of the city, the nation's capital where news happens 24/7. One thing's for certain. She'll divorce her unscrupulous husband as soon as possible.

She chats up the bartender—Raimi is his name—while he pours vodka and Bloody Mary mix into a tall glass, garnishing it with a stalk of celery and a lime. He tells her a little about the history of the restaurant, and when she quizzes him about the menu offerings, he volunteers his favorites—spicy chicken tenders and the quarter pound cheddar burger.

"We're having a golf-themed happy hour this afternoon in honor of the Masters Tournament. Starts at six. I won't be here, though. I get off at five."

Is he flirting with her?

Raimi leaves her to attend to several other groups of patrons seated at the bar. When he returns to take her order a few minutes later, she tells him he needs help.

He smiles, his gorgeous eyes lighting up. "Anna will be here around one."

Maggie mentally punches the air. *So, Anna does work here. But is Anna really Reese?*

"If I didn't know better, I'd think someone has a crush on Anna," Maggie says in a teasing tone.

He chuckles. "I love Anna, but not in a romantic way. She's like a sister to me."

His response reminds her what the guy from the record store said. *She lives with one of our church families.*

A patron at the other end of the bar motions for Raimi and he scurries off.

Maggie glances at her watch. Forty minutes until Anna is due at work. Her chicken tenders arrive within minutes, and she eats slowly. When her Bloody Mary is gone, she asks for a beer to alleviate her guilt over occupying a barstool in the busy restaurant. She grows antsy as one o'clock draws near. What if Anna isn't Reese? Or what if she's changed so much, Maggie can't tell if it's Reese. But the young woman who arrives promptly at one o'clock is undeniably Reese Carpenter. She's much prettier than her photograph with pale-gray eyes beneath heavy brows and a kilowatt smile she bestows upon Raimi. Maggie gets further confirmation when Anna pulls her hair back in an elastic band, revealing *rock 'n' roll* tattooed in script behind her right ear.

Discreetly, before Reese can get a good look at her, Maggie summons Raimi, pays her check, and leaves the tavern. With plenty of time to kill until happy hour, she decides to play tourist. Stopping for a look at the White House along the way, she walks the National Mall before heading to the Tidal Basin where the Cherry Blossom Festival is in full steam with giant food tents and souvenir vendors. It's a glorious day, mid-seventies with clear blue skies. She camps out on the steps of the Jefferson Memorial for hours, basking in the warmth of the sun and watching the crowds coming and going. The diversity of people is extensive with seemingly every nationality and ethnicity represented. Once again, as she has many times since arriving in DC, Maggie experiences an overwhelming feeling of belonging.

When she returns to Reveler's Tavern at six that evening, the downstairs room is packed, and she has to wait fifteen minutes for a seat to open up at the bar. Raimi has gone and an older, giant of a man has taken his place alongside Reese, who's currently working the opposite end of the bar.

Maggie gives her order to the male bartender for a Bloodline Blood Orange Ale, one of the cheapest draft beers on the menu, and watches the end of the third round of the Masters Golf Tournament on the television behind the bar.

It's eight o'clock by the time the crowd thins, and Maggie gets a chance to speak to Reese. "Busy night."

Reese smiles. "Every night's busy around here. We usually have a lull around now. The dinner crew has moved on and the partiers are pregaming somewhere else. They'll start arriving around ten and stay until closing at three."

Maggie's heart sinks. Will she have to stick around until closing to talk to Reese in private? Not that Reese would be in any frame of mind to confront her past after working twelve-plus hours.

Offhandedly, as though making idle conversation, Maggie says, "That's awful late. I hope you don't have to work until then."

"No, thank goodness," Reese says. "I get off at nine tonight. I worked the late shift last night."

While Reese straightens up behind the bar—restocking glasses on shelves and wiping down counters—they talk for a few minutes about the rowdy crowds Reese sometimes sees late at night.

For the second time that day, Maggie pays her bill and leaves the restaurant. She waits on the sidewalk for Reese to emerge at five minutes past nine and steps inline beside her heading in the direction from which she'd come that morning.

Reese shoots her a sideways glance. "What're you doing? Are

you stalking me? I'm sorry if I gave you the wrong impression, but I'm not gay."

"Neither am I. My name is Maggie Wade. I'm a trained investigator sent by your mother to find you. Is there somewhere we can talk?"

*R*eese increases her pace. She thinks about running. She knows the area well. She can ditch this woman with relative ease. But she's tired of hiding. The time has come for her to own up to the past.

"I know a place a few blocks up," Reese says, and they continue in silence to Jack Rose Dining Saloon.

A young couple is vacating a table by the window in the main room downstairs when they enter the pub. They snag the table and Reese summons the waiter, Jimbo, a guy who frequents Reveler's Tavern on his nights off. She orders her usual—a twelve-year-old Johnnie Walker Black Label—and Maggie, seemingly perplexed by the menu, asks for the same.

Reese looks closely at Maggie for the first time. She's stunningly beautiful with glossy mahogany hair and flawless skin. Reese detects both kindness and sadness in Maggie's brown eyes.

"So, you're an investigator," Reese says.

"Technically, I'm an investigative journalist. But this isn't about my career. I'm here as a favor to your mother. We're neighbors and friends. My husband and I moved in across from her on West Avenue back in January."

This surprises Reese. She's certain her mother would've moved. "How is she?"

Maggie's smile is warm, and Reese can tell she's fond of Eva. "She's doing well. At least she seems to be. I haven't known her long enough to make a judgment. She misses you. I know that much. And I get the impression she's lonely, although she has the shop to keep her busy."

"I'm glad she still has the business. So, she never remarried."

Maggie shakes her head. "As far as I know, she doesn't even date."

Reese feels a pang of guilt. She doesn't need this right now. She needs to focus on Bella. "How'd you locate me?"

"I went to the college. Pete Lambert is on staff there now. He told me he thought something was going on between you and Trey McDaniel at the time of your disappearance. Since it was the only lead I had, I decided to track Trey down."

"I assume you found him."

Maggie nods. "He told me he'd seen you working as a bartender, but he couldn't remember where. Locating you took some legwork. He also told me you showed up at his house after the accident, wanting to borrow money. Why didn't you meet him at Starbucks the day after Christmas as planned?"

"It's a long story."

Jimbo arrives with their drinks. Once he's gone, Maggie says, "I'd like to hear it, if you're up to talking about it."

As she sips her whiskey, Reese contemplates how much to tell this woman. Reuniting with her mother is inevitable. And now that Maggie has found her, she can't very well disappear again. Might as well confess all. "Did Trey tell you I was pregnant with his baby?"

If this shocks Maggie, she doesn't let it show. "He left that little tidbit out."

"Figures," Reese says, staring down at the amber liquid in her glass.

"So that's why you ran away from the accident, because you were pregnant?"

Reese clinks the ice in her glass. "Yep."

Maggie's eyebrows become one. "I have so many questions, I don't know where to begin."

Reese sighs. "Then maybe I should back up and start at the beginning." She runs her finger around the lip of her glass. "My teenage years were pretty bad. Going away to college was an enormous relief." She tells Maggie about the band and her friendship with Franny, her crush on Trey, including their one night together, and then finding Franny and Trey in bed together the night of the deb party in Philadelphia. When she gets to the part about the accident, she says, "I should never have told Dad about the baby while he was driving. And, I was too distracted by my problems to notice he wasn't wearing his seat belt. It's my fault he died."

"He was an adult, Reese. The parent, not the child. He should've been reminding you to buckle up. He should've pulled over, waited until he calmed down to continue driving."

"Nothing you say will lessen my guilt, Maggie. I'll live with it until I die."

"Okay, then. Let me ask you this." Maggie plants her elbows on the table. "If you were going to tell your father about the pregnancy, why'd you run after the accident? Why not confide in your mother?"

"Because Mom's parting words on the morning I left for college were, 'If you get pregnant, don't you dare come crying to me. I'm done raising children.'"

Maggie mouths an O, and Reese can tell this surprises her about Eva.

"It was wrong of me not to get in touch with my mom, to let her know I was alive. But I was young and afraid. Trey wanted me to have an abortion. That's why I didn't show up at Starbucks.

I just needed time to figure out what was best for me and the baby."

"And what did you do about the baby, if you don't mind me asking?"

"I gave her up for adoption." Reese tells Maggie about Raimi finding her on Christmas Eve, and Clara taking her in and finding a home for the baby.

"That must have been difficult, giving up your baby. I'm glad you had Clara and Raimi to support you. I met him earlier, by the way. At the tavern. I didn't tell him I was looking for you, but we had a friendly chat. He seems like a nice guy. He mentioned you. Said you're like a sister to him."

"Yeah, we're pretty tight." Reese drains the rest of her whiskey and sets the glass on the table. "Let's stop beating around the bush, Maggie. What exactly do you expect from me? Is my mom paying you to look for me?"

"She gave me a little money for expenses. But she didn't have much to spare. She's struggling financially. Although she probably wouldn't want me to tell you that." Maggie smiles. "I hope you'll come back to Richmond with me, to see your mom. She's going to be beyond excited to see you."

"I'm not ready to face her, Maggie. I can't leave DC. Not yet."

Anger flashes in Maggie's eyes. "I'm not suggesting that you *leave* DC. Why can't you at least visit her? It would mean so much to her."

Reese considers telling Maggie to mind her own business. But Maggie has gone to a lot of trouble to find her, and it's unfair of Reese to hold anything back. When the noise in the restaurant increases with the arrival of a large group, she says, "I can't talk about this here."

"Where else we can go?" Maggie asks, already pushing back from the table.

"My apartment is only a few blocks away," Reese says, flagging Jimbo down for the bill.

They walk in silence as they fight their way through throngs of bar hoppers on the sidewalks. When they arrive at her apartment, Reese removes a bottle of Ketel One vodka from the freezer, pours two fingers into a glass, and hands it to Maggie, motioning her to the sofa. Reese rarely has more than one drink. She's lived up to her long-ago vow not to turn out like her mother.

She puts Van Morrison's *Moondance* album on the turntable and crosses the sitting room to the window. The lyrics and melody of "And It Stoned Me" calms her.

"Raimi used to live in this apartment," Reese says. "He brought me here when we first met. I remember standing in this very spot, looking out at the lights on Christmas trees in the other houses on the street. It reminded me so much of West Avenue. As lost and alone as I felt that night, I knew I couldn't go home. My relationship with my mother was that bad." She turns away from the window. "Why are you doing this, Maggie, if you're not getting paid?"

"When Eva told me about your disappearance, I couldn't stop thinking about you, and . . ." Her voice trails off. "Let's just say I needed an excuse to leave town."

Reese moves to the sofa, sitting down close to her. "I told you my story. Now I'd like to hear yours."

"I guess that's fair. But I warn you, it's not a pretty one." Maggie relaxes back against the cushions. "My marriage was a mistake. The man. The timing. I was rebounding from a relationship with a guy I'd been dating for eight years. Daniel was my soul mate. I thought we would grow old together. In hindsight, I saw what I wanted to see in Eric—handsome, good provider, family man. I certainly never thought he was capable of this." She pulls down the neck of her short-sleeved turtleneck, revealing a line of fading bruises. "He attacked me on Monday night. I walked out on him the next day. I went to Claudia's Closet to see Eva, to tell her I'd decided to try and find you."

Reese's heart goes out to Maggie. "So, you know what it feels like to be on the run."

Maggie nods. "Unfortunately, yes. Unlike you, I have a solid relationship with my mom. She's my rock. I've pushed her away these past few months, though, because I was too proud to admit I'd made a mistake in marrying Eric. I should've called her sooner, but like you, I needed some time to figure out my life, to make the decisions that are right for me."

"And have you? Figured out your life?"

"I'm nowhere near it," Maggie says, her face full of hurt and sadness. "There's more. I learned some disturbing information about my husband from the police chief in Mapleton. But I'm having a difficult time wrapping my mind around it and would rather not get into it that now. Suffice it to say, looking for you has been a blessed distraction."

Reese scrunches her face up in concern. "So, if your husband is still living in your house, which is across the street from my mother, is she in danger?"

"Honestly, Reese, I can't guarantee she's not. But Eric doesn't know your mother and I are friends. And I sent Eva a text warning her to call the police immediately if he threatens her." Draining the rest of her vodka, Maggie gets up and retrieves the Ketel One bottle from the kitchen counter, refilling her glass almost full. She sits back down and sets the bottle on the lamp table beside her. "Your mother's a wonderful person. She's suffered a lot. You can give her some happiness. She'll be so proud to learn you put yourself through college. She wants nothing more than to put all that bad stuff behind you and start over. If you'll let her, she can give you some happiness as well."

Reese questions whether that's even possible, but she owes it to herself and her mother to find out. With the possibility of Eva being in danger, Reese is tempted to head off to Richmond tonight, but she has Bella to think about. "I'm willing to give it a try. But I have urgent unfinished business I need to sort out before I go anywhere."

"What kind of business?" Maggie asks, and when Reese hesitates, she adds, "You can trust me, Reese. I only want what's best for you."

While trust doesn't come easy for Reese, she feels a bond with this young woman. Not only are they about the same age, they have a lot in common. "You're an investigator. Maybe you can help me. It has to do with Bella, the baby I put up for adoption. I've been keeping tabs on her all these years. Knowing she's loved and being well taken care of has given me peace of mind. Until recently. I now have reason to believe she's being neglected, possibly even abused."

Maggie gasps. "That's horrible."

Reese walks Maggie through the events of the past few weeks, from when she first noticed a change in Bella until Friday morning when the teacher chased her away from the playground.

"You get bonus points for perseverance," Maggie says.

Reese moves to the edge of the sofa. "Can you help me, Maggie? If we put our heads together, we can find out what's going on with my child."

Reese's own words echo in her mind. *My child.* In all these years, she hasn't stopped thinking of Bella as her child. Reese starts to cry. She can't go on like this. If it turns out she's mistaken and everything is fine in Bella's family life, she'll leave DC and never come back. But if something is wrong, if *her child* is being abused, she'll not stop fighting until she gets her to safety.

Maggie shakes her head. "I wish I could, Reese. I really do. But I'm flat broke. I don't even have enough money for another night at the hotel where I'm staying."

"I'll pay your expenses. Better yet, you can stay here with me. My sofa pulls out into a bed." Reese jumps to her feet. "We'll go shopping and stock the refrigerator. I can take a few days off from work, and the two of us can figure this thing out in no time."

Maggie closes her eyes for a painfully slow minute without saying a word. Finally, she looks up at Reese. "I'll help you on one condition."

"Name it," Reese says, as eager as a dog waiting for its owner to give it a bone.

"Regardless of the outcome, you have to promise to visit your mother. And I don't mean next week or next month. I mean right away."

"I promise." Reese places her hand over her heart. "I don't own a car, but I'll get on the very next train to Richmond."

EVA

$\mathcal{S}$ometime during the busy day on Saturday, Eva's purse disappears from behind the checkout counter at Claudia's Closet, and she doesn't discover it missing until closing time. While her phone was in her back pocket at the time of the theft, her keys and wallet were stolen. She has Annette's key to lock up the shop, but she has to Uber home.

She's relieved to see Ian and Mack lounging on the front stoop with martini glasses in hand. Thanking her driver, she gets out of the car and crosses the yard to greet them.

"I'm sorry to interrupt your cocktail hour, but I need to get my spare key from you. Someone swiped my purse from under the counter at the shop."

Mack frowns. "That's a bummer!"

Handing his martini to Mack, Ian rises from his metal glider. "I'm sorry to hear that, Eva. Did you have much cash in your wallet?"

"No, I don't usually carry cash."

When she follows Ian inside, she's surprised to see the traditional furnishings in his living room. The eclectic assortment of pieces he inherited from his grandparents have been replaced by animal skin rugs and leather upholstery. "I love what you've done with the place. Add a few horses, and you'll have a bona fide dude ranch."

"Ha-ha." With arms akimbo, he says, "All of this belongs to Mack."

She nudges him playfully with her elbow. "Does this mean he's here to stay?"

Ian's fair skin blushes scarlet from his neck to his receding hairline. "I think he might be the one."

She offers him a sincere smile. "Good for you, Ian! You deserve some happiness."

"As do you, Eva. Any word about Reese?"

She restrains herself from blurting out anything about Maggie's investigation. She's often wondered if Reese ever confided in Ian about her troubles at home. Even if she had, he would never break Reese's trust in him. "No. I'm afraid not."

He hangs his head. "Reese has been on my mind a lot these past few days. Having the woman across the street go missing has brought it all back to me. I'm telling you, that husband, Eric Jones, is a strange one. I wouldn't be surprised if he killed his wife and buried her in the backyard." His face falls. "I'm sorry. That was insensitive of me. I know you were friends with her."

Eva manages to keep a straight face. "Whatever gave you that idea?"

"I saw her leaving your house a few times. I just assumed . . ."

Fear grips Eva's chest. If he saw Maggie leaving her house, others on the street may have seen her as well. As though suddenly struck by the memory, she says, "Oh right. There was that one time when she borrowed some coffee from me. We talked for a few minutes. She seemed nice enough, but we really don't have that much in common. She's much younger than me."

Ian snickers. "You mean younger than us." He opens the drawer of a console table and removes her brass house key. "Do you have a spare key to your car?"

Eva nods. "If I can remember where I put it." She turns to leave. "I better be going. I need to call the credit card companies."

"Good luck with that." Ian walks her out of the house to the edge of the lawn. "Let me know if I can do anything else to help."

Eva waves at him in response.

Inside the house, she pours her vodka and soda, spends thirty minutes reporting her credit and debit cards stolen, and scours the house for her spare car key, which she finally locates in the back of the junk drawer in the kitchen.

That night, for the first time in years, she drinks her dinner and goes to bed drunk.

She wakes the following morning with a splitting headache. "Serves you right," she says to her reflection in the mirror as she pops two Advil.

She brews a large cup of coffee and heads on foot to Carytown to retrieve her car. The warm sunshine and gentle breeze do little to improve her mood. Not only will it take at least a week for her new credit and debit cards to arrive in the mail, she will also need to get replacements for her driver's license and health insurance card. She will have to cash a check at the bank to buy groceries and pay miscellaneous expenses. Wondering if she should report the incident to the police, she decides to wait and call the nonemergency number on Monday morning.

When she returns home with her car, she goes to work in the yard, raking leaves out of flower beds bordering her small brick patio. The physical labor helps take her mind off of stolen purses and missing persons. Breaking only for a turkey and swiss sandwich around noon, she spends the remainder of the afternoon pruning shrubs and planting two flats of pink impatiens she purchased earlier in the week from Lowe's around the corner. By the time she finishes, it's nearing five o'clock.

In the kitchen, she's surprised to find the counter and sink spotless. She's positive she left a knife smeared with mayonnaise on a cutting board after lunch, but she finds both items in the dishwasher. Blaming it on aging memory, she goes upstairs to her room. After luxuriating in a long shower, her concern deepens when she finds plaid Bermuda shorts and a pink polo have replaced the denim cutoffs and Tar Heels T-shirt she's absolutely certain she laid out on her bed.

Is she losing her mind? She considers the possibility of early-onset dementia, then convinces herself she's simply distracted. She hasn't heard from Maggie since she arrived in Washington on Thursday.

Eva dresses in the Bermuda shorts and polo and goes downstairs. Mixing a cocktail, she stands at the living room window. Eric's car is parked on the street in front of Maggie's house, but there's no sign of movement from within. Then, as if she willed it to happen, he appears in his upstairs bedroom window. Despite the distance, the hatred in his evil eyes strikes her like a laser.

Fear steals her breath with an audible gasp. Is it possible Eric stole her purse? Is he trying to torment her by making her think she's losing her mind? A chill travels her spine at the thought of him in her house. While she was in the shower, no less. He's an abusive man. She's seen the bruises on Maggie's neck with her own eyes.

Racing up the stairs, she retrieves the gun safe from the top shelf of the master bedroom closet. She then works the combination and removes the revolver, tucking it into the waistband of her shorts. On her way back to the living room, her phone vibrates her hand with an incoming text from Maggie. It dawns on her that she'd left her phone on the bedside table while she was in the shower. Even if Eric saw it, he couldn't access her contact information without her password. Maggie's prepaid cell number is safe. For now. Eva will have to be more careful with her phone in the future.

Her heart sinks as she reads Maggie's text. Just checking in. The investigation is moving along. I'll call you when I know more.

Moving along how? Why is Maggie being so evasive? Maybe she has bad news and doesn't know how to break it to Eva. Or maybe she's on the cusp of finding Reese and is afraid to get Eva's hopes up. The waiting, the not knowing, is torture.

Eva microwaves a bag of popcorn for dinner and chases it down with four more vodka and sodas. Despite her alcoholic haze, she's keyed up and needs an Ambien to sleep. Around four in the morning, she's startled out of a deep slumber by a loud crashing noise downstairs. She snatches up her phone and gun from her nightstand and grabs her robe from the foot of the bed. She tiptoes down the hall and the stairs. As she nears the bottom, the living room comes into view. Light from the streetlamp streams in through the front window, casting a pale glow across the room. The frame with Reese's senior photograph is turned facedown on the table beside the leather recliner and the shattered remains of Eva's beloved porcelain Scottie figurine are scattered across the fireplace hearth.

She freezes. *Is someone still in the house?* She backs slowly up the stairs. At the top, she darts down the hall to her room, closing and locking the door behind her. Crouched down in the corner behind the door, she calls 9-1-1.

"Someone's in my house," she whispers to the emergency operator.

"I'm sorry, ma'am. You'll have to speak up."

Her tone is low but urgent. "Someone's in my house! Send the police. Hurry," she says and provides the woman with the address.

"I'm dispatching the police now. Stay on the line with me until they get there."

The sound of fingers typing on a keyboard comes across the line.

"Ma'am, did you actually see someone in your home?"

"No. But I heard a noise. I found a broken porcelain figurine. It didn't get broken by itself."

"Where are you now?"

"Locked in my bedroom. I can feel his presence. I know he's still in the house."

"I know you're frightened but try to remain calm. The police should be there soon."

Five agonizing minutes pass before the sound of loud knocking reverberates throughout the house. "They're here now."

The operator says, "They've explored the exterior of your home, and report no visible sign of a break-in. Do you feel comfortable letting them in? I can stay on the line with you. Or do you want them to bust down your door?"

"I'll let them in." Scrambling to her feet, with phone tucked beneath her chin and gun held in trembling outstretched hands, Eva makes her way quickly to the door. Through the peephole, she identifies two uniformed officers, both middle-aged males of average height, one as thin as the other is plump. Slipping the revolver into the pocket of her robe, she unlocks the bolt and throws open the door.

"Thank goodness you're here, Officers." She steps out of the way to let them in. "There's someone in my house." She tells them about the photograph and broken figurine. "In here." When she shows them to the living room, the black Scottie figurine stands intact beside Reese's upright photograph. "I don't understand. Minutes ago, the figurine was in a million pieces." She drops to her knees, running her hands across the brick hearth, but they come up clean.

Officer Knight, the thin officer, helps her to her feet.

Eva scrubs her face. "I know you think I'm crazy, but I know what I saw."

"We checked all the windows and doors from the outside. They all appear to be locked. With your permission, we'll check again from the inside, to make certain nothing is amiss."

"Please."

Knight's partner, Officer Kelley, leaves Eva and Knight standing in the center of the room. While he's gone, Eva tells

Knight about her stolen purse and the incidents that happened earlier in the day.

"Everything is locked up tight," Kelley reports when he returns.

"That's because he let himself in," Eva says. "I told you he stole my purse. He has a key to my house."

Kelley and Knight exchange a look. "Who is *he*, ma'am?" Knight asks.

"Eric Jones, my neighbor across the street. He's trying to make me think I'm losing my mind."

Kelley narrows his brown eyes. "What reason would he have for doing that?"

Eva blurts out, "Because he's an abusive psychopath. His wife is missing, and he's convinced I know where she is."

"And do you? Know where she is?" Knight asks.

Eva has backed herself into a corner. She has no choice but to lie. "Of course not. I barely know her. We only met once or twice."

"You've made some serious allegations against Mr. Jones," Kelley says. "Do you have any proof?"

Eva lets out a sigh. "No. I'm sorry to say, I don't."

Knight tilts his head to the side as he studies her. "Have you been drinking, ma'am?"

"I had a couple of drinks earlier in the evening." She waves the drinks off as insignificant. "But that was hours ago."

"What about drugs?" Kelley asks. "Have you taken any tonight, prescription or otherwise?"

"I took a sleeping pill around midnight." Eva realizes her mistake too late. She watches Knight's face as he puts the pieces of the puzzle together. He thinks he's solved the crime.

"What was the name of the sleep medication?" he asks.

"Ambien," she admits. "I'm well aware of the potential side effects, but I've taken Ambien as needed for sleep for years. I've never experienced any bazaar behavior. I don't mow the grass naked or anything like that."

"There's always a first time." Knight moves toward the front door. "We'll be back in touch after we do a little digging."

Locking the door behind them, she settles herself in Stuart's recliner with the gun resting on her lap until the first rays of sun peek through the clouds. She waits until eight o'clock before calling around to area locksmiths. On the fifth try, she finds one who can come right away. Regardless of what the police think, she knows Eric Jones has been in her house. If the police won't protect her, she'll have to protect herself. She owns a weapon, and she's not afraid to use it.

MAGGIE

Maggie strides up and down the sidewalk, gripping the leash she purchased earlier in the day while pretending to look for her lost dog. The homes lining the street are attractive brick colonials—old but mostly renovated and well maintained. She's only interested in one of them, a gray-framed house with pots of pink geraniums flanking the yellow-painted front door. A silver minivan swings into the driveway. In a din of laughter, three little boys and their parents tumble out. The children scurry inside while the parents unload a picnic basket and tote bag stuffed with balls and Frisbees and plastic baseball bats from the trunk. They appear to be a nice family returning from a pleasant Sunday afternoon at a nearby park. Unfortunately, they're not the right family.

Maggie leaves the quiet neighborhood and heads to the Cleveland Park Metro Station where she rides a Red Line train one stop to Woodley Park. Claiming her suitcase from the desk clerk at her hotel, she walks the half mile to Reese's apartment.

Reese is unpacking groceries when she arrives. Placing a carton of mint chocolate chip gelato in the freezer, she slams the door and turns to Maggie. "How'd it go?"

"It's not them. The family who lives at the address you gave me is African-American with three children—all boys."

"So I had reason to worry." Reese sags against the counter. "I can't remember when the last time was that I saw the Neilsons at that house. Every time I've been by there, no cars have been in the driveway." She frowns. "This means Nora and James have moved. Washington is a big city with lots of neighborhoods. They could be living anywhere."

"But wouldn't Bella have to live within a specific area to attend the same school?"

"Technically. But James and Nora may have conveniently"— Reese uses air quotes—"neglected to tell the school they've moved. What do we do now?"

"Plan B," Maggie says. "But it'll have to wait until the morning." She parks her suitcase in a corner and plops down on the sofa.

"I hope you like sushi," Reese says, setting a tray of assorted sushi rolls on the coffee table in front of Maggie.

"I haven't eaten since breakfast, and I love sushi."

Reese returns to the kitchenette for plates, napkins, wine glasses, and a bottle of pinot grigio, and joins Maggie on the sofa. "I hope you don't mind. I accepted an invitation for us to have dinner with Clara tomorrow night. I told her about you, and she's dying to meet you."

"Will Raimi be there?" The words tumble off Maggie's lips before she can stop them.

A smirk appears on Reese's lips. "Maybe. Do I detect a spark of romantic interest?"

"Who? Me? No way. I'm staying away from men for now. Maybe forever. I'm asking for your sake." She points at Reese. "I have a hunch there's something going on between the two of you."

Reese burst out laughing. "I can say with absolute certainty there is nothing resembling romance between us. Raimi and Clara are my fam. I love Raimi like a brother."

Maggie's heart skips a beat, and she reminds herself that her last rebound relationship didn't turn out so well.

While they eat, and for hours afterward, they talk about a host of topics, including but not limited to Eva and Eric and Bella. Maggie and Reese come from different backgrounds, but both are driven to succeed within their chosen professions and hope to one day marry the right man and start a family. They also identify with the trouble in their lives and make a pact to see each other through to better days.

Night is beginning to fall and the room has darkened when Maggie says, "I need to call Eva, but I have no idea what to say to her. I hate lying to her."

"Then don't call her. And don't lie to her. Text her that the investigation is moving along, and you'll know more soon."

Maggie thumbs off the text and tosses the phone on the sofa cushion beside her.

"How much do you know about my mom?" Reese asks.

Maggie hesitates before answering. "I know she'll do just about anything to find you." She can tell by Reese's pained expression that she's about to hear an earful.

"My mom's a hypocrite, Maggie. At least she was back then. She was always waiting up for me when I got home at night, accusing me of being drunk or stoned or sleeping around. Ironically, she's the alcoholic. She's the one who cheated on my dad." Retreating to the corner of the sofa, hugging one of the throw pillows to her chest, Reese reveals vivid details about Eva that Maggie never would've believed had she not been hearing them from Eva's own daughter.

Maggie's gaze travels to the nearly empty wine bottle. While they were talking, Reese refilled Maggie's glass twice but she's barely taken a sip of her own wine. "What you must think of me," Maggie says.

Reese waves her hand, as if to say, No worries. "I'm a bartender. I don't cast judgment. I love seeing other people enjoy themselves. It's just not for me. I made a mistake in college and ended up pregnant."

"I admire your convictions. You're one formidable young woman."

Reese ignores the compliment. "I'm sorry if I ruined your opinion of my mother. But it's important to me that you understand why I stayed away so long. Do you know? Is she still drinking? Your answer won't affect my decision to visit her. I promised I'd go, and I will. But I need to mentally prepare myself for what I'll find."

"I can honestly say, I've never seen her drunk. And she's never given me reason to suspect she was hungover. We shared a bottle of red wine the first afternoon we met. But it was during a snow storm and seemed like a festive thing to do. After that, we only had an occasional drink together."

Reese stands and stretches. "I hope that means she's gotten her drinking under control. Because, I'm going to be honest with you, Maggie, I can't go through all that again."

For a long time after Reese goes to bed, Maggie lies on the sofa trying to imagine what *all that* had been like for Eva and Reese. She cares a great deal about both mother and daughter. She believes that, despite their past differences, Reese and Eva owe it to each other to try again. And Maggie will do everything within her power to make that happen.

A few minutes before nine the following morning, Maggie is seated on a bench across the street from Cleveland Park Elementary, observing the parade from behind the Monday edition of the *Washington Post*. Families arrive by foot and in luxury SUVs— mothers and fathers waving and blowing their darlings goodbye kisses. She scrutinizes the faces of every parent, but none of the mothers or fathers resemble the Facebook pictures Reese showed her. The bell rings and the last car pulls away. Maggie waits ten more minutes, stands, and tucks the folded paper under her arm. She's rounding the corner at the end of the block when she spots Nora and Bella coming toward her from the opposite direction. Lowering her head, with her eyes peeled to the sidewalk, Maggie waits until they've passed her by before risking a backward glance. Bella's brown hair is a tangled mess, the seat of her white shorts is streaked with dirt, and she walks as though carrying the weight of the world on her tiny shoulders.

Maggie ducks behind a neighbor's hedgerow and hides, crouched down, until Nora returns, alone, ten minutes later. Stepping out from the bushes, Maggie trails her at a respectable distance to the Metro. On the Red Line train to Glenmont, she steals glances at Nora who's seated across the aisle from her. Her cheeks are hollow and dark circles rim her blue eyes. Despite the warm weather, she's wearing a hoodie and sweatpants. Reese has loaned Maggie her cell phone for the purpose of taking photographs. When Nora pushes up her sleeve to pick at a scab, Maggie, pretending to check messages on the phone, snaps a pic of the bruises and track marks in the crook of her arm.

At the Farragut North Metro Station, Nora departs the train and Maggie follows at a reasonable distance on the neighborhood sidewalks to Q Street. Nora disappears inside a two-story house with peeling aqua-blue paint on the facade and bars on the windows and doors.

Maggie waits two hours for Nora to emerge again. And when she does, she's wearing a sunhat and carrying a small round basket. Backtracking to Seventh Street, Nora turns right, walks two blocks, and plants herself in the alcove of an abandoned building with her basket on the pavement in front of her.

Maggie can hardly believe her eyes. This woman, who'd been

an elementary school teacher when she adopted Reese's baby nine years ago, is now a drug addict and a beggar.

Maggie rounds the next corner and leans against the side of a building while she works out the best way to approach Nora. It takes less than five minutes to devise a plan.

Strolling at a leisurely pace, pretending to window shop, Maggie leans down as though to place a folded five-dollar bill in Nora's basket. When Nora looks up from where she's seated cross-legged on the pavement, Maggie asks, "Can I buy you a hot meal?"

Nora snorts. "I'd rather have the five."

"I'll make a deal with you. If you eat a hot meal, I'll give you the five."

"Keep your money," Nora says, slapping Maggie's hand away. "Why do you care, anyway? You're just looking for a way to feel better about yourself."

"I have a sister in your situation. I'd like to think someone is looking out for her." Lying is part of Maggie's job. She no longer thinks of it as morally wrong. It's a means to an end, a way to extract the information she needs.

"Oh really?" Nora asks in a challenging tone. "Where does she live?"

"In Portland, Oregon. She's homeless and addicted to heroin."

Nora harrumphs. "I'm not homeless."

"But you are addicted to heroin."

"Not that it's any of your business." Nora glares at her. "I used to be pretty once like you. It can happen in a flash, you know? Your whole life can simply fall apart."

Yeah, I know. It happened to me—an abusive husband and not a cent to my name. The money I'm offering you isn't mine. "But there are people who can help you put your life back together."

"Let me guess. You're one of them," Nora says.

Maggie extends a hand to her. "I can be, if you let me."

REESE

*R*eese slips her hand in the front pocket of her backpack for her phone, then remembers she gave it to Maggie. She risks a glance at the wall clock behind her. In fifteen minutes she'll sneak out of class so as to make it home in time for a Skype interview at noon with a Nashville music producer. She's struggled all morning to stay focused. Her mind is on Maggie, not the old material her professors are reviewing. She has As in all her classes. Next week's exams are the least of her concerns.

Reese has faith in Maggie's abilities as an investigator, and believes Maggie will eventually track Nora down. But what will happen then? What if Nora or James is in trouble? Reese is prepared to get involved, even going to the police if necessary, in order to protect Bella.

Although Reese has known her for only a couple of days, she can tell that Maggie sees the best in everyone she meets. Which explains why she married an abusive nut job. Maggie deserves better. Someone like Raimi. Reese bites down on her lip, suppressing a smile. *Actually, why not Raimi? I can't think of anyone I'd rather have as a sister-in-law than Maggie.*

Reese looks around the room at her classmates. She's struck up friendships with a few of them over the years, relationships based solely on their mutual interest in music. She's never had coffee after class or joined them for lunch in the cafeteria or socialized with them on the weekends. She won't miss them. She will shed no tears on graduation day. After going to school part-time and working full-time these past six years, she's ready to move on with her life, whatever that entails.

At twenty-five minutes past eleven, she slips out of class unnoticed. With a stroke of luck, the Metro trains are running on time, and she makes it back to her apartment without a minute to spare. When she opens her laptop on the kitchen counter, her Skype app is buzzing with the incoming call. Clicking accept, she's surprised to see that Grant Gardner is much younger than she'd anticipated. By the professional, almost stilted, tone of his emails, she'd judged him to be at least sixty, but the good-looking guy with blue-gray eyes staring out at her from her computer is not much older than she. Early thirties is Reese's best guess.

"I'm so sorry. I'm running late. I just got out of class," Reese says, dragging a barstool across the floor to the counter.

"No worries," Grant says, his lips parting in a soft smile. "We've got plenty of time. Take a minute to catch your breath."

Reese inhales and exhales until her breath steadies. "There. Now. That's better."

Grant clasps his hands together on the desk. "As you know, I'm quite fond of your music. The last batch of songs you sent were your best yet."

Reese smiles and crosses her fingers. "I'm glad you like them."

"I have some exciting news to share with you, and I'm glad to have the opportunity to do it face to face."

"I'm intrigued," she says, nodding for him to continue.

"June Tucker has selected you to write the songs for her new album."

Reese's mouth falls open. "June Tucker? Are you kidding me?"

she says, her professional manner forgotten. "She's, like, the hottest country music vocalist. Her songs are topping the charts."

Grant chuckles. "I'm aware. I helped put her there."

Remembering who she's speaking with, Reese collects herself. "Of course, you did."

"While June is a gifted singer and entertainer, her talent as a songwriter leaves much to be desired. But she absolutely adores your work. She's already chosen a few of the songs from your portfolio, but she'd like to work with you directly to develop the rest. She has great lyrics, but no idea how to write a composition using them. We're talking a multilevel collaboration. It would be helpful if you'd move to Nashville. We'd pay all your moving expenses, of course."

Bella pops immediately into her mind. "Move to Nashville? Wow. I hadn't expected that."

Grant clears his throat. "By no means is moving a deal breaker. Although, I dare say, living in Nashville will ultimately open more doors for you going forward."

Reese tucks a strand of hair behind her ear. "In the interest of full disclosure, I have some personal issues I need to sort through in DC before I can consider moving to Nashville."

"I understand. I can tell I've caught you by surprise. Take some time to think about it. We can fly you down for a visit. You might find you like Nashville. I know, I do. I've lived here all my life."

"I'll give it some thought."

"Great! We can talk more about you moving to Nashville later. I need to make a few adjustments to our offer, and I'll email it to you in a matter of minutes. I think you'll be pleased with our terms."

Reese smiles. "I'll be waiting for it."

"Don't hesitate to reach out if you have any questions or reservations," he says, and the screen goes black.

Reese slides off the barstool, fills a glass of water from her

Brita pitcher, and crosses the room to the window, observing her neighbors hustle back and forth on the sidewalk below. She knows a few of them by name, none of them well. Not enough to miss them if she moves. Washington has been her home for all of her adult life. What will it be like to start over in a new city? After looking over her shoulder for ten years, it'll be a relief to come out of hiding. But can she simply go back to being Reese? And why not Nashville? Even if her reconciliation with Eva goes well, she has too many bad memories from her youth to move back to Richmond. Home for Reese is Mama Clara's house with the aroma of something delicious cooking in the oven. She can always come back and visit, though. She doesn't have to continue living in a city she doesn't love.

Turning away from the window, she's setting her water glass in the sink when her computer pings with an incoming email from Grant. She clicks on the email and scrolls down, her eyes growing wide at the mid-five figure his company is willing to pay her for ten songs plus all expenses should she decide to move to Nashville. Throwing her arms in the air, Reese victory dances around her apartment. Her hard work is finally paying off.

Flutters of excitement take up residence in her belly and stay there all afternoon.

"You're in a good mood," Raimi says when he hears her humming her latest work-in-progress tune. The lunch crowd has died down, and they are restocking for happy hour.

"Is it a sin for a girl to be in a good mood?"

"Not at all," Raimi says, shaking his head. "I just wasn't sure what to expect. Mom told me about Maggie. I know you have mixed emotions about reuniting with your mama."

"I do have mixed emotions about that. I have a lot to tell you, Raimi. But you'll have to wait until dinner. I want to tell you and Clara at once." She twirls her dish towel and pops him on the butt.

"Ouch! That hurt. You're gonna pay for that." Grabbing her

from behind, he squeezes his arms tight around her, lifting her off the ground.

"Put me down," she squeals.

She wiggles out of his arms and pushes him away and they double over with laughter.

When the laughing fit ends, Reese collapses against the counter. "What would you say if I told you I was thinking of moving to another city?"

"So, you *are* moving back to Richmond?" Raimi returns his attention to the rack of clean glassware he was unpacking onto the shelves.

"Not Richmond. Somewhere new."

He fist-punches the air. "I'd say go for it. I'll miss you like crazy, but I'll come visit you wherever you land."

"I'm terrified though, Raimi. What if I can't make it on my own?"

Leaning against the counter beside her, Raimi gives her a half hug. "What're you talking about? You made it on your own a long time ago."

"If you hadn't rescued me that Christmas Eve, I would've starved to death, maybe even been kidnapped and murdered. And Mama Clara. Think of all she's done for me. She gave me a place to live, nurtured me through pregnancy and childbirth, and organized the adoption."

"That was in the beginning. Think about what you've accomplished since. You've worked a full-time job while putting yourself through school. You've come into your own. You don't give yourself enough credit. Spread your wings and fly. You've earned this chance. Go for it. And don't look back."

She wraps her arms around his neck, hugging him tight. "You're the best fam brother a girl can have."

MAGGIE

*a*cross the booth from her, Maggie studies Nora as she picks at her hamburger. The attractive woman she once was—petite features in a heart-shaped face—is evident beneath her dry, cracked skin. Her natural wheat-colored hair, which would've shined like gold in healthier days, now frames her face in greasy clumps. The woman reeks of sweat and urine and booze. The odors drift across the table and assault Maggie's nose, taking her breath away. And her appetite. Her bagel remains untouched in front of her.

Maggie pushes the bagel away. "Do you have any family that can help you?"

"Nope. Both my parents are dead, and my sister lives in the wilds of Alaska. She offered for my kid and me to come live with her, but she's not much better off than I am. Neither of us has the money for airline tickets. Not that I'm particularly interested in living in Alaska." Nora shivers. "Too cold."

Maggie sits back against the red leather bench and sips stale coffee from a white ceramic mug. "If you're willing to talk about it, I'd like to hear how you arrived at this juncture in your life."

Nora stuffs a french fry into her mouth. "I had a perfect life.

Married my college sweetheart. Lived in a house with a picket fence. We both had successful careers. I was a second-grade teacher and James an IT specialist with a local firm. We hit our first bump in the road when we had trouble getting pregnant. After five years and $50,000 in fertility treatments, we decided to adopt a child. The good Lord blessed us with a beautiful baby girl. Bella. We were happy." A dreamy expression crosses her face. "So very happy." The dreamy expression subsides. "Until my husband grew distant and the arguments started. He wanted a child of his own. He blamed me for our fertility problems and accused me of pressuring him into adopting Bella. One day he came home from work and told me he was leaving me for another woman. An administrative assistant at his firm who was pregnant with his child. He divorced me and moved out to California. I've yet to receive a single dime of the child support the judge ordered him to pay." Tears spill from Nora's eyes and she snatches a napkin from the dispenser to wipe them.

Once again, Maggie is reminded of life's volatility. Nora is an educated woman who's fallen on hard times. Just like herself. "I'm so sorry."

"It was a difficult time for me. I wasn't myself. My emotions were all over the place. One day, about six months after we separated, one of my students was acting up, and I grabbed her by the arm, so tight I left bruises." Choking back a sob, Nora covers her mouth with a trembling hand. "The child told her mother what happened and, understandably, I was fired from my job."

Maggie shakes her head in dismay. "That seems like an unreasonably harsh punishment. You were under a great deal of stress."

"That's no excuse. Teachers are expected to be perfect at all times regardless of the circumstances." Nora takes a minute to collect herself. "No school would hire me after that. I tried to find another job. Although, admittedly, my attempts weren't hard enough."

Nora shifts her attention to her paper napkin, shredding it into pieces and rolling them into tiny balls.

When Nora doesn't continue, Maggie asks, "How'd you get into drugs?"

Nora looks up, as though surprised to find Maggie sitting across from her. She sweeps the mountain of napkin balls onto the floor and sits back on the bench. "One night last summer, my daughter was spending the weekend with a friend at the beach. I was so lonely. When the walls began to close in on me, I left my house. I walked for hours. It was hot as hell, one of those nights when the temperature never drops and the humidity sucks the life out of you. I got thirsty, so I stopped in at a local bar for a beer. I met Todd that night. I'd never used drugs before meeting him, never even smoked weed. I was addicted from the get-go. I couldn't get enough of the high, the escape. I was already behind on my mortgage payment. Not long after that night, the bank foreclosed on my house. With nowhere else to go, I had no choice but to move in with Todd."

"What does Todd do for a living?"

Nora rolls her eyes. "Whatta you think? He's a dealer."

Maggie dreads telling Reese her biological child is living with a drug dealer. "How is he with your daughter?"

"He tolerates her, I guess. He helps out when I'm in a bind. Like today, he's picking her up from school so I can go to the dental clinic to see about a toothache." She raises her hand to her face, cupping her cheek.

"Is Todd abusive to either of you?"

Maggie knows she's gone too far when Nora's expression hardens, and her hand falls away from her face. "That's none of your business. Who are you anyway? You said you wanted to help me. Are you a social worker or something?"

"No, I'm a journalist. I'm working on a feature about women like you who are—"

"Junkies?"

"Women who are in crisis. I've just begun my research, but my goal is to help women, like you, get treatment for their addictions. To help you on your path to a better life." Maggie isn't lying. She's been batting around the idea for the feature since arriving in DC.

Nora glares at her. "And who do you think will take care of my daughter while I'm getting this treatment?"

"Foster care, until you get your feet back on the ground." Not an ideal situation, Maggie thinks, but certainly better than having Bella live with Todd.

"I might never get her back, and I can't take that chance." Nora's lips part in a devilish grin as she lifts Maggie's purse from under the table and dangles it in front of her.

Maggie pats the empty bench beside her where she'd placed her purse. "How'd you—"

"Desperate people do desperate things." Nora removes Maggie's wallet and withdraws a five-dollar bill, stuffing it into her bra. Pushing the bag across the table to Maggie, she slides out of the booth to her feet. "I may be a drug addict, but I'm not a thief. Your two twenties are safe in your wallet. Heroin hasn't stripped me of everything. I still have a shred of decency left."

Maggie stares at the grimy glass door long after Nora disappears through it. She doesn't want to end up on the streets like Nora. Unlike Nora, she has a family to turn to for help. As soon as things are settled with Reese and Eva, she'll reach out to her family for support. She'll return to Richmond, make certain the police throw the book at Eric for his past and present sins, file for divorce, and get what's rightfully hers—the meager amount from the sale of her car and the savings she'd so readily handed over to him.

Maggie thinks about Nora stealing her purse from under her nose. While she feels an undeniable connection with the city, she has much to learn about its inhabitants. And, even though she only knows one person here, she's certain she wants to make DC her home. What better place to be an investigative journalist than the nation's capital? She'll use her article about the down-trodden street people as sample material when interviewing for jobs.

Realizing it is nearly two o'clock, she pays the bill and rushes back across town to the elementary school, arriving just as a thin man with tattoos decorating his shaved head emerges with Bella from the front entrance. He grabs hold of the little girl's hand and drags her across the street and down the block. Bella runs alongside him, struggling to keep up with his long strides. When she trips on a crack in the pavement, he jerks her arm, lifting her in the air and setting her back on her feet.

The crossing guard motions for Maggie to stop, and she watches Todd and Bella disappear out of sight. She's seen enough for today. For now, she needs to find a way to tell Reese what she's learned.

Because Reese is working the afternoon shift at the tavern, Maggie doesn't see her until that evening when they meet at Clara's for dinner.

"You're an answer to my prayers," Clara says to Maggie when she greets her at the door. "For years, I've been asking the Lord to send someone to carry this child home to her mama."

Reese pats Clara on the back as though humoring a child. "I'm not going anywhere yet, Mama Clara. I have some unfinished business in DC first."

The freckles dotting Clara's nose grow wide as a smile spreads across her face. "Graduation! Of course. You should ask your mama to join us for the celebration. She'll be so proud of what you've accomplished." She turns back to Maggie. "I bet she was beside herself when you told her you'd found her baby girl."

Reese steps between them. "Maggie hasn't told her yet, Mama

Clara. I promised to call my mother as soon as I've sorted out my business. Which, by the way, has nothing to do with graduation."

Clara's body grows still. "Please tell me this isn't about the Neilson child."

"We'll talk about it after we eat." Reese sniffs. "I'm starving. And something smells delicious. What's for dinner?"

"Fried flounder, cheese grits, cornbread, and coleslaw."

When Clara leaves them for the kitchen, Maggie holds Reese back, briefly explaining the events of the day. Reese, although understandably distraught, keeps a stiff upper lip.

"What do we do now?" Reese asks.

"I'm fresh out of plans. I suggest we ask your family for help."

"Let's get through dinner first." Reese spins on her heels and heads out of the room.

Maggie trails her through the living and dining rooms to the kitchen, noticing that Clara's furnishings are circa 1980s, and her home is clean and tidy and inviting.

They find Raimi, spatula in hand, attending a sizzling cast iron skillet on the stove. Reese stands on her tiptoes, peering over his shoulder at the fish. "Who put you in charge? Clara usually fries the fish."

His eyes remain glued to the skillet. "She's been running around here like a crazy person, getting ready for your company." When he casts a glance at Maggie, recognition registers on his face and he does a double take. "Hey! I know you from the tavern."

Maggie feels flushed. When she opens her mouth to speak, the words tumble out jumbled and incoherent. "When I met you at the bar, I had no idea Anna was Reese. Or Reese was Anna. I mean, I hoped she was, but I had no way of knowing for sure. And I certainly didn't know the two of you were so close. It's just that I had this lead, and I needed to track it down. And I suspected I was close to finding Anna. I mean Reese."

When Raimi continues to stare openmouthed at Maggie,

Reese snatches the spatula away from him and hip-bumps him out of the way of the frying pan. "You're burning the fish, bro."

Maggie squirms under Raimi's gaze. The light bounces off the gold flecks in his green eyes, electrifying them. She finds him sexy as hell and has to remind herself she's technically still married. "I only want what's best for Reese," Maggie goes on. "Eva loves her so much and misses her. I'm sorry. I didn't mean to deceive you."

Raimi, a soft smile on his lips, holds up his hand to silence her. "No need to explain. We're on the same side. Reese will always have a home here, with us. But she should've contacted her mother a long time ago. She must first reconcile with the past before moving on with the future."

"Stop talking about me as though I'm not here," Reese says as she forks the flounder filets, one at a time, from the skillet to the layers of paper towel on the counter.

Maggie smiles over at Reese. "She's shared a lot about her past with me. And I respect the decisions she's made."

"All right now," Clara says. "We agreed to table that discussion until after dinner." Shooing them out of the way, she removes a pan of steaming cornbread from the oven. "Table's all set out on the patio. Here, you take this." She gives Maggie a bowl of coleslaw. "And you take the grits." She hands over the hot pads and casserole dish to Reese.

Maggie follows Reese out the back door to the screen porch. The picnic table is set for four with pink gingham placemats and floral plates, which Maggie suspects belonged to Clara's grandmother. Beyond the porch, a patch of lawn is surrounded by a privacy fence, lined with rose bushes in full bloom.

Clara and Raimi sit on one side of the table with Maggie and Reese opposite them. They bless the food and serve their plates. Maggie manages a few bites in between answering numerous questions about her family in Portland and her life in Richmond. They don't ask about Eva, and Maggie avoids the subject of her marriage. The conversation eventually transitions to a young member of their church who recently committed suicide, allowing Maggie the opportunity to finish her dinner.

Raimi and Reese clear the table and bring out plates of strawberry shortcake with homemade whipped cream.

"We can't ignore the elephant on the porch any longer," Reese says. "Maggie, please tell Clara and Raimi about your encounter with Nora today."

As Maggie walks them through the day's events, expressions of disbelief settle on Clara's and Raimi's faces.

When she finishes talking, Raimi lets out a loud exhalation. "I owe you an apology, Reese. I thought you were being melodramatic."

"You're forgiven," Reese says with a sad smile. "Honestly, it's worse than even I imagined."

"That poor child," Clara says. "Shame on Nora for letting this happen."

"Addiction is a disease," Reese says. "But Bella shouldn't have to suffer because of it."

"What're you gonna do?" Raimi asks.

Reese shakes her head. "I have no idea. Me being the birth mother complicates things. We need advice from the professionals." Her gaze shifts to Clara. "Mama Clara, you're the most well-connected person in our community. Is there someone you can call?"

Clara closes her eyes and nods her head. "There are several people I can call. I will get on it first thing in the morning."

EVA

*A*fter changing the locks on her West Avenue home, the locksmith follows Eva to work and repeats the process at Claudia's Closet. Monday mornings are always quiet, and Eva uses the time to reset the showroom after the busy day on Saturday. Customers begin to trickle in around noon, and by one o'clock, when Helena arrives, Eva is swamped and grateful for the extra set of hands. While her new partner has a special knack for choosing the right clothes for their customers, Helena is having a hard time getting the hang of processing a credit card transaction.

"The racks look sparse," Helena says during a break in the flow of customers.

"Because most of your mother's clothes have sold," Eva says. "Which is a good problem to have but we need more inventory."

"Funny you should mention that." A broad smile spreads across Helena's face. "Three of my friends challenged each other to clean out their attics over the weekend. I told them to be here around two thirty." She glances at her watch. "Any minute now, actually."

Eva's excitement at the prospect of new merchandise is short-lived. "All three of them? Today? At once? But where will we put everything? The stockroom is only so big. It takes time to check in merchandise, Helena. We have a process. Having them come one at a time would work much better."

"What can I say? They're eager to get rid of the junk."

Junk? An image of Fred Sanford flashes through her mind. "We're not junk collectors, Helena."

"Whatever. You know what I mean." Helena waves a tube of lipstick at her before running it across her lips. "Anyway, their cars are already packed. I can't very well tell them to put everything back in their attics. You don't need to worry. I've got it all figured out. I created a spreadsheet for them to catalog their inventory. What doesn't fit in the stockroom, we'll store at your house."

"At my house?" Eva says, placing a hand on her chest. "Are you joking?"

Helena drops the tube of lipstick into the pocket of her gray knit blazer. "It'll only be for a couple of weeks, until we take possession of the new store. We're expanding our business, Eva. It's normal for us to experience growing pains."

A customer enters the store, cutting short their conversation. Eva forces a smile on her face and goes to welcome the newcomer.

Helena's friends arrive promptly at two thirty. Eva forgets their names as soon as they're introduced. They're attractive middle-aged women—fit and trim with time and money to burn.

Helena says to Eva, "If you can handle the showroom, I'll help them unload."

"Unload?" one of the women says with a gasp. "I thought you were hiring a muscle man for that."

"I'm not dressed for physical labor," another says of her slinky wrap dress and high-heeled shoes. "I just came from a luncheon."

"It won't take long if we all pitch in." With a wink in Eva's direction, Helena corrals her friends through the stockroom and out the back door.

As Eva predicted, the stockroom fills up fast. As best she can tell, the items are of high quality, and she reluctantly volunteers to store the rest in her home. She gives Helena her house key and off they go.

When Helena returns to the shop around four thirty, Eva asks, "Did everything fit in my guest bedroom?"

"Well . . . not exactly. We put the overflow in your dining room." Helena appears genuinely apologetic. "I'm sorry, Eva. I know it's not ideal, but we got some really great stuff."

At least it's stuff now and not junk, Eva thinks. "What kind of *stuff* did we get?"

"We left most of the clothes here. Some beautiful cashmere sweaters and Tory Burch handbags. And took the household items to your house. Lots of lamps, some rugs, artwork, and a bunch of small pieces of furniture."

"And I was worried about filling that enormous showroom we leased," Eva says in a sarcastic tone.

"Have no fear! I have plenty more friends who've promised to clean out their attics."

Eva admires Helena's endless enthusiasm. Did Eva ever feel so optimistic about her business?

At five minutes till six, Helena and Eva are preparing to lock up for the night when a policeman enters the shop. Not Officers Kelly and Knight from the previous evening but Castillo, the policeman Eva remembers who's investigating Maggie's disappearance.

Eva comes from the back of the store to greet him. "Good evening, Officer. What brings you in?" Despite her racing heart, she manages to appear calm as she extends her hand to him.

Castillo's handshake is cold as are his deep-blue eyes. "In case you've forgotten, I'm investigating Maggie Jones's disappearance.

I've learned some things that contradict what you told us about your relationship with your missing neighbor."

Cold dread ripples through her. "Like what?"

"Like Greg, the bartender at the Village Cafe, where we now know Maggie has been working part-time, says you and Maggie were good friends."

Eva is caught off guard. "Well . . . I don't know what to say . . . he's mistaken."

"I don't think so, Mrs. Carpenter. Not only did he call you by name . . ."—Castillo consults the small notepad cupped in his hand—"he referred to you as the woman who owns the second-hand store."

Eva experiences a flash of anger. "It's vintage, Officer. Not secondhand."

"My apologies," Castillo says. "Anyway, it's the bartender's word against yours, and I'm inclined to believe the bartender."

"Oh? And why is that, Officer Castillo?"

"Because, my investigation has unearthed some concerns about you, Mrs. Carpenter. According to my sources, you were recently institutionalized. On two separate occasions, as a matter of fact. Once for an emotional breakdown, and the second time for substance abuse."

Eva casts a nervous glance at Helena who is in the back of the store returning garments to hangers. With her eyes still on Helena, she lowers her voice. "Is it necessary to have this discussion here? In my place of business?"

Following her gaze, Castillo reaches for the door handle. "Point taken. Why don't we step outside."

On the sidewalk, Eva turns on him. "I was not institutionalized, Officer. I admitted myself voluntarily. And neither time was recent. The first was in February of 2010. I had a mental breakdown two months after my husband was killed in a car accident and my daughter went missing."

He chuckles. "People have a way of going missing around you, don't they, Mrs. Carpenter?"

The blood drains from Eva's face. "You're way outta line, Castillo. I'm going to pretend you didn't say that."

He ignores her. "And the second time?"

"As if you don't already know, it was in October of 2014 for alcohol and drug rehabilitation." She refuses to explain further. If he wants details, he can get a subpoena for her medical files. "What is it you really want from me?"

He steps close to her, intimidating her with his large presence. "I want the truth, Mrs. Carpenter. I know you're holding out on me. Where is Maggie Jones?"

Eva feels sweat streaming down her back. He knows that she knows more than she's saying. But she needs a little more time. Maggie needs a little more time. "You're barking at the wrong squirrel up the wrong tree. Stop wasting my time and start investigating Maggie's husband."

Eva doesn't give him a chance to respond. Spinning away from him, she heads back inside to face Helena, who is waiting just inside the door.

"I'm so sorry, Eva. You've been through so much. I wish I'd been a better friend to you."

"I have friends, Helena." *One at least,* Eva thinks. Oh, how she misses Annette. "But I appreciate your concern." She brushes past Helena on her way to the checkout counter.

Helena follows her. "Are you stable now? Mentally, I mean."

"I'm fine," Eva says in a strangled tone that suggests she's not fine at all. "But if you have concerns about my sanity, we should reconsider our partnership. I can't work with someone who doesn't trust me."

Helena appears flustered. "That came out all wrong. I open my mouth, but I have no idea what's going to come out. My mother always said I have—"

"Impulse control issues," Eva says with a little laugh. The years fall away, and they are children again. On many occasions, Eva had gone home in tears from a playdate with Helena, only to have Helena apologize later for unintentionally hurting her feelings.

"If it's any consolation," Eva says, "I haven't seen that side of you since we started working together."

"I'm much better than I was back then, although my husband often accuses me of having no filter."

They share a laugh.

"Listen, you have every right to be concerned about my mental stability. Having the police show up like that is disturbing. But it's all a big misunderstanding. I owe you an explanation, which I'll be happy to give you once it's sorted out."

"I don't need an explanation. Unless it makes you feel better to talk about it." Helena places a hand on Eva's arm. "I want you to know that I trust you implicitly. I want this partnership to work."

With the chance now to reinvent their friendship, Eva suddenly realizes how much she needs and wants Helena in her life. "Me too," she says, her tone sincere.

"I'd better be going. Roger and I have a dinner thing tonight. But I'd like to come in early tomorrow to get a head start on organizing the new merchandise. Do you have an extra key to the shop?"

"Of course!" She retrieves the spare key the locksmith provided from the cash register drawer and hands it to Helena. "Text me on your way here, and I'll meet you."

Eva walks with Helena to the back door, closing and locking it behind her. Boxes stand stacked all around the room while hanging garments jam rolling clothing racks. Staying busy has always been her salvation, and with Evil Eric lurking nearby, the last place she wants to be is alone at home. She begins to organize the boxes, but instead of distracting her from her problems, she becomes more antsy. She can't stop thinking about the visit from Officer Castillo, and wondering why Maggie hasn't called,

and imagining what fun and games Eric Jones has in store for her
next.

When she sees the disorder Helena left in her home, something
inside Eva snaps. The *junk* clutters not only her dining room, as
Helena indicated, but her living room and center hallway as well.

She makes her way through the assortment of odds and ends
to the kitchen, pours two fingers of vodka into a glass, and
downs it in one gulp. She sets the glass on the counter and picks
up the bottle. She takes swigs of vodka, staring out the window at
her courtyard garden and waiting for the booze to work its
magic.

Minutes later, when the awaited sense of calm finally washes
over her, she turns away from the window. Bottle in hand, she
strolls through the maze of consignment items. There are so
many lovely things. Needlepoint pillows. A brass banker's lamp
with an emerald-green glass shade. A watercolor of a schooner
gliding across the calm waters of what appears to be the Chesa-
peake Bay. Eva has little knowledge of home furnishings. She's
better with clothing and accessories. Although she imagines the
same principle applies to both. *One person's trash is another person's
treasure.* Despite the popular contemporary lifestyle of the day, a
surprisingly large number of people still prefer the timeless and
beautifully crafted to the trendy.

She circles the downstairs to the living room, grateful to find
no clutter. She plops down in Stuart's chair, setting the vodka on
the table beside her, and struggles to free her phone from her
back pocket. She calls Maggie, but she doesn't answer. She
doesn't send a text. Why is Maggie keeping her in the dark about
the investigation? If it's bad news, Eva is prepared to hear it. But
she needs an update, and soon, before she loses her mind. Eva is
only mildly comforted by the new locks on the doors. Evil Eric

will continue to harass her until she tells him where Maggie is. She has her gun, next to her in the drawer of the table beside her chair.

Eva turns on the TV, tuning into a news channel, and nurses vodka until she passes out drunk sometime around midnight. Hours later, a loud popping noise jerks her out of her alcohol coma. More popping brings her bolt upright in the chair. Realizing the sound is coming from the news station—gunfire from a segment about a street fight in Chicago—she powers off the TV and sinks back against the cushions.

She drags her tongue across her lips. Her mouth is so dry. Gripping the arms of the chair, she pushes herself up and stumbles to the kitchen for a glass of water. Her heart skips a beat when she sees an assortment of pills in a variety of colors and shapes scattered across the counter. Someone has been in her house. Someone may still be in her house. Dropping to her knees, she crawls on all fours back down the hall to the living room.

Retrieving her gun from the drawer, she races around the house, checking the locks on all the windows and doors. When she sees the side window in the dining room is partially cracked, allowing the cool night air to drift in, she slams it shut and engages the lock. She recalls Officer Kelley checking the windows the previous night and declaring them all locked. Had he missed this one? Or was it cracked that afternoon when Helena was there with her friends? Any one of them could've done it to let in fresh air.

Locating a flashlight in her pantry, she searches the house from top to bottom until she is absolutely certain no one is hiding in any of the closets or under any of the beds. She's returning the flashlight to the pantry when the pills once again attract her attention. There are so many of them. She sets the gun down and scoops them up in her hands. She imagines the high. A few worry-free moments of bliss. What if she takes all of them at once? She uncurls her fists and stares at the pretty pills. She would die and her suffering would end. No one would miss her. She's left explicit instructions in her will that she's to be buried at Hollywood Cemetery beside her husband. Annette would arrange the graveside service. Helena would be the only other person in attendance.

Life would go on as if Eva had never lived. Helena would continue with the expansion plans for the store. No one would remember that Eva was once the proprietress. What exactly had she accomplished in her life? Nothing noteworthy for sure. God had blessed her with her greatest gift, Reese, and she'd blown it. She'd taken motherhood for granted. Instead of nurturing her quirky daughter into the person she was meant to be, Eva had tried to mold her into someone else. Reese never cared about being popular or athletic or smart. It was Eva who'd wanted all those things for her only child. Their last years together were unbearable, not because of anything her teenager did but because of Eva's dissatisfaction with her own life. Her irrational and unjustifiable accusations against Reese had driven her away. Her child deserved so much more. With her talent, if she'd had her mother's support, Reese could have achieved greatness. Eva wishes for two things. That Reese has somehow managed to achieve that greatness on her own, and that Eva will one day have the opportunity to make amends with her only child.

Eva lets the pills fall onto the counter and sweeps them into a Ziplock bag, which she places in her utensil drawer for safekeeping. For later, in the event Maggie's investigation doesn't end well.

REESE

$\mathcal{R}$eese lies awake most of the night, imagining the unimaginable being done to sweet Bella. While she's grateful to Clara for offering to help, proceeding through the proper channels could take days, if not weeks. And Reese has a sick feeling Bella doesn't have a moment to spare.

Just after dawn, she rolls out of bed and throws on a pair of jeans and a sweatshirt. Careful not to disturb a sleeping Maggie, she sneaks out of the apartment. Stopping in at the nearest Starbucks for a large coffee, she sets out on foot with no particular destination in mind. An hour later, she finds herself in front of Bella's school. The students have yet to arrive, but the crossing guard is in position at the corner and a team of teachers wait under the portico in the drop-off circle. Leaning against what Reese now thinks of as her tree, she pulls her hood over her head and nestles her chin into the collar of her sweatshirt. The air is crisp, a reminder that winter is not far in the rearview mirror, but the sun is bright, a promise of a warm day and even warmer months ahead. Peering out from under her hood, she watches the students arrive one-by-one, but Bella isn't among them. The trail of cars dwindles and the last mother on foot, with a dog on a leash, drops off her child. Reese's heart sinks, and her gut instincts warn that something is wrong. Bella is in trouble.

Removing her phone from her pocket, she clicks on Maggie's number as she takes off down the street. A groggy Maggie answers with a muffled hello.

Reese increases her pace to a jog. "I'm leaving the school. Bella didn't show up today. I need you to text me Todd's address."

Maggie's voice is now alert. "What're you planning, Reese?"

"I won't know until I get there. Please, Maggie. Don't argue with me. Just text me the address. I have a bad feeling. And I can't ignore it."

"I'm coming with you," Maggie says, her tone now desperate. "Stop by here on your way. Or I can meet you somewhere."

"There's no time. Just text me the address."

Maggie lets out a sigh. "It's 1351 J Street. I took a picture of it with your phone. I took several pics, actually. I meant to show them to you after dinner at Clara's but forgot."

"Okay. Thanks." Ending the call with a decisive click, she engages her GPS app and enters the address, which is located in the hip area of the city known as Shaw. Phone gripped in hand, she takes off running to the Metro stop. Boarding the Metro train and finding a seat, she accesses her photos app and scrolls through the images Maggie took—the one of Todd's rundown row house and of Nora with track marks and bruises on her arms, looking decades older than the young woman Maggie gave her baby to nine years ago. Heroin. Reese gave her daughter to a woman who sticks needles in her skin. Does she get high in front of Bella? What kind of lasting impact will Nora's behavior have on that poor child? Will Bella be traumatized just like Reese had been by her mother's alcoholism?

The train slows to a stop, the doors part, and Reese exits the train station. Her anger mounts with each step as she makes her way to J street. She locates Todd's house, marches up the brick steps, and pounds on the front door. A man with a tatted-up bald head opens the door. Gauged earrings stretch his earlobes to the size of a half dollar, and a patch of beard is trimmed close on his chin. He's not tall, about the same height as Reese, but he's sinewy, and a voice inside her head warns her not to underestimate his strength.

He eyes her from head to toe. "Who are you?"

An adrenaline surge gives Reese courage, and she brings herself to her full height. "A friend of Nora's. Is she home?"

"Nah. Sorry. She ain't here."

Reese can see past him into the living room where Nora—both eyes bruised and swollen, blood crusting the nostrils of a broken nose—is curled up in a tight ball at one end of a large brown sofa.

Heart pounding against rib cage, Reese brushes past Todd and hurries to Nora's side. "Oh my God, Nora! Are you okay? Where's Bella? We need to get you some help."

She tries to lift the battered woman off the sofa, but Nora jerks her arm away. "You need to leave. You're only gonna make it worse."

Crossing the room, Todd towers over Nora. "Who is this bitch? Why is she here?"

Nora's eyes grow wide and she cowers back on the sofa. "I swear, Todd. I didn't invite her here. Make her leave."

He takes Reese by the arm. "You heard her. You have no business here."

"I'm Bella's birth mother. I have every right to be here," Reese says to him, and then to Nora, "I gave you my daughter in good faith. You promised to take care of her."

"I am taking care of her," Nora says in a weak voice.

Reese stares openmouthed at her. "Are you kidding me? Have you looked in the mirror lately? You live with a drug dealer. A drug dealer who beat your face to a bloody pulp."

"Let her have the kid," Todd says. "One less mouth for me to feed."

Yanking her arm free of Todd's grip, Reese makes a dash for the stairs. She's greeted on the second floor by the overpowering stench of urine and marijuana smoke. She runs from room to room, throwing open doors and looking under beds, until she finds Bella hiding behind a row of hanging clothes in the front bedroom closet. The child's face is wet with tears and her left arm is tied around her neck in a makeshift sling.

Reese kneels down in front of her. "Don't be afraid, sweetheart. You don't know me, but my name is Anna, and I'm going to help you."

From the hallway, she hears footfalls on the hardwood floors followed by Nora's voice. "Please, Todd! Put the gun away. She's not here to cause trouble."

Reese freezes.

"The hell she ain't," Todd says.

Pulling her phone from her sweatshirt pocket, Reese quickly thumbs off a text to Maggie. I'm inside the house. He has a gun. She slips the phone back in her pocket, and as Todd and Nora enter the room, she stands to face them, shielding the child with her body.

"I beg you," Nora implores. "Leave now, and no one will get hurt. Forget you saw anything."

"It's too late for that, you dumb bitch!" Todd backhands Nora, sending her reeling across the room. She slams into the wall and drops to the floor.

Aiming the revolver at Reese with his right hand, he holds his left out to her. "Give me your phone."

"I don't have one," Reese says in a defiant tone.

"Do you think I'm stupid or something? Of course, you have a phone." He cocks the gun's hammer. "Give it to me."

Retrieving the phone from her pocket, with all her might, she throws it at his feet. It crashes onto the hardwood floors, shattering the screen.

Picking up the phone, Todd fiddles with it but he can't get it to power on. "The police can still track it, which means we have a problem." Pocketing the phone, he produces a roll of duct tape from the top drawer of the dresser. He spins Reese around and forces her facedown on the bed. He wrenches her arms behind her back and then tapes her wrists and ankles. Rolling her over, he tears off a length of tape with his teeth and seals her lips.

Todd gets to his feet. "There. Now." He stares down at her. "The police won't be able to get a search warrant without probable cause. If they even come, they'll never know you're here."

Reese silently prays that her text to Maggie will be the probable cause the police need. But if the text didn't go through, she and Bella are screwed.

Todd tapes Nora's wrists, ankles, and mouth, and then locks Bella in the closet, bracing a chair under the doorknob. He lowers the blackout shade in the window and closes the door behind him, leaving them in the pitch darkness.

Reese screams at Nora, "What is wrong with you? How could you let this happen?" With her mouth taped shut, her words come out as loud moans.

She thrashes around on the bed until her energy is spent. As she lies still, panting, she tells herself to think smart. Her life depends on it. If she rolls off the side, she'll go crashing to the floor. While the impact will be painful, the thud of her body landing on the floor will be audible in the living room below. The doorbell rings downstairs. She may get only one chance. Her timing will have to be perfect.

MAGGIE

*M*aggie arrives on J Street as two uniformed policemen wearing aviator sunglasses are ringing Todd's doorbell. Both officers sport crew cuts, one blond and the other dark headed, Greene and Walsh respectively according to their name tags.

"I'm Maggie Jo—um . . . Wade. Maggie Wade. I'm the one who called 9-1-1. I was in the Metro when I placed the call, and we got cut off before I could tell the operator that the man inside has a gun."

Officer Greene says, "Move away from the house, ma'am. This is a police matter."

"But Officer . . ." Maggie holds her phone out to show him Reese's text.

Peering over the top of his glasses, he silences her with a glare.

Maggie backs down a step but remains on the stoop with them.

Walsh rings the bell two more times before Todd finally answers. The sight of him gives Maggie goose pimples. The tattoos. Stretched earlobes. Malicious glint in his eyes.

Todd rubs his eyes and yawns as though he just woke up. "What's with the racket, Officers? I'm trying to catch some Zs."

Maggie isn't buying his act. He's fully clothed with damp armpits in his dark T-shirt and cowboy boots on his feet.

"We received a call about a domestic disturbance at this residence," Walsh says.

"Sorry. Wrong house. There's no domestic disturbance here." Todd moves to close the door, but Walsh blocks it with his foot.

"Is your house number thirteen fifty-one?" Walsh asks.

Todd gestures at the metal numbers on the wooden facade in front of them. "Can't you read, bro?"

Stepping toward him, Walsh says, "I'm not your bro." The officer is a good six inches taller than Todd, and has beefier shoulders.

"Sorry, dude." Todd runs his hand across his tattooed head. "But I told you. I been sleeping. I don't know nothing about no domestic dispute."

"Does anyone else live here with you?" Greene asks.

Todd shakes his head. "Nah, man. I live alone."

"He's lying," Maggie interjects. "His girlfriend, Nora, and her nine-year-old daughter, Bella, live here with him."

Todd jerks his neck back as he notices her for the first time. "Who the hell are you?"

"A friend of Nora's," Maggie says.

Todd raises an eyebrow. "And I'm Donald Trump. Nora don't got no friends."

Walsh and Greene exchange a look. "We're a little confused, here. Do you or don't you have a live-in girlfriend?"

Todd leans against the doorjamb, as though bored with the conversation. "She lives here. What I meant was, she ain't here right now."

"Oh really? Then, where is she?" Greene asks.

"She went to take the kid to school," Todd answers.

A loud thud sounds over Todd's head, and four sets of eyes travel to the ceiling.

"What was that?" Walsh asks.

"I thought you were home alone," Greene says.

Beads of sweat dot Todd's upper lip. "That was my cleaning lady."

"Right," Greene says with a smirk. "And I'm Donald Trump."

"If I didn't know better, I'd think you were lying to us," Walsh says. "What's going on here?"

Maggie elbows her way onto the top step. "I've been trying to tell you that. My friend Anna, who is also a friend of Nora's, was worried about Bella when she didn't show up for school today. Anna came here, to this address, to check on Bella. She sent me a text saying she was inside the house and Todd, this man, has a gun." She shoves her phone at Greene. "That's why I called you guys. He's holding them hostage."

Greene looks down at Reese's text and back up at Todd. "Step aside, sir. We're coming inside."

"Not without a search warrant, you're not." Todd slams the door in their faces and seconds later a shot is fired from inside the house.

"Take cover!" Walsh shouts.

The officers grab Maggie and run down the sidewalk with her. The threesome crouch behind the patrol car as Greene speaks into his headset. "Unit five-five calling for backup. Shots fired. We have a hostage situation here."

Within minutes, dozens of patrol cars appear. Uniformed officers wearing bulletproof vests, helmets, and face masks barricade the streets and notify the neighbors of the situation. One of the armed officers whisks Maggie off to one end of the block where a crowd of spectators has begun to gather.

Maggie calls Clara and Raimi who arrive together within thirty minutes.

"How on earth did this happen?" Clara asks. "I thought we agreed to proceed through the proper channels."

"I thought so, too. I was still asleep when she left the apartment this morning. She called around nine fifteen and woke me up. Without thinking, I gave her Nora's boyfriend's address." Maggie tells them about calling the police after receiving Reese's text that she was inside the house, and then the police arriving and their confrontation with Todd. "I made matters so much worse. I should've kept my mouth shut and let the police handle it." The enormity of the situation hits home, sending tremors through her body.

Raimi pulls her in for a half hug. "Don't blame yourself, Maggie. When Reese gets something in her head, there's no stopping her."

"If anyone's to blame, it's me," Clara says. "I let her give that baby up for adoption when I knew it was the wrong choice for her."

Raimi wraps his other arm around Clara. "You didn't let Reese do anything. She agonized over the decision, and she made the right choice for her at the time. She was only nineteen, too young to raise a baby, even with your help. Compare the person she's become—self-sufficient and determined to succeed—to the naive girl she was back then." He kisses Clara's forehead. "Sure, she's missed her baby. That's normal. But she's never regretted her decision. At least not until recently, when she began to fear Bella was in trouble."

Maggie bites down on her lower lip to stop it from quivering. "Should I call Eva?"

Raimi massages Maggie's shoulder. "That's a good question. How do you think she might react?"

"Knowing Eva, she'll jump in the car and drive up here. But she'll be worried and upset, and I don't want her on the highway. To answer my own question, I think I'll wait until we find out more."

Squeezing her eyes shut, Clara clasps her hands together in prayer. "By the grace of God, you'll have good news to tell her when you make that call."

REESE

*R*eese lies on the floor in the pitch dark, her ears ringing from the gunshot downstairs. *Did he shoot whoever was at the door? What if it was Maggie?* Her mind races with thoughts of escape. She hears soft crying behind the closet door. Her arms ache to hold Bella. Her mind drifts back to moments alone she had with her daughter right after her birth. Bella's fingers were so tiny, although her grip was already strong. Reese remembers the feeling of the baby's downy skin against her lips when she kissed her forehead. She'd planned to never see the child again. But she'd been unable to stay away. She'd vetted the young couple who'd been so eager to adopt her baby. James and Nora had promised they'd take care of Bella. *We love her already,* they said time and again during the pregnancy. They'd attended every doctor's appointment and been in the delivery room during the birth. She'd put her faith in them, and they'd let her down.

In the upstairs hallway outside the room, hurried footfalls on the steps precede Todd's sudden burst through the door. With a flip of the wall switch, light fills the room. He's sweating profusely and his wild eyes bounce off the walls and ceiling before falling on Reese. Holding the gun steady with both hands, he aims it at her. "You, bitch! You've ruined my life." He kicks her hard, the tip of his boot landing in her side. The sound of Reese's scream is suppressed by tape. When the pain finally subsides enough for her to breathe, she looks to Nora for help. But Nora looks away.

Todd, massaging the back of his neck with one hand while brandishing the gun with the other, paces the floor in front of Reese's face. "What am I supposed to do now? I'm screwed and it's all your fault." He kicks her again, the toe of his boot jabbing deep into her thigh muscle.

Agony wrenches her gut and she feels as though she might vomit.

He looms above her, the gun trained on Reese's head. "If I kill you, I'll go to prison for murder. If I let you live, the police will discover all the smack I have hidden in this house, and I'll be facing major trafficking charges. Either way, I'm looking at a life sentence." He crouches down beside Reese, driving the barrel of the gun into her forehead. "Might as well kill you. At least that way, I'll get some satisfaction."

Reese squeezes her eyes shut and prays to God he doesn't shoot.

A voice, amplified by a bullhorn, resounds from the street below. "Todd, this is Detective Alex Hammer, hostage negotiator for the Metropolitan Police Department. I'd like to work this thing out. There's no reason for anyone to get hurt."

Todd flies to the window, throwing open the shade and the lower sash. He fires a series of shots into the air, slams the window shut, and ducks down between the bed and the wall. The sound of Bella's screams come from within the closet.

Todd crawls over to Nora. "Babe, do you remember what we talked about, what we agreed we'd do if the going ever got too tough."

Nora bobs her head up and down.

"Are you sure you can go through with it?"

More head bobbing from Nora.

He dangles two small bags of white powder in front of her nose, and Nora's eyes plead with him to give it to her.

Todd removes the tape from her wrists and mouth but not her ankles. He spreads syringes, spoons, and cigarette lighters on the floor between them. Their actions are fevered as they liquefy the white powder and fill their needles. Nora has the perfect opportunity to jab Todd in the eye with her needle, but she injects it in the skin in the crook of her elbow instead. They repeat the procedure a second time. They're on the third round when Reese begins to comprehend. They aren't just getting high. They are intentionally overdosing.

"Stop!" Reese screams beneath the tape.

Todd and Nora laugh at her in response.

A contented expression settles on Nora's face as she rests her head against the wall. Within minutes, her head sags to the side, her breathing slows, and her lips begin to turn blue. It takes a fourth round to knock Todd into unconsciousness. Seconds later, he vomits all over himself. Reese needs to try and save them. Death is the easy way out. They should go to prison, to suffer for what they've put Bella through. Wincing from pain, she writhes her way to the window. Struggling to her feet, she stares down at the police cars parked haphazardly on the street below. While no officers are in view, she knows they're there, hiding, waiting for an opportunity to take a shot. Closing her eyes, she head-butts a window pane, cracking the glass. Pain shoots through her brain and blood floods her face from a deep gash in her forehead. Punching out the glass with her elbow, Reese lets out muffled screams until dizziness overcomes her and everything goes black.

EVA

*E*va's hangover gets the best of her around one o'clock on Tuesday afternoon. She goes to the stockroom for a cup of tea and promptly falls asleep with her head resting on the table.

Helena nudges her awake sometime later. "Do you not feel well?"

Eva stands and stretches. "I'm fine. I didn't sleep well last night."

Frown lines dip between Helena's blue eyes. "Why don't you go home? I can manage the store until closing."

This is music to Eva's ears. The perks of having a partner. "Are you sure? We can close early if need be."

"That's not necessary. But, if you don't mind, I have a young friend I can call to help. I worked with her on a benefit last year and found her to be a whiz at organization. She's looking for a part-time job. And, if we're entertaining the idea of hiring someone in the future, I think she might be a good fit."

"By all means, call her. At the rate we're expanding, we should consider hiring someone anyway."

In her car, instead of making a right out of the parking lot, Eva takes a left and drives to the nearest liquor store in Carytown. She purchases the largest size available of vodka, forcing back the temptation to drink it until she's safely at home. Inside her front door, she unscrews the cap and chugs, feeling immediately better. Until she sets her eyes on the cluttered hallway.

With the afternoon stretching ahead of her, she sets about sorting Helena's friends' donations. She moves all the boxes to the hallway, stacking them neatly and creating a pathway from the front door to her kitchen, and then sorts the remaining items in her dining room into sections based on type—lamps, blankets, pillows, and so on. She rewards herself periodically with sips from the vodka bottle, and by the time she finishes two hours later, she's more than a little drunk. She fills a glass with vodka and takes it to her storm door, staring out across the street at Eric's car. He hasn't left his house all afternoon. She knows he's up to something. She can feel it in her bones.

She empties her glass and goes to the kitchen for a refill. When she returns, he's standing in his bedroom window, looking down on her. He waves at her with his condescending finger wiggle, and she steps back, closing and locking the solid door. She drains the vodka in one gulp. She needs something stronger, and a tremor passes through her body at the thought of the bag of pills in her utensil drawer. *Don't go there, Eva,* she warns herself. She needs help, and she knows only one person who can give it to her.

Leaving her empty glass on the kitchen counter, she takes her phone outside to the terrace. Tears well in her eyes at the sound of her best friend's voice. "I'm in trouble, Annette."

Annette sighs. "Oh, honey, I was afraid you might be. You haven't returned any of my calls."

It's true. Eva's been avoiding Annette for days. Or has it been weeks? "I know. And I'm sorry." She wipes the snot from her nose with the back of her hand. "So much has happened. I don't know where to begin."

"Start at the beginning."

Eva tells Annette about Eric and Maggie, about Eric abusing Maggie and Maggie going into hiding while she investigates Reese's disappearance. She intentionally leaves out the part about Eric stalking her. That information would send Annette to the airport to catch the next flight to Richmond. While she wants nothing more than to see her best friend, she refuses to intrude on her new life.

"The not knowing is driving me crazy," Eva admits. "I'm afraid to hope Reese is alive. If only Maggie would call."

"Have you been drinking, Eva?"

There it is, the dreaded question. She hesitates.

"Are you taking pills?"

"No!" Eva answers emphatically.

"I warned you, Eva, your one-drink-a-night would eventually catch up with you." Her tone is both stern and sympathetic.

"I know," Eva mumbles, thinking how she'll have to quit drinking completely if she ever expects to recover. And she's never been willing to do that.

Annette says, "Assuming Maggie finds Reese, and I pray that she does, this might be your one and only chance to make things right with your daughter. Don't blow it. I'm sorry if this hurts your feelings, but I need to say it, and you need to hear it. The last thing you want is for Reese to come home to the same drunk mother she ran away from ten years ago."

"What should I do?" Eva asks in a shaky voice.

"For starters, you need to get yourself together. Sober up. Pour what's left of the vodka down the drain. Then you keep yourself busy until you hear from Maggie. You can do this, Eva. Chin up. Head high."

They talk for a few more minutes before saying goodbye. Closing her eyes, Eva tilts her head back, lifting her face to the warm afternoon sun. Annette is right. *If I don't stop drinking, I'll blow my chance to reconcile with Reese, and it will be my own fault. My drinking is not Eric's fault. He's tormenting me, preying on my weaknesses, and I'm letting him get away with it.*

A surge of energy drives her to her feet. She can't give up without a fight. She's got nothing to lose and everything to gain. As she walks in circles around the patio, she formulates a plan to beat him at his own game. But before she can put her plan into motion, she needs to sober up.

She goes inside to the kitchen and pours the remaining vodka down the drain, stuffing the empty bottle in the trash can under the sink. She's climbing the stairs, on her way to shower, when the doorbell rings. She's so lost in the possibility of seeing Reese again, she doesn't stop to consider who might be at the door. Hurrying back down the stairs, she throws the door open and comes face to face with Eric. She cracks the storm door. "What do you want?"

"You know what I want, Eva," he says, his lips pursed in a self-satisfied smirk. "Let's stop this little cat and mouse game we're playing. Tell me where my wife is, and I'll leave you alone."

"I already told you, I don't know where she is." Fear takes hold of her body, squeezing out a hiccup.

He narrows his aqua eyes. "Have you been drinking?"

She brings her hand to her mouth as another hiccup escapes.

"You have! You're drunk, aren't you? I bet you're high on Oxy, too. I thought you might like the goodies I left for you last night." He palms his forehead as though he can't believe his luck. "You're making this so easy for me." Taking a step forward, he sticks the toe of his loafer in the storm door so she can't close it. "If you don't tell me what you know about Maggie, I'll torture you until you do."

Kicking his foot out of the way, she slams the storm door and turns the lock.

He presses the tip of his finger against the glass. "I'm coming for you, Eva."

From somewhere deep inside, she summons the courage to look him straight in the eye. Through the glass pane, she says, "Bring it on, Eric."

MAGGIE

*C*lara's medical background wins her the opportunity to ride in the ambulance with Reese. Maggie and Raimi follow behind in Clara's Ford Flex wagon with Raimi at the wheel. As he weaves in and out of traffic, Maggie asks, "Did you speak to Reese? Did she say anything?" Raimi had walked beside the gurney as the EMTs wheeled Reese out of the house to the waiting ambulance.

He takes his eyes off the road and risks a glance at Maggie. "She begged me to find out where social services is taking Bella."

Maggie relaxes in her seat. "She's gonna be fine."

"Exactly." Raimi's smile is short-lived. "I certainly didn't tell her that social services whisked that child away so fast we may never see her again."

Maggie stares out the window at the blur of office buildings. "It doesn't seem right, the way Reese risked her life to save Bella."

Raimi's expression becomes grim. "Some will undoubtedly argue she put the child in danger by showing up at Todd's like a cannon with a short fuse."

He rounds Washington Circle to Twenty-Third Street and enters George Washington University Hospital's parking deck.

They locate a spot on the third level and race back down the stairs to the emergency room entrance. The waiting room is hopping, with all ages and ethnicities, and noisy with a cacophony of babies crying and people moaning in pain. Raimi makes his way to the reception desk where he's promptly told to have a seat, that someone will be with him soon. They don't have to wait long before an elderly couple vacates two chairs near the reception desk in front of a pair of locked doors, which Maggie assumes lead to treatment rooms. Raimi texts his mother and stares at the phone, waiting for her response. When she doesn't respond within a few minutes, he's back at the reception desk.

"I'm freaking out here," he tells the nurse. "My sister was held hostage by a deranged gunman earlier today. She could've been killed. I need to see with my own eyes that she's okay. She's back there with my mother." He aims his thumb over his shoulder at the double doors. "Can't I go check on them?"

With her lips pressed tight, the nurse says, "I'm sorry about your sister, sir. But you'll have to wait until someone calls you."

His face darkens, and Maggie thinks he's about to explode when the double doors swing open and Clara emerges from the back hallway. He hurries over to her. "Well? How is she?" he asks.

"Ornery," Clara says. "She wants to see you. But hurry. They're taking her for a CT scan soon."

Raimi disappears through the double doors and Clara lowers herself to the seat beside Maggie.

"How bad are her injuries?" Maggie asks.

"She has a concussion, several broken ribs, and a laceration on her forehead. The CT scan will make certain there is no internal bleeding and determine the extent of the brain trauma. Best case scenario, she has a concussion. Fortunately, they have a plastic surgeon resident on call to stitch up her forehead."

"And how are her spirits?"

"Naturally, she's worried sick about Bella," Clara says. "And furious with Nora, even though the poor woman is probably dead."

Raimi returns, and Clara jumps to her feet. "That was fast."

"They took her for her CT scan." Raimi shakes his head. "That girl's a red-hot mess. They need to sedate her."

"Let me see what I can do," Clara says and is once again swept up by the double doors.

Raimi massages his forehead. "I need some coffee."

"Want me to go to the cafeteria?" Maggie asks.

He's standing again. "No. I'll go. One of us should stay here, and I could use the distraction. Do you want some?"

Maggie nods. "Please. I drink it black. Thanks."

Grateful for a moment alone, Maggie crosses her arms over her chest, closes her eyes, and focuses on her breathing. She's replaying in her mind the events of the day when a familiar voice interrupts her thoughts. "We wondered what happened to you. We looked for you at the crime scene."

Her eyes shoot open and she's surprised to see Officers Walsh and Greene staring down at her.

"Oh. Hi." She rises to greet them. "I waited it out at the end of the block with Anna's family. Do you know anything about Nora's condition?"

A solemn expression crosses Walsh's face. "She died before they could get her in the ambulance."

Greene adds, "Todd is still alive. But barely. The doctors refused to let us question him. They say he's suffered significant brain damage. He'll be a bigger burden to taxpayers in a comatose state than he would be in prison."

Maggie is suddenly aware of people nearby eavesdropping on their conversation. "I'd like to walk with you if you're on your way out. I have something I'd like to run by you."

"Certainly," Greene says, motioning for her to go ahead of them.

Outside, the air is thick with moisture and dark clouds hang low in the sky above the rooftops of the surrounding buildings. She stops twenty feet from the emergency room entrance and turns to the policemen. "I wanted to ask you about the little girl, Nora's daughter, Bella. Do you happen to know where social services has taken her?"

"I'm sorry, ma'am," Greene says. "We don't have that information."

"Did you know that Anna is the child's biological mother?" Maggie asks.

Walsh and Greene exchange a look that tells Maggie this is new information for them.

She continues, "After Bella was born, Anna gave her up to Nora and her ex-husband for adoption. Although Anna never had any aspirations of getting the child back, she's kept tabs on Bella throughout the years to make sure she was being properly cared for. But over the past months, certain aspects of the child's behavior have given her reason for concern. What happened today legitimizes her worries. Anna has a right to know the child is in good hands."

"I know one of the social workers who was at the scene," Walsh says. "I'm happy to make a phone call."

Maggie bounces on the balls of her feet. "Would you, really? That'd be so great."

"I'm not making any promises," he says in a cautionary tone.

"I understand. I'll give you my number and Anna's in case you find out anything."

Withdrawing a notepad from his shirt pocket, he jots down Maggie's and Reese's numbers as she recites them.

He hands her a business card. "In case you need to reach me."

She slips the card in her bag. "Thank you so much."

Raimi is waiting for her with a steaming cup of coffee when she returns. "Looks like it might storm," Maggie tells him.

"Storms cause accidents, which drive folks to emergency rooms. As if this one isn't crowded enough already. Why don't you go home, Maggie. There's no reason for all three of us to stay."

"No way," Maggie says, shaking her head with vigor. "I'm not leaving."

"Suit yourself." Crossing his legs, Raimi slides down in his chair, settling in for a long wait. "Tell me, Maggie, why isn't a pretty woman like you married?"

Maggie's heart flutters at the compliment. "I actually am married. Biggest mistake I ever made."

Raimi grunts. "You too, huh?"

She leans in close to him. "I'll tell you mine, if you tell me yours."

For the next hour, while a storm with howling winds and driving rain rages outside, they share their lives with each other. Raimi's expression transitions from anger to anguish as he speaks of the wife who divorced him because she fell out of love with him and the son he obviously adores but doesn't get to see nearly enough. When it's her turn to talk, Raimi angles his body toward her, focusing his undivided attention and those killer green eyes on her. The chaos around them slips away and it's as though they are alone on a deserted island.

When she finishes, he says, "You're pretty calm for a woman with a deranged husband, a potential murderer, on the loose."

"I've been looking over my shoulder since I left him. But I learned a lot about courage from Reese today. Seeing how much you and Clara care about her has reminded me of the importance of family. In a day or so, when Reese is feeling better, I'm going to call my parents and my brothers. I'll need my family by my side when I go to the police in Richmond about my husband."

Raimi and Maggie have no shortage of subjects to talk about during the coming hours. The storm finally dies down and patients come and go from the emergency room. At dinnertime, they go to the cafeteria for sandwiches and more coffee. They don't see Clara again until nearly nine o'clock when she comes to tell them Reese is being released. The day has taken its toll, and Clara appears exhausted with her slouched posture and dark circles under her eyes.

"The doctor wants to keep her overnight for observation," Clara says. "But our hard-headed girl insists on going home. She'll sleep better in her own bed. I can stay the night with her at her place."

Raimi rests a hand on Clara's back. "You look exhausted. You've been with her all day. I'll take the night shift."

The old woman cuts her eyes at him. "You know better than to tell a woman she looks exhausted."

He laughs. "I merely speak the truth."

"It's been a long day," Maggie says. "We should all sleep in our own beds. Which, at the moment, for me, is Reese's couch. It only makes sense that I take the night shift."

An attendant dressed in blue scrubs pushes Reese's wheelchair through the double doors.

"I'll go get the car," Raimi says, already on his way out of the building.

Maggie and Clara wait with Reese and her attendant just inside the entrance. When Raimi pulls up to the curb, they wheel Reese out to the sidewalk. They are helping her in the car when Maggie's phone rings with a call from Eva. With all the commotion, she lets the call go unanswered. Five minutes later, as Raimi is navigating the traffic toward Reese's apartment, she receives a text from Eva. I'm sick with worry. Are you safe?

Maggie takes a minute to decide how to respond. I'm fine. I have good news. I promise to call you in the morning.

EVA

*E*va stays in the cold shower as long as she can stand it. Much to her relief, her head feels clearer when she gets out. She dresses in a pair of drawstring khaki pants and an old chambray shirt and returns to the kitchen where she brews a pot of coffee and makes herself an omelet.

She remains at the table long after she's finished eating. She considers alternatives to her plan, but there are none. This is about survival of the fittest. She must protect not only herself but Maggie and Reese as well.

The coffee works its magic, and by the time the last bit of daylight fades away, she's well on her way to being sober. She turns off all the lights and takes position in Stuart's chair with her revolver in her lap. She's facing a long night, but she'll wait forever, if necessary.

Minutes drag by. Then an hour. Keeping her eyes open is agony, like staying awake on the highway during a long drive, but she doesn't dare shut them for fear of falling asleep.

Around nine o'clock, she calls Maggie, but Maggie doesn't answer. She waits five minutes. When Maggie doesn't call back, Eva thumbs off a text. Maggie responds a minute later. Eva reads the last sentence again and again. Good news can only mean one thing. Maggie has found Reese. Eva can hardly believe it. She'll get to see her daughter soon. Or will she? What if Reese refuses to come home? Then Eva will go to her.

Stay focused, Eva. Get through the night first.

For the next three-plus hours, she daydreams about Reese's homecoming and the party she wants to throw in her honor. She can hardly sit still from the excitement, and when she hears the sound of crashing glass at her back door just after midnight, she leaps to her feet. She takes three steps toward the hallway and stands with feet slightly wider than shoulder width. She extends her arms out in front of her with elbows locked and revolver gripped in hands. She hears a creak in the floor. Eva knows it well. It's just inside the hallway from the kitchen. Eric moves into view. Streetlight from the front window falls on him, and she can see that he's dressed from head to toe in black, including the stocking cap on his head. Light glints off the butcher knife in his hand.

"Hello, Eric. How good of you to come. I've been waiting for you."

If Eric is surprised to see her, he doesn't show it. He laughs at the sight of the gun. "Seriously, Eva. Is that a toy?"

She releases the safety and engages the hammer. "Not hardly."

"Ha. You're too much of a coward to shoot me."

"I am not a coward," she says, but as he takes a step toward her, she takes a step backward. *Stand up to this prick, Eva.* She straightens, steadying the gun as she aims it at his head. "You deserve to die for what you did to Maggie. What you've been doing to me."

"So it's my knife against your gun?"

"Correction," Eva says. "It's you against me."

He rushes her and she fires off a single shot to the head. She was a good target in her gun safety class, and she has not lost her touch. The bullet shatters his skull, splattering blood and brain matter on the wall and all over her face and clothes. His body crumples to the floor with a loud thud, his fingers relaxing the grip on the knife still in his hand.

Panic renders her paralyzed. She's killed a man. In cold blood. In her living room. A guttural scream comes from deep inside her body, echoing throughout the house. With trembling hand, she taps 9-1-1 on her cell phone and manages to choke out to the operator that she's killed an intruder. Dropping the gun, Eva is out the front door and vomiting violently in the bushes beside her porch when the first responders arrive.

She feels a hand on her back, hears a voice whispering, "There now, Eva. Everything's going to be okay."

With his arms supporting her, Ian helps her straighten and walks her to the edge of the yard where her lawn meets his. She collapses against him and sobs into his chest, crying until his shirt is soaked through with tears and Officer Knight pries her away.

"We need to ask Mrs. Carpenter some questions. If you'll give us a minute, please."

"She's obviously in shock, Officer," Ian says. "Can I stay with her?"

"I'm sorry, sir. We need to speak with her in private."

Taking her by the arm, Knight guides her back to her front porch where Kelley is waiting for them. Through the storm door, she sees a team of crime scene workers hovering over Eric's body.

Kelley asks, "What happened here tonight, Mrs. Carpenter?"

Be strong, Eva. You've done nothing wrong. You killed this man in self-defense. "Eric Jones broke into my house, and I shot him. I tried to tell you he was stalking me, but you wouldn't listen."

"It wasn't that we didn't believe you," Kelley says. "Without evidence to prove your claim, there was nothing we could do."

Knight eyes her suspiciously. "Have you been drinking tonight, ma'am?"

"I had a few drinks this afternoon, but nothing after about five o'clock," she says in a tone of voice that suggests, It's no big deal.

A man in a white hazmat suit comes to the door. He's clenching the necks of two empty bottles of vodka in his right hand and holding the bag of pills in his left. He lifts his arms. "I found the bottles in the trash can and the pills in the utensil drawer."

"Have you taken any painkillers in the past twenty-four hours, Mrs. Carpenter?" Kelley asks.

"Those aren't mine. Eric left them scattered on my kitchen counter when he broke in last night."

Knight raises a brow in question. "Last night? We weren't notified of a break-in at your home last night. At least, as far as I know."

"Because I didn't report it. It would've been my word against his. And since I have a past history of pill addiction, you would've believed him over me."

A white-clad crime scene member moves out of the way, giving them a direct view of the mangled remains of Eric Jones's brain.

She shields her eyes. "Can we finish this discussion somewhere else?"

"I think that's a grand idea, Mrs. Carpenter," Knight says. "We'll continue our questioning downtown, at the police station."

MAGGIE

aggie's prepaid phone vibrates on the pillow beside her head. She snatches up the phone and accepts the call. Her friend would not be calling her in the middle of the night without reason. "Eva?" she answers in a questioning tone.

"Maggie!" Eva cries. "Your husband is dead! Eric is dead! I killed him."

Maggie shakes her head as if she misunderstood. *Eva killed Eric? How can that be?* "Say again. I don't think I heard you correctly."

"You heard me. Eric broke into my house, and I shot him," Eva says, her voice nearing hysteria.

There must be some mistake. Maggie remembers what Reese said about her mother's drinking problem. "Where are you?"

"At the police station."

The police station? Maggie is on her feet, raking her hands through matted hair as she paces the length of the sofa. "Listen to me, Eva. I want you to start at the beginning and tell me everything."

The sound of Eva taking a deep breath comes over the line,

and when she speaks, her voice sounds calmer. She recounts the events leading up to Eric's death—from his stalking her for days through her shooting him in self-defense.

Waves of emotion crash over Maggie. Astonishment. Guilt for bringing Eva into her problems. Relief is abundant. Sadness is noticeably absent.

Eva sniffles. "I'm so sorry, Maggie. Despite what he did to you, he was still your husband."

Maggie's head spins, and she lowers herself back to the sofa. She takes a minute to let it sink in that Eric is dead. That all her troubles are over. "I'm the one who is sorry, Eva. I put your life in danger when I dragged you into my marital problems. Eric was a vicious man. I'll explain when I see you, but I've learned even more horrible things about him since I left Richmond. God may strike me dead for saying this, but I'm not sorry he's gone. He got what he deserved." It dawns on Maggie that Eva may be holding something back. "Wait a minute. This appears to be a clear case of self-defense. Why are you at the police station?"

"Because the police don't believe me. And no wonder. When they were investigating your disappearance, I lied to them about our friendship. I told them I'd only met you a couple of times on the street. I told them the truth tonight, after the shooting, about you going undercover to find my missing daughter. But they think it's far-fetched. They want to talk to you, Maggie. In person. I need you to come back to Richmond."

Maggie considers the logistics. How will she get to Richmond? She can't leave Reese unattended. She'll have to call Raimi or Clara. "I'll get there as soon as I can, although it may not be until tomorrow morning."

The line goes silent, and Maggie is about to hang up when Eva says, "I hate to ask you this, Maggie. Especially after what I just told you. But I can't bear the suspense any longer. I need to know, Maggie. Did you find my daughter?"

Maggie's heart goes out to Eva and all she's been through. It's not fair to keep her in the dark another second. "Yes, Eva. I found your daughter. I'm with Reese now, in her apartment. We've had our own share of excitement. I'll explain everything when I see you, but I need to go now," she says, and hangs up before Eva can pressure her for more answers.

She taps on Raimi's number. He answers in a husky whisper on the third ring. Her words are jumbled, her explanation for the call makes no sense, but Raimi derives enough information to know there's an emergency.

"Hang tight," he says. "I'll be there in a few minutes."

Throwing on jeans and a gauzy black sweater, Maggie is standing at the kitchen counter with Reese's laptop, booking an Amtrak train to Richmond, when Raimi arrives fifteen minutes later.

"There's a train leaving at 7:20 that arrives in Richmond at 10:03. But I don't have enough money for the fare. Could you loan me thirty-eight dollars?"

"I can do better than that," Raimi says. "I'll loan you my car."

Reese appears in her bedroom doorway. "Why are you loaning her your car? Where are you going, Maggie?"

"To Richmond," Maggie says. "But it's nothing for you to worry about. Just a little misunderstanding I need to clear up."

Reese crosses the living room to the kitchen. "Is this about your husband? Or is my mom in some kind of trouble?"

Maggie considers lying, but she is sick of the lies. She tells Reese an abbreviated version of the situation.

When she finishes, Reese says, "I'm going with you."

"No way!" Raimi says. "You're in no condition to travel."

Reese stares him down. "I can sleep in the car. I'm going, and that's final. You're not talking me out of it, but you can help me pack."

He follows her into the bedroom like a dutiful brother.

Maggie gathers her belongings, stuffing them into her suitcase, and goes to the bathroom for her toiletries. Reese is inspecting her battered face in the mirror. Both eyes are now black from the laceration on her forehead. "Maybe I shouldn't go, after all. I haven't seen my mom in ten years. I'll scare her to death if I show up looking like this."

Maggie locks eyes with her in the mirror. "Your mother will see past the bruises, Reese. All she cares about is that you're alive. If you feel up to the trip, you should definitely come with me."

Reese turns away from her reflection. "Then let's get on the road."

Raimi insists on carrying both suitcases down the stairs. He tosses them in the trunk of his two-door sports car and helps Reese into the passenger side while Maggie squeezes into the back. Speeding through the deserted streets of downtown, they arrive at his apartment within minutes.

Raimi hops out of the car, folding the driver's seat forward and giving Maggie a hand out. He wags his finger at her. "If you need me, you call me. I'll either catch the next train or borrow Mom's car."

"Thanks for the offer," Maggie says. "But we'll be fine."

"You've had quite a shock tonight, Maggie." Raimi's eyes are full of concern. "Are you sure you're okay to drive?"

"I'm fine," Maggie says. "I promise. I have a lot to think about on the drive."

He places a hand on each of her shoulders. "Take care of my girl. She means the world to me." His lips brush her forehead. "And take care of yourself."

She smiles at him. "Will do." She gets behind the wheel and drives off, waving at Raimi in the rearview mirror.

Reese falls asleep before they get on the highway. Maggie debates whether to call her mother in Portland. With the three-hour time difference, it's only midnight there. Late by some standards but not for her mother, who often reads suspense novels until the wee hours of the morning. Gripping the steering wheel with her left hand, Maggie keys in the number with the thumb of her right. The line rings and rings. She's not surprised her mother isn't accepting a call from a strange number. Maggie has her thumb on the end call button, prepared to try again, when her mother answers.

"Who is this?" she says.

"It's me, Mom. Maggie."

"Maggie! I've been trying to get in touch with you for days. Why haven't you responded to my calls and texts?" Her tone is a mixture of anger and concern.

"I know, Mom. And I'm sorry. A lot has happened this week. The past few months, actually." Maggie confesses everything to her mother. "I tried, Mom. I really tried to make it work with Eric. But when the abuse started . . . and then I find out he's somebody else, possibly a murderer."

"Oh, honey. Why didn't you call us? We would've come right away."

"And that's exactly why I didn't. You all warned me about Eric. But I married him anyway. I made a huge mistake, and I wanted to figure it out myself. If it's any consolation, I was planning to call you in the morning. I'd made my mind up to go back to Richmond, to press charges against Eric and get a divorce. I was going to ask you to come with me."

"You know I would have," her mother says. "I'll come to Richmond now, if you'll let me."

Maggie has always been able to count on her mother's support, but hearing the words warms her heart and brings tears to her eyes. "I would love that. I need you here, more than ever, to help me through the next few days."

"Do you want your dad to come with me?"

Maggie has given this a lot of thought. "Maybe later. Right now, can it just be us?"

"Of course, it can. Let me get on the computer and book a flight. I'll text you the information as soon as I have it. Drive safely, darling. And be strong when you talk to the police."

Maggie smiles. Her mother is always telling her to be something. Be patient. Be brave. Be kind. Be careful. "Yes, ma'am," she says and ends the call.

The tension drains from her body at the thought of seeing her mother. She settles back in her seat and sets the cruise control. The traffic is light, but the drive seems endless just the same. She is eager to get to Richmond, to put this whole episode of her life behind her.

The sky is pink with the first rays of dawn, and they're nearing the outskirts of Richmond when Raimi calls to check on them. "Piece of cake," she says about the trip. "Reese has slept the whole way."

Raimi chuckles. "Poor thing is exhausted." He makes Maggie promise to call him after they leave the police station. "Hang in there. You've got this."

Maggie knows that now is not the time to be contemplating a relationship with Raimi, but she can't help herself. He is thoughtful and caring, just the kind of man she'd like to spend the rest of her life with.

The downtown streets are quiet, and when she arrives at the police station, she gently nudges Reese awake.

Reese brings her seat upright and winces as she stretches her body. "I'm sore all over. I feel like I got run over by a train. And my head is killing me."

Maggie removes a bottle of Tylenol from her bag. "Here. These might help." Maggie snaps the cap and shakes two out in Reese's palm. "But I'm afraid it's gonna get worse with what we're about to face."

Inside the police station, they present themselves to the receptionist. A rookie officer leads them down a maze of hallways to a small conference room where Eva awaits them. Pushing her chair back from the table, she jumps to her feet and hurries over to them.

When she moves to embrace her, Reese holds her hand out to stop her. "Sorry, Mom. No hugging. Broken ribs."

"What happened to your beautiful face?"

"That conversation will have to wait until later." While Reese's manner is all business, Maggie can tell she's fighting back her emotions.

Eva gently runs a finger down her daughter's cheek. "I've waited a long time for the opportunity to tell you how sorry I am for being such a rotten mother to you. I don't blame you for staying away all these years. What matters is that you're here now. If you'll let me, I'd like to try and make it up to you."

Reese's gray eyes glisten with unshed tears. Her chin quivers, and when she opens her mouth to speak, no words come out. Nodding, she swipes her eyes and lowers her head.

Eva turns to Maggie. "Thank you for bringing her home to me."

Maggie smiles. "My pleasure."

Eva and Reese are escorted from the room by the same rookie cop who'd escorted them there. Two men in plainclothes then join Maggie and introduce themselves as Detectives Fleming and Franklin. Sitting opposite her at the rectangular table, Fleming says, "Well now, Mrs. Jones, we'd like to hear your version of events as they pertain to the death of your husband."

She tells them about her friendship with Eva and about her marriage to Eric. When Maggie describes the physical abuse her husband dealt her, Franklin asks if she can provide any evidence to support her claim.

"I can, actually. Call Chief Marshall at the police department in Mapleton, Ohio. Not only will he share what he learned from his research into Eric's past, he can give you the photographs his coworker took of the bruises on my neck from where my husband tried to strangle me the night before I left him."

"I'll get on the phone with him right away," Franklin says.

"It's just a formality, but would you be willing to identify your husband's body?"

Maggie starts to object, but then realizes she needs to see her husband's dead body, to see for herself that he is no longer a threat to her. "I can do that."

Reese is brought into the room, and Maggie ushered out. When Reese emerges some fifteen minutes later, the detectives inform the three women they are free to leave.

The stop at the medical examiner's office is brief. Maggie's stomach hardens into knots when the attendant lifts back the white sheet, revealing her husband's lifeless body, his gray face and the mass of exposed tissue on top of his head that was once his brain. She has no parting words for Eric and feels nothing for him except pity. A wasted life.

Thirty minutes later, she navigates Raimi's sports car onto West Avenue and parks behind Eva's wagon. None of them has spoken during the drive, and no one makes a move to get out of the car.

Eva breaks the awkward silence. "I don't think I can go inside. There was so much blood everywhere."

Maggie stares at her hands gripping the steering wheel. "We can go to my house, although I'm not sure I'm ready to face the memories of the awful things that happened to me there."

"Is there somewhere else we can go?" Reese asks. "A hotel, maybe?"

"That's not a bad idea." Maggie has her hand on the ignition key when Eva's storm door bangs open and Ian comes barreling out. The sight of Reese in the car brings him to an abrupt halt on the sidewalk, his hand flying to his mouth and his eyes growing wide. He then jumps up and down, punching the air with balled fists.

A wide smile stretches across Reese's face. Her broken ribs momentarily forgotten, she jumps out of the car and runs into his arms. Maggie and Eva join them on the sidewalk.

"I can't believe our baby girl has come home. I'm throwing a party tonight to celebrate, and everyone's invited." His eyes fall on her. "Including you. You must be Maggie. Please say you'll come."

"I appreciate the invitation, but my mother's flying in from Oregon. Her flight arrives around six."

Ian flicks a wrist at her. "Bring your mama, too. The more the merrier. Let's say seven o'clock. Or whenever you get home from the airport. I'm not taking no for an answer." Starting across the yard toward his house, he turns back around. "Oh, and Eva, Mack and I cleaned up as best we could."

Eva blows him kisses. "I love you, Ian. You're the best."

"By the way, what's with all the stuff in there?" Ian asks. "Are you planning a yard sale?"

Eva laughs. "Sort of. I'm expanding the business."

They watch until he disappears inside. Reese casts a sideways glance at her mother. "Did you redecorate my room?"

"I haven't changed a single thing." Eva motions Reese toward the house. "Shall we?"

Placing a hand on the small of Eva's back, daughter and mother start up the sidewalk together. Reese glances back at Maggie. "Aren't you coming?"

Maggie waves them on. "The two of you need some time alone."

Retrieving her bag from the car, Maggie is crossing the street when Reese and Eva step in line on either side of her.

"Mom and I will have plenty of time together." Reese smiles over at Eva, who beams back at her. "We can't let you face your ghosts alone. We're fam now, Maggie. You've had our backs this past week, now we've got yours."

EVA

*J*an and Mack greet Reese and Eva at the door with sombreros and margaritas. Ian toasts Reese's homecoming. "Sure, a lot of bad stuff has happened, but there's plenty to celebrate as well."

Eva is envious of the way Reese and Ian resume their friendship as though the past ten years had never happened. She reminds herself to be patient. She and Reese have a lot of bad baggage to work through.

Maggie's mother's flight is delayed, but mother and daughter arrive when everyone is sitting down for dinner. Valerie Wade is every bit as lovely as her daughter in both appearance and personality. Ian seats Eva and Valerie together at the table, and by the time they've finished dessert—heavenly slices of chocolate caramel turtle flan—they've become fast friends.

Exhausted after the celebration, Eva and Reese sleep until the persistent ringing of the doorbell wakes them around eleven the following morning. Eva finds Helena on her front porch with shopping bags from Stella's Grocery in each hand. She'd texted Helena the previous afternoon with the news of Reese's homecoming, asking if Helena can manage the shop while Eva takes a few days off.

Helena holds the bags out to her. "I wasn't sure what you like, so I bought a little of everything."

"This is unnecessary, but much appreciated," Eva says taking the bags from her.

"By the way, I have great news," Helena says. "I convinced the owner to let us start moving into our new building early. If it works for you, I'll schedule the moving crew to come to your house this afternoon around three."

Eva glances back at the boxes in her hallway. "That will be wonderful. I can't wait to have my house back. I'll make a point of being here at three."

Much to Eva's delight, Reese chooses to stay in Richmond for the next ten days. Reese's professors exempt her from exams, allowing for proper recovery time from her injuries, and Raimi assures her that he can do without his car until she returns.

Eva and Reese spend a lot of time with Maggie and Valerie, which helps alleviate the tension between Eva and Reese. The foursome take long walks in area parks and on hiking trails along the James River. They linger over lunch at trendy new restaurants and favorite old establishments.

Reese spends hours on end holed up in her room, lovely music from her guitar drifting from within. In the late afternoons, Eva and Reese sip herbal tea on the terrace and talk. While much is shared about their lives from the past ten years, much about the past remains unspoken. Eva tells Reese about confessing her affair to Stuart and getting marriage counseling, and then how they'd planned to tell her about it at the homecoming celebration that never happened.

On Reese's third night home, after finishing the dishes and

locking up the house, Eva stops in to wish her daughter pleasant dreams on her way to bed. "I know it was silly of me to save your Christmas gifts all these years," she says when she spots the unopened presents stacked in a corner of Reese's room. "By holding on to them, I was holding on to the hope that you were still alive."

"I was going to ask you about them." Reese slides off the bed to the floor. "Can I open them now?"

Eva sits down beside her on the rug. "Sure. Most are clothes. But this one is special." She removes a square-shaped package with silver wrapping paper and a red bow from near the top of the pile.

Reese rips off the paper, takes the lid off the cardboard box, and removes a leather-bound scrapbook. She turns to the first page where a series of snapshots of Reese's birth are arranged around her hospital identification bracelet and a lock of honey-colored hair. "You finally got around to making my baby book."

Eva smiles. "It's more than a baby book."

Reese thumbs through the pages of memories from throughout her childhood until she arrives at a photograph of Stuart dancing with her at the Christmas cotillion. It was her sixth-grade year in middle school, when they were still a relatively happy family, before Eva's depression took a turn for the worst.

Eva hears a sniffle and pulls her daughter to her, holding her close. Taking the book from Reese, she returns to the beginning, and they go through page by page, crying and laughing. Remembering.

Reese softens somewhat toward her after that, but they still have a long way to go. Eva is beginning to accept the past ten years will forever exist as a void between them. Whether they can start anew remains to be seen.

The subject of Bella is strictly off limits for Eva, although Reese carries on endless phone conversations regarding the child's future with Clara and Raimi and the social worker in charge of her case. Reese also speaks frequently with someone named Grant Gardner. From the tone of Reese's voice and dreamy expression on her face, Eva suspects he may be a love interest. But she doesn't ask. Reese will eventually tell her. Or not. Eva will not push her. She's content with whatever tidbits of her life Reese is willing to share.

The ten days fly by way too fast for Eva's liking. "It won't be the same without you," she says as she walks Reese to Raimi's car.

Reese tosses her suitcase into the trunk. "But we'll see each other in two weeks, when you come for my graduation."

Then what? Eva wants to know but doesn't ask. Reese has ignored Eva's subtle hints about her moving home to Richmond. Washington is only a two-hour drive, even though traffic congestion on I-95 often adds another hour. For some people, a hundred miles is no big deal. But for Eva, it feels like a continent. She doesn't want to miss another day of her daughter's life.

Eva hasn't drunk a drop of alcohol since the night Eric died. She's been tempted, of course, although Reese's presence has helped reduce her craving. Even so, as she watches her daughter drive away, she yearns for a drink, can taste the vodka on her lips. Grabbing her car keys, she heads off to the liquor store, but on the way, she makes a detour to Claudia's Closet.

She hasn't been to the store since Reese's homecoming, and she marvels at the improvements Helena has made. While she's transported all the excess inventory to the new location, she's incorporated enough home accessories to give the store a cozy, inviting feel.

Eva makes a lap around the showroom, careful not to disturb the handful of customers scattered about. When she stops in front of a display of decorative pillows, Helena comes to stand with her.

"I love what you've done with the place," Eva says.

Helena's pride is obvious in her expression. "I can't tell you how thrilled I am to hear you say that. You've been doing this so long, I was worried about overstepping my boundary."

"We're partners now, Helena. You are free to try anything new. You've inherited your mother's excellent taste. Claudia's Closet will benefit from your elegant style."

Debra, the new part-time employee who's been working full-time in Eva's absence, arrives at noon. She and Eva hit it off right away. In between waiting on customers, they work for the remainder of the afternoon on plans for the official grand opening at the new storefront, which is scheduled for the Wednesday after Reese's graduation.

At six fifteen, Eva locks the back door and gets in her car, but she doesn't start the engine. Going home to an empty house holds no appeal. Fighting the urge to drive to the liquor store, she places a call to an old acquaintance who is a recovering alcoholic.

"Lydia, this is Eva Carpenter. I'm looking for an AA sponsor. I don't know how the process works, but I would appreciate your guidance."

Lydia is all business. "Are you sober now, Eva?"

"I am. But it's taking every bit of self-control I can summon not to go to the liquor store."

Lydia says, "If you feel comfortable driving, meet me at the Starbucks at the bottom of River Road in ten minutes. You've taken the first step toward recovery. It's a long journey and it won't be easy. At times, it'll be hard as hell, but you are on the path to changing your life for the better."

For the next two weeks, Eva attends at least one, sometimes two AA meetings a day. Now that she's been given a second chance with Reese, she's determined to be a model mother. And grandmother, if Reese is granted custody of Bella. With her confidence growing every day, Eva, after ten years, finds herself mentally prepared to move on with her life. She books an airline ticket for the end of June to visit Anette in Florida, and, with Reese's blessing, she puts the West Avenue house on the market. She has her eye on a two-bedroom condominium in the charming Libbie and Grove neighborhood near the new store.

On Friday, the day before Reese's graduation, Eva and Maggie drive to Washington in Eric's BMW. Riding in his car gives Eva the shivers.

"Is it weird for you to drive his car?" Eva asks.

"Are you kidding me? I can't wait to trade it. Who knows? Maybe I won't even need a car in DC."

Surprisingly, and much to Maggie's relief, Eric left a will naming her as sole beneficiary. While the majority of their assets are in his name alone, her attorney made certain she has enough to live on until his estate settles and she's free to sell the house and car and do as she pleases with the money in the brokerage account.

"Speaking of which, how's the job search coming?"

"Great! I added another interview to the two I already have for Monday." When these interview opportunities presented themselves, Eva volunteered to take the train home to Richmond on Sunday afternoon, so Maggie can stay in DC to meet with potential employers the next day.

"Are you sure that moving to DC is what you really want? You've been through so much recently. Maybe you should take some time to think about it."

Maggie risks a quick glance at Eva. "I'm absolutely certain this is what I want. This move is necessary for my mental stability. Some days are better than others, but I'm struggling. I'm so angry at myself for falling victim to him. In his own words, he picked me out of a crowd for his twisted little game of life. Worst part is, I let him."

"You were on the rebound, Maggie. You were vulnerable and you made a mistake. Take it from someone who knows, don't let that mistake dictate the rest of your life. Put your foot in the stirrup and get right back in that saddle."

"I'm trying," Maggie says with a sigh. "I wish the circumstances were different, because Richmond is a wonderful place. Unfortunately, the city holds nothing but bad memories for me."

The city holds bad memories for Eva as well. While part of her wants to move to Washington, she doesn't want to cramp Reese's style. Eva ponders her nearly nonexistent social circle in Richmond. Several women from AA, who routinely get together for dinner after their meetings, have invited her to join them on several occasions. So far, she's invented a reason to say no. Next time they ask, she'll say yes.

Maggie goes on, "I'd planned to wait until I sell the house, but I've decided to go ahead and look for an apartment in DC next week. It'll be easier to search for a job if I'm actually living there."

"That makes sense. But I'm not worried about you finding a job. I predict you'll have multiple offers to choose from."

"I've finished my first piece in a series on the homeless. It's good, Eva. Really good. Even if I say so myself. My creative juices are flowing. I have ideas for several more stories."

Eva smiles. "Your enthusiasm, alone, will get you the job. It doesn't hurt that you're beautiful and intelligent."

"You're biased. But I hope you're right." Maggie slows the car as they pass a fender bender on the side of the highway.

Once they return to the speed limit, Eva says, "I haven't seen you since Reese left. I know you're coping with a lot. How're you holding up?"

"I'm okay. The evening hours get kinda lonely. You know how that is. To occupy my time, I've been helping out behind the bar at the Village Cafe this week. But my days have been busy with writing and packing for the move. Which reminds me of something I've been meaning to ask you. I donated all Eric's clothes and the baby stuff from the nursery to Goodwill, but I was wondering if you'd consider consigning the furniture and decorative items. They are too contemporary for me. They may be too contemporary for Claudia's Closet as well."

"Not at all," Eva says. "Helena and I agree we should branch out to attract more customers. Everything in your house is certainly high quality."

They discuss briefly which items in Maggie's house will sell the best before circling back to the topic of the graduation festivities ahead of them. Upon Reese's suggestion, Eva and Maggie are staying at a boutique hotel near Reese's apartment. And Mama Clara—Reese's surrogate mother whom Reese obviously adores —has organized a celebratory dinner for that evening at the hotel's purportedly posh restaurant. The honor of hosting graduation parties typically belongs to the parents of the graduate, but when Eva offered to take everyone to dinner the night before or brunch following graduation, Reese turned her down.

"I can't wait for you to meet Clara and Raimi," Maggie says.

"I'm looking forward to dinner," Eva lies. She's dreading it— not only the temptation to have a drink but also meeting the two people Reese loves most in the world. No telling what Reese has told Clara and Raimi about her. What they must think of her?

As if reading her mind, Maggie says, "They're really good people, Eva. I promise, you have nothing to worry about."

Eva inhales a deep breath and straightens in her seat, holding her head high. She can do this. Her daughter is alive. The focus of this elaborate dinner will undoubtedly center around the consumption of alcohol. While her craving for a drink is fierce, Eva will not embarrass herself and her daughter by getting drunk.

"I never thought I'd see my daughter again, let alone attend her college graduation. And I owe it all to you, Maggie. I don't know how I'll ever be able to thank you."

Maggie smiles over at her. "No thanks are needed. Only your friendship."

REESE

$\mathcal{R}$ eese rarely fusses over her appearance, but she's gone the extra mile for her graduation celebration dinner. She even had her hair cut into long layers and purchased a new dress—a sleeveless black sheath with a considerable slit up her right thigh. As she climbs the lobby stairs at The Line Hotel, she catches a glimpse of her reflection in the gold leaf mirror in the corner of the stairwell. The confident young woman staring back at her has come a long way from the pregnant runaway of ten years ago.

The hotel is housed in the converted building of a hundred-plus-year-old church, and the restaurant, A Rake's Progress, occupies what used to be the balcony seating area of the sanctuary. A marble bar stretches down one side of the restaurant under an arched milk-glass window, and an enormous chandelier fashioned out of the original pipes from the church's organ hangs from the ceiling in the center of the room.

Reese asks Maggie to meet for a drink before dinner to discuss a proposal she has for her. Maggie is already seated at the bar, studying the drinks menu of fruit and herb-based cocktails, when Reese arrives. She kisses Maggie on the cheek and slides onto the vacant barstool next to her.

"You look fabulous, girlfriend." Maggie pinches Reese's chin in between two fingers, rotating her head back and forth as she examines her face. "All the bruises are gone, and I can barely see the scar on your forehead."

Reese lifts back her new bangs to show Maggie the angry red scar. "It's still there. But the plastic surgeon promises it will fade in time."

They place their order with the bartender, and while they wait for their drinks to arrive, Reese tells Maggie her plan. "It's perfect!" Maggie says. "I absolutely love it."

The bartender delivers their drinks—a concoction of Ketel Vodka, muddled blackberries, and honey served in bell-shaped glasses and garnished with blackberries.

Reese holds her glass out to Maggie. "Then we have a deal?"

"Deal," Maggie says, clinking her glass.

When the others begin to arrive, they get up and go to the top of the stairs to greet them. Reese crosses her fingers and says a silent prayer that everyone gets along during dinner and that awkward moments are few.

When Reese introduces Clara to Eva, Clara takes Eva's hand in both of hers and says, "I'm delighted to finally meet you. I've heard so many wonderful things about you."

Reese observes the relief on Eva's face. She knows how difficult this must be for her mother, especially now that she's admitted to being an alcoholic and joined AA.

After greeting Eva with a handshake and hug, Raimi announces that their table is ready.

The maître d' seats Clara at one end of a cozy rectangular table. Reese sits at the opposite end with Eva on her right and Raimi and Maggie together on the banquette to her left.

Clara says, "I've taken the liberty of ordering wine and an assortment of small plates for starters."

Two servers clad in black pants and crisp white shirts appear, one holding a bottle of red wine and the other a bottle of white. As they are circling the table, a third server arrives with a virgin cocktail—a cherry-blueberry soda—for Eva. The smile on her face expresses gratitude to Mama Clara for ordering a special cocktail for her.

Once everyone has a glass in hand, Reese says, "I'd like to thank Clara for organizing this dinner. It means so much to have all the members of my extended family here to help me celebrate my graduation. I have three exciting pieces of news to share with you."

She pauses while her gaze travels from one expectant face to the next, lingering on Eva's. She's wearing a capped-sleeve swing dress in a geometric print of muted colors that accents her healthy glow. Sobriety agrees with her. Reese prays she can keep up the good work.

Raimi rolls his eyes. "Enough with the theatrics already. Tell us the news."

Reese sticks her tongue out at him. "I'll start with the serious news. After a great deal of soul-searching, I've decided not to pursue custody of Bella."

The table erupts in a chorus of buts and whats.

Reese lifts a hand to silence them. "Hear me out. I've made this decision with Bella's best interests at heart. Not mine. Bella's social worker, Emma—who, by the way, is inspirational—has found the perfect parents to adopt her. I haven't met them. I don't even want to know their names. After years of unsuccessful fertility treatments, they've decided to adopt. Because they are both in their early forties, they want to give an older child a home."

Skepticism crosses Clara's face and Reese meets her gaze. "I know what you're thinking. We thought Nora and James were the perfect couple. But this man is a foreign dignitary and his wife is a stay-at-home mom. He's currently stationed in another country. I didn't ask which one. Again, I don't want to know. Emma has successfully placed a lot of kids over the years, and is convinced this is a 'match made in heaven,'" Reese says, using air quotes.

Raimi focuses his attention on Reese, as though they are the only two people in the room. "Are you sure you're ready for a permanent separation?" He brings the side of his hand down on the table like a meat cleaver. "You won't even know what country she's living in."

"She'll have two parents, a mother and father, who've been married for fifteen years. And they're extremely wealthy. She'll get to travel all over the world. Think of the doors they can open for her. She was never meant to be my daughter, Raimi. It's taken me ten years, but I finally realize that. And I believe it in my heart."

Servers deliver small plates of artfully presented salads and vegetables and crab dishes for the table to share.

Clara says a quick blessing, thanking God for the food and companionship, and orders everyone to dig in.

"I can't wait for you to tell them your good news," Raimi says, as he stuffs a forkful of strawberry and beet salad into his mouth.

Clara snorts. "Wait a minute? You told Raimi before you told me?"

Reese laughs. "I knew him first."

"By twelve hours." Clara's face is serious, but her tone is teasing.

"I had to tell him," Reese says. "Because I need him to drive the U-Haul for me. I'm moving to Nashville on Monday."

Reese watches closely for their responses. Eva's jaw drops, and Clara touches the tips of her fingers to her chin, mouthing, "Thank you, Jesus."

Reese shifts in her seat toward Eva. "I know this is a shock.

And I'm sorry it's happening so soon after our reunion. But I've been offered an incredible opportunity. I just signed a contract to write the songs for June Tucker's next album."

Eva's jaw drops open a second time. "You mean *the* June Tucker?"

"The one and only. I flew to Nashville for a couple of days last week to meet with Grant Gardner, the music producer. He showed me around, took me out for a night on the town. Nashville has this incredible vibe. It's the perfect place for a music artist like me." She looks down the table at Clara. "You've been after me for years to make a fresh start. Now that I'm finally ready, I have to admit it feels really good." She comes out of her seat a little. "I'm so excited, I can hardly stand it."

Raimi's eyes glisten when he says, "I'm really gonna miss you, fam. But you've worked hard for this, and I'm proud of you."

Reese playfully punches his arm. "I'm gonna miss you too, fam." She reaches for her mother's hand. "Please be happy for me, Mom. If it's any consolation, I've rented a two-bedroom apartment. You can come visit any time."

Eva smiles at the invitation. "I'm almost afraid to ask what the third bit of news is."

Reese locks eyes with Maggie. "I'll let you tell them."

"Well." Maggie sets her wineglass down and dabs at her lips. "This bit of news pales in comparison to the rest. But I'm excited about it. I'm taking over Reese's apartment when she moves out. And Raimi has offered to stop in Richmond, on his way back from Nashville, to help me move my stuff."

"That's perfect," Clara says. "I've always loved that apartment."

"Raimi lived in the apartment before me," Reese explains to Eva. "You'll have to come see it tomorrow after brunch."

"I'd like that," Eva says in a soft voice.

"So, Reese." Maggie has mischief in her eyes. "Tell us about Grant Gardner. You got all goo-goo eyed when you mentioned him just then."

Reese's face beams red. "Sorry, Mags. I never kiss and tell."

Raimi nudges Maggie, his conspirator, with his elbow. "So, there *was* some kissing going on."

"Hmm-mm, Raimi," Maggie says. "You'd better check Grant Gardner out when you go down there next week."

"Have no fear," Raimi says. "I intend to."

The main courses arrive—platters of grilled pork loin, soft-shell crabs, fillets of fish, and pan-seared scallops. Reese's move to Nashville and the graduation festivities the following morning dominate the conversation while they eat. Champagne—sparkling cider for Eva—is served with baked Alaska for dessert, and the toasts to Reese drag on and on.

Finally, Reese raises both hands to silence them. "Your congratulations and best wishes are much appreciated, but enough already. Eat your dessert."

"You don't have to tell me twice," Raimi says and sinks his dessert fork into the mound of meringue.

Reese takes several bites and sets down her fork. "A few weeks ago, Raimi asked if I thought of myself as Anna or Reese. I couldn't answer him at the time, but I've thought about it a lot since. The truth is, I don't think of myself as either. I think of myself as me. It's too complicated for me to change my surname back to Carpenter after legally being Anna McKenzie for ten years. But going forward, when I meet new people, I plan to introduce myself as Anna Reese."

Eva repeats the name. "Anna Reese. I like that."

Clara nods. "It's very pretty. Feminine."

Raimi eyes her suspiciously. "What are *we* supposed to call you?"

"Whatever you want to call me. I'll be Anna to those of you who know me as Anna and Reese to those of you who know me as Reese."

Raimi glances over at Maggie as if looking to her for approval. She nods, as if granting it, and he shrugs as if to say, If you say so. There is no question but that love is in the air for these two.

A few minutes later, when Clara is paying the bill, Reese smiles to herself when she overhears Raimi whisper to Maggie, "I need to drop my mama at home first, but do you want to go out for a nightcap afterward?"

A lovely glow washes over Maggie's face. "I'd love to."

After dinner, as the group is migrating to the lobby, Reese makes a point of speaking with each of them in turn. To Maggie, she says, "I've only known you a short time, but it already feels like we're best friends." She moves in close to her ear. "I'm praying that you'll one day be my fam sister-in-law."

Maggie blushes red. "I may never be your in-law, but I'll always be your fam."

Reese turns to Raimi, play-punching him in the gut. Wrapping his arms around her, he lifts her off the floor until she squeals for him to put her down. Laughing, she places her hands on his cheeks, bringing his face close to hers. "That Christmas Eve seems like so long ago. I'm not sure I ever properly thanked you for rescuing me that night."

"Having you in my life is the only thanks I need."

She wants to tell Raimi how much she loves him, but she doesn't trust her voice.

He presses his finger to her lip. "I know. You don't need to say it. I will always have your back."

Clara is standing beside Raimi, and Reese falls into her arms. "You've always known me better than I know myself. You taught me so much about life and love. And family." She whispers the last so Eva can't hear. She doesn't want to hurt her mother's feelings.

Wiping her eyes, Reese offers her elbow to Eva. "Come on. I'll walk you to your room."

Eva takes hold of her arm, but instead of going to the elevator, she drags her toward the exit. "Let's go outside for a minute. I could use some fresh air."

They sit side by side on the top of a dozen steps. The sounds of car horns, sirens, and roaring engines fill the warm night air. Reese will miss this town. But she isn't saying goodbye to DC. The people she loves most in the world still live here.

They sit in silence for a long while, before Reese asks, "Are you okay? I threw a lot at you at once. Not just with all my news but in meeting Clara and Raimi as well. It was insensitive of me. I know how hard you're working to stay sober."

"I admit I was looking forward to being a grandmother." The monotone quality of Eva's voice gives nothing away, and Reese can't tell if she's serious or joking.

"You'll be a grandmother one day. When the time is right."

"When the time is right," Eva repeats with a nod. "Watching you interact with Clara and Raimi got to me. They are truly your family. More than I ever was. Funny thing, though, instead of feeling jealous, I am grateful to them. They obviously love you so much. You've grown into an amazing young woman, Reese. And it's because of them."

"That's not true. I owe them a lot, for sure. But the values you and Daddy instilled in me as a child are part of the reason I am who I am today."

All the unpleasant memories—the torture her mother had put her through in high school, and the pain she'd caused her mother by running away and staying silent for ten years—are best left out. *Let those memories go. Focus instead on your overall sense of happiness as a child on West Avenue.*

She angles her body toward Eva. "I have plenty of room in my heart for all of you, Mom. We've been given another chance, and I, for one, am looking forward to creating new memories with you."

"What do you say we wipe the slate clean and forge a new relationship based on friendship?"

Reese's heart explodes with love. "There's nothing I'd like more."

ACKNOWLEDGMENTS

I'm grateful to the many people who helped make this novel possible. First and foremost, to my editor, Patricia Peters, for her patience and advice and for making my work stronger without changing my voice. A great big heartfelt thank-you to Kathy Sinclair, criminal investigator with the Bartow County Sherriff's Office, and good friend Alison Fauls for giving me honest and constructive feedback on my works in progress. To my daughter, Cameron, and her adorable friends—Emma, Hayes, Fran, and Margaret—for giving me the lay of the land in DC. And to my behind-the-scenes team, Geneva Agnos and Kate Rock, for all the many things you do to manage my social media so effectively.

I am blessed to have many supportive people in my life who offer the encouragement I need to continue the pursuit of my writing career. I owe a huge debt of gratitude to my advanced review team, the lovely ladies of Georgia's Porch, for their enthusiasm for and commitment to my work. Love and thanks to my family—my mother, Joanne; my husband, Ted; and the best children in the world, Cameron and Ned.

Most of all, I'm grateful to my wonderful readers for their love of women's fiction. I love hearing from you. Feel free to shoot me an email at ashleyhfarley@gmail.com or stop by my website at ashleyfarley.com for more information about my characters and upcoming releases. Don't forget to sign up for my newsletter. Your subscription will grant you exclusive content, sneak previews, and special giveaways.

ABOUT THE AUTHOR

Ashley writes books about women for women. Her characters are mothers, daughters, sisters, and wives facing real-life issues. Her goal is to keep you turning the pages until the wee hours of the morning. If her story stays with you long after you've read the last word, then she's done her job.

Ashley is a wife and mother of two young adult children. She grew up in the salty marshes of South Carolina, but now lives in Richmond, Virginia, a city she loves for its history and traditions.

Ashley loves to hear from her readers. Feel free to visit her website or shoot her an email. For more information about upcoming releases, don't forget to sign up for her newsletter at ashleyfarley.com/newsletter-signup/. Your subscription will grant you exclusive content, sneak previews, and special giveaways.

ashleyfarley.com
ashleyhfarley@gmail.com

CPSIA information can be obtained
at www.ICGtesting.com
Printed in the USA
LVHW051728030320
648855LV00005B/1049